What

MW01141487

"*In His Majesty's Secret Service* is ab: about courageous young people who risked their lives to smuggle Bibles into communist Romania during the revolution in 1989. I read it in one sitting. I could not put it down."

—Lyle W. Dorsett, Ph.D.
Billy Graham Professor of Evangelism, Emeritus
Beeson Divinity School
Samford University

"Patrick Bell hits the target with his award-winning first novel *In His Majesty's Secret Service*. Young adults 16 and older will enjoy the mystery and action in this adventure about a group of Bible smugglers who travel throughout Romania before the fall of the Soviet Union. The novel is chock full of historical information as the authentic characters brave some frightening escapades. Readers will enjoy learning more about the persecuted church through this fictionalized account. Fast moving and well written, the characters and plot engage and deliver."

—Pippa Davies
Director, HCS Blended Learning Commons
Heritage Christian Online School
Kelowna, British Columbia

"Patrick Bell takes us on a stirring, memorable, and historic journey in the book *In His Majesty's Secret Service*. As a long-ago former Bible Courier myself, I can viscerally relate to the emotions of anxiousness, uncertainty, hope, and joy that cycle in every chapter. Patrick vividly describes the remarkable witness of believers behind the Curtain, the honor of those from the West who served the Church in the East, and the staggering suffering that despots like Romanian dictator Nicolae Ceaușescu unleashed on millions of his own countrymen. Reading the book is not only a riveting experience, it's a first-hand exposure to one of the most momentous global events of the second half of the 20th century."

—Craig Glass
Peregrine Ministries
www.peregrineministries.org

"Read the amazing, exciting fictional account of Bible couriers going through the Romanian revolution. Feel the pain and the joy of those that suffer for their faith. See how God works His plan for our good and His glory!"

—Dr. R. Mark Beadle
CEO, Sevenstar LLC.

"I loved this novel! Each page brings adventure, intrigue, heroism, and deep faith. Author, Patrick Bell, lived this incredible story in real life. It's a must read."

—Jim Burns, PhD
President, HomeWord
Author of *Doing Life With Your Adult Kids: Keep Your Mouth Shut and the Welcome Mat Out*

"Having traveled myself through Romania and other former Iron Curtain countries, I was looking forward to reading Patrick Bell's new book, *In His Majesty's Secret Service*. This action-packed thriller has a masterful blend of history and fiction; a real page-turner! Patrick's character development is so superb that I was drawn quickly into this intriguing adventure. A fun, must read!"

—Jerry Lewis
Former Director, Mount Hermon Conference Center
California, USA

"As a bible courier in the late 1980's, Patrick Bell was not just a front-row observer of the momentous collapse of the communist regimes of Central & Eastern Europe, he was right in the mix of things. So even though *In His Majesty's Secret Service* is a fun, action-packed work of fiction, Patrick has managed to capture the tension, uncertainty, and exhilaration of that time and place. Reading through this page-turner brought back to mind many of the places, people, conversations, naiveté, and soul searching I remember from my own experience as a youthful 'bible smuggler.'"

—Greg Reader
International Teams, Canada
Former Bible Smuggler

"What a treat! Just finished reading *In His Majesty's Secret Service* in one sitting. I could *not* put it down. The detail, the character development, the weaving of stories...incredible!"

—Darlene Unrau, MA
Educational Coordinator, True To You

"Patrick Bell is a master storyteller. You'll feel like you are there in Eastern Europe in the years around the collapse of Communism. You get a sense for the things that Christ's Ambassadors see in the parts of the world where the Church is politically powerless, and it isn't pretty. I hope this book calls out the best courage and faith in another generation who will spread the Good News to those who have no access to it."

—D. C. Keane
Mission Mobilizer
Phoenix, AZ

"I like fictional books if they

- Let me learn something that I did not know, or
- Leave me wanting to know what happened after the story ends, or
- Make me wish that I had been present when the story occurred, or
- Create within me a desire to visit the location of the story, especially if it is a foreign country.

In His Majesty's Secret Service did all of these, which makes this a book I consider worth reading."

—Sandy Davis
Newport Beach, CA

"Based on true events, *In His Majesty's Secret Service* delivers unpredictable twists and turns and will leave you thoroughly engrossed. You will be transported to another world. But this book is more than an adventure. It is also a testament to the awesome power of God in a troubled time, and you will be drawn closer to Him in every page."

—Nigel Paul
Founder and International Director, MoveIn

"From the very first page of the book, I had a hard time putting it down. It is such a blessing to read a book about how God can move through people in mighty ways if they truly put Him first every minute of the day. It was a real inspiration to me to seek more of the will of God in my life."

—Janet Rainbow
Former Academic Director, Heritage Christian Online School
Kelowna, BC

In His Majesty's ☭ Secret Service

Bible smugglers, Romanian believers, and the Secret Police become entangled in an epic struggle. Who will survive?

Jared !

May your faith be inspired ! ☺

PatBell

Patrick D. Bell

IN HIS MAJESTY'S SECRET SERVICE
Copyright © 2018 by Patrick D. Bell

Printed in Canada

ISBN: 978-1-4866-1754-8

Word Alive Press
119 De Baets Street, Winnipeg, MB R2J 3R9
www.wordalivepress.ca

MIX
Paper from
responsible sources
FSC® C016245

Cataloguing in Publication may be obtained through Library and Archives Canada

Dedication

To my amazing wife Holly,

From our first date in Vienna,
To Romania through the Revolution,
California,
Japan,
Kenya,

And around the world.

And to our incredible children,
Grace, Sam, and Mark
Who carry the mantle of faith and the spark of creativity

May our adventures together continue!

Acknowledgements

Every work of historical fiction is a combined effort. I'd like to acknowledge and thank the following:

My Dad and Mum, Jim and Ruth Bell: From our early days in Africa, you created in me a thirst for adventure. Dad, thanks for your gift of story and the tremendous help you leant to the novel. (Who knew that you could tell someone how to get through a barbed-wire electric fence?) And Mum, thanks for all the edits. I love you both tons!

Holly Bell: What would I ever do without you? You lived the adventure with me, you cheered me on as I finished the novel, and you encouraged me to pull the manuscript out of a box after a quarter century and try once again to have it published. Every step of the journey with you.

Greg Reader: You invited me to come to Europe to smuggle Bibles. Thank you! We had a lot of conversations about Romania, the ethics of smuggling, how to behave in various cultures, and not a few about certain members of the fairer sex. You also gave me a lot of content for the novel. (And you get to be Nick in this book, though I probably made Nick a bit smarter and better-looking than you deserve.)

Gary Amato: We travelled extensively together through Romania and you were the first to encourage me to write this novel. "Start with a bang and go from there!" you said.

Ted Gerk: Sometimes simple acts of kindness are the measure of true greatness. Thank you for scanning a dusty four-hundred-page manuscript and encouraging me along the way.

My former team of Bible smugglers at International Teams: We slept in parking lots, lousy hotels, and tents across Eastern Europe. And now we look back and remember how amazing it was.

Radio Free Europe: I consumed your research reports on Romania. Thank you for the work you are still doing.

Anita Dyneka and Joseph Ton: You taught me once about Romania at the Slavic Gospel Association outside of Chicago. And Joseph, we stood together in your pulpit on your first day back to Oradea, Romania after the revolution. You've probably forgotten, but it was inspirational to me.

The Christians of Romania: Thank you for standing strong through the years and being the real catalyst for the revolution. And to those who contributed insights into this novel and answered so many of my questions, I appreciate the gift you gave me.

Word Alive Press: Thank you for choosing *In His Majesty's Secret Service* as your annual contest winner. May this be the first of many projects together!

Sara Davison: As my editor, you're "genius heaped upon genius." (And no, you don't get to edit that statement.)

Thank you, Lord, for your gift of faith and courage that allowed us to travel behind the Iron Curtain without fear so that we might bless your persecuted church.

And thank you for being with me as the journey of faith continues.

Europe 1989

Romania 1989

Prologue

September 3, 1989
Romania

The distant pounding of an AK-47 assault rifle brought each person to a standstill. Petru's eyes locked with those of their leader Emil. Emil shook his head slightly, warning him not to move or speak. The six men and four women listened, hesitated, then, when Emil gestured for them to continue, followed him through the dense brush in the dead of the night. A murky, cold canal stretched before them, barely visible through the trees. One hundred yards beyond, they would be challenged by the heavily-patrolled fence, its top lined with twisted coils of barbed wire. This was the Yugoslavian frontier, which signaled freedom and escape from Romania.

Petru, tall and bulky with an unruly tangle of brown, curly hair, brought up the rear; his huge hand gripped a length of cord, nearly invisible in the darkness. He strained to see, but could barely make out their guide as Emil moved on carefully and silently in front of them. He wouldn't abandon them, would he? Petru felt a tug on the cord and kept close to the group, anxious not to be left behind.

A yellow moon rose at the edge of the forest, outlining Emil. The forest came alive with the movement and sound of small animals and insects. Frogs trilled their chorus between the reeds of the canal; crickets chirped their reply among the grass and leaves. Then, as suddenly as they had begun, both the frogs and the crickets fell silent.

Petru froze. Beyond the tree line, a border guard near the edge of the canal strode towards Emil. "Stop," Petru hissed at the others. They promptly drew back into the brush, crowding together out of sight of the guard. Petru tensed, ready to run.

The guard uttered a sharp, "Halt. Stand still." Emil lifted both arms. The cord in Petru's fingers went limp.

"You are under arrest," the guard shouted. "Turn around and put your hands on your head." A beam of light flashed across Emil's body, settling on the side of his face.

"My bicycle broke down and I thought this was a short cut to the village," Emil declared loudly. "I have my papers in my inside jacket pocket."

The guard shoved the muzzle of his AK-47 into the small of Emil's back. Without hesitation, Emil spun to his right, pinning the rifle barrel between his body and his right arm. With his left hand, he grabbed the knife strapped to the back of his neck. A quick slash with the blade stifled a cry from the guard. Petru watched as the two men toppled over and disappeared with a noisy splash into the dark waters of the canal.

Petru drew closer to the others. "Emil is finished."

"Maybe not," one of the other man replied. "We must wait and see. I haven't heard an alarm."

They waited for nearly an hour, huddled together, growing colder as the minutes past. A branch rolled as a woman shifted her foot, which drew a round of harsh stares from the others. She didn't move again.

The hairs on the back of Petru's neck stood on end as a twig cracked behind him. He turned his head slowly and sighed with relief when he spotted Emil moving between the darkness and shadows only ten feet away.

The others spun to face Emil, who held a finger to his lips. "Come now," he whispered, "it's time to go. The guard forgot to release the safety lever on his rifle. I didn't give him a second chance."

"Where *is* the soldier?" a woman asked. "Why weren't you watching out for him? We each pay you two hundred dollars American and you run into a trap. You're not a professional."

"Be quiet," Emil muttered. "Did you see any other guards?"

Petru shook his head.

"Be quick then." Emil spun on his heel. "Let's get out of here before another patrol comes."

Emil led off, this time at a faster pace. The woman who had complained struggled to keep up and mumbled something inaudible. Petru followed closely behind the last of the group members, ducking the low branches that scratched at his face.

He reached the canal bank only moments after the others. Anxious to keep moving after their close call, he tore off his coat and boots and eased himself into the dark water, holding his bundle over his head. *What was that?* His leg brushed against something in the water and his hand instinctively shot out to protect himself. What *was* it? Something bumped his leg again. Petru jumped forward then lost his footing and fell shoulder deep into the murky canal. A military cap floated by his head. He grabbed it and flung it behind him before surging forward against mounting fear. *Please don't let me encounter the body of that dead guard.*

On the far side, he put his boots back on and hurried to catch up to Emil and the others. He grasped his coat firmly in one hand; it was only a short distance to the border.

Petru slowed his pace, stopping occasionally to listen. He detected no sound above his own heartbeat and the suppressed breathing of the others. Emil pushed forward again with the rest of the group, but Petru hung back. Something wasn't right. Would one soldier patrol alone? Wouldn't there be others with him?

Petru stopped and looked back over his shoulder. Should he turn back? He shook his head. It was too late. The police would be looking for him back home. He had to escape this country. Once he was free, he could arrange for his family to leave and then they would all enjoy safety. He hurried forward and caught up to the others who waited at the edge of the final clearing. The fence was just ahead!

"Oh, Lord Jesus," Petru prayed, "please take us safely across."

He saw no one in sight as he and the others began their final dash to freedom. He tightened his grip on his coat, ready to throw it over the barbed wire. His heart drummed in his chest. Adrenaline surged through his veins.

Without warning, two heads appeared from a ditch by the fence and two gun barrels were leveled in their direction. The first staccato burst caught Emil and one of the young women. Both were flung backwards off their feet, their bodies shattered and their blood-soaked clothing turning black in the dim moonlight.

Something tugged at Petru's shirt sleeve. He lost his balance and plunged head-long into the short grass. Someone crashed over him, slamming into the ground just a foot away. Petru stared at the dead man, catching a glimpse of a face frozen for eternity in a mask of terror and disbelief. *God, why did it have to end this way? We've come so close to our freedom. Now my dreams are nothing. Don't you care about me?*

Footsteps thudded behind him. A heavy boot rolled him onto his back. Petru opened his eyes and cried out in terror, "Oh God, help me."

"This one's still alive, Ian," the soldier said in Romanian to his comrade.

"We could shoot him and no one would know," his companion replied. "See if he has any money on him. I'll check these others for loot."

"We'd better let our superiors deal with him. Perhaps when the *Securitate* finish talking to him, he'll wish he had died tonight."

Chapter One

December 8, 1989
Bratislava, Czechoslovakia

The night fog swept into the city on leopard's feet, unpredictably swift. The mists swirled, changed form, and slipped down a dimly-lit cobblestone street. One hundred yards up the street to the north a bus squealed brazenly to a halt and a dozen or more people stepped out. The fog moved in and encircled them.

Jim Barham glanced past his partner, Kirsten Frey, in the direction of the bus. He could vaguely make out figures coming towards them and he waited no longer. He turned the brass handle on the iron-barred glass door of Number 12 Klemensova Street, and together the two entered the dark building. They left the cold blackness of the night, which darkened even more as clouds descended upon the city and obliterated a three-quarter moon, along with a kaleidoscope of stars. Jim was thankful that few people walked the streets, although it was not yet ten o'clock. Hopefully most were curled up in their beds, so he and Kirsten could complete their evening mission.

Jim and Kirsten crossed the foyer silently and climbed the stairs. Ignoring the elevator to their left, Jim headed for the second level which, in Europe, was considered the first floor. At the top of the stairs, he looked across the courtyard and discovered a problem. If anyone stood at his door, whoever it was could easily see nearly every other apartment across the courtyard, and he and Kirsten could not allow themselves to be seen. *This is crazy. This is crazy. This is crazy.* His thoughts raced. *Why did Nick have to send me? I'd rather be sitting in the van.*

Kirsten closed her eyes briefly. Was she praying?

His stomach in knots, Jim turned to his right and walked along the open corridor. The first door he encountered bore the number 113 on a small metal plate. Kirsten had gone the opposite direction, but came back, her brow furrowed.

"I didn't see number 27. Did you?"

Jim shook his head.

"Great." Kirsten threw her arms in the air. "Where to next?"

"Let's go up one more," Jim replied.

Together they retreated to the staircase, started up, then stopped. Jim's breath caught in his throat. Below them, on the ground level, a door slammed, and the distinct tapping of a pair of shoes across the unkempt tiled floor echoed upwards. Kirsten moved first, taking the stairs two at a time, with Jim close behind, wiping perspiration from his forehead. At the second floor, she took the corridor to the right.

Jim followed. *Hope this is the right choice.* "I wish the building planners knew how to count," he muttered.

Kirsten stopped so abruptly he nearly slammed into the back of her. Apartment 27. The tense muscles across Jim's shoulders relaxed slightly. To the left of the metal plate on the door frame, a cardboard tag bore the name MIROLEK, JAN, and under that, a buzzer button. Kirsten pushed it three times. Jim strained to hear. Someone moved inside.

On the stairs below, the footsteps grew louder, a methodical *tap, tap, tap.* The stranger would reach the second floor in seconds. "Answer," Kirsten hissed, stabbing at the buzzer again.

Someone inside the apartment approached the door. *Hurry. Hurry.* Jim glanced down the hall. The footsteps on the stairs had stopped.

The door opened and Jim, not waiting to introduce himself, brushed past the person still holding the knob and yanked Kirsten in after him by the arm. The door swung silently behind them and closed with a click.

In a low voice, Jim addressed the man in English. "Good evening. Is Jan here?"

Outside, at the top of the stairs, a man propped a shoulder against the wall and drew slowly on a cigarette. Who were these Westerners and what were they doing in Apartment 27? He had heard two sets of footsteps, but by the time he had emerged from the staircase had only caught a glimpse of one person. Even a dark scarf could not hide the wisps of blonde hair that escaped around the woman's eyes. She was one he would remember.

Taking a half step forward, he studied the other apartments on the second floor, his eyes scanning for anything out of place, his ears tuned for a sound. Only silence.

After a long minute, the man shrugged and dropped the remainder of his cigarette to the floor, crushing it with the sole of his shoe. In this present time of political revolution, it probably mattered little now. The Communist Party was on its way out in Czechoslovakia; his services might never again be necessary here in Bratislava. He turned and continued up the stairs, contemplating a career move back to his homeland of Romania. His abilities might be better used by Romania's own Secret Police.

☭

Inside the apartment, Jim faced the man who had opened the door for them.

The man smiled. "Greetings my friends, my name is Mirolek." He held out an arm to a woman who stood smiling near the door to the kitchen. "This is my wife, Anica. And you are … ?"

Jim reached out to shake his hand. "Max."

"And you?" Jan offered his hand to Kirsten.

"Cathy." She used her code name, as Jim had, since they both knew that someday it might protect all of them.

"You have Bibles for me?" Jan rubbed his hands together.

Jim shook his head. "Only medicine. We heard you needed this for your heart." He pulled four boxes of *adalat retard* from the pocket of his sheepskin coat and handed them to Jan.

"Thank you, brother. Thank you, sister. I have great need of this." Jan paused. "You have no Bibles for me?"

"I'm sorry, Jan. We gave our books to a brother in Prague. Perhaps we can bring you some Bibles on our next trip."

Mirolek nodded. "Thank you, brother. Thank you, sister," he repeated. "You come from West Germany, yes? You are from America?"

Is he probing or just being friendly? "From the West, yes." Jim weighed each word before speaking. "How have things changed for you since the Communists were recently thrown out? We still try to be cautious."

"Everything is fine now. There is no need to worry." Jan raised his hands in the air and looked up. "We are free. Thank you, Lord Jesus. Praise you, Lord."

"Amen," Kirsten said.

Jan took her by the elbow. "Can you come in for something to eat? Perhaps a cup of coffee or tea?"

Kirsten smiled at Jan and his wife and removed the scarf from her head, allowing her long, blonde hair to fall past her shoulders. "Yes, that would be nice. A cup of tea please. But we can't stay long. We have a transit visa and we must be out of the country tonight. And we have a friend waiting for us in our vehicle, keeping an eye on things outside."

☭

Lying motionless across the middle seat of their blue imported Chevrolet van, Jim stared at the dots on the roof's upholstery, allowing them to play tricks with his eyes. Only ten minutes had passed since the hour-long border crossing between Czechoslovakia and Hungary. He was exhausted from the day's activities, but knew he could not sleep until his mind sifted through these new experiences. The rolling and rocking motion of the van over a fairly good Hungarian road had a soothing effect on his body and the tension slowly drained from his muscles.

Jim listened to the profound lyrics of a Michael Card song that drifted from the cassette player on the front panel. *"How can a man be father to the Son of God?"* He shifted on the seat. *What a concept!* Jim struggled to comprehend the meaning of the words. Occasionally, the hushed voices of Kirsten and his best friend Nick Conrad rose above the notes.

Jim reflected on how he had arrived at this moment in time. *Here I am in Hungary tonight, Romania tomorrow, throwing another wrench into the crumbling machine of the Eastern Bloc. It's Nick's fault of course. Nick always has the crazy ideas.*

His thoughts went back to the small Canadian city of Peterborough, where he and Nick grew up. They had attended the same church, gone to the same high school, even played on the same football team. The summer of 1981 at Joy Bible Camp he and Nick met Kirsten, a girl from California who was staying with cousins for the summer. Neither he nor Nick were deterred by the fact that Kirsten was three years younger. She was not only beautiful, she was a lot of fun and easy to get along with.

Jim's friendship with Kirsten grew at about the same rate as her relationship with Nick. Thankfully, their own friendship did not evolve into a jealous rivalry. Not irreparably, anyway. For that one week each summer, the three remained inseparable. Sometimes Nick appeared aggravated at his presence, but Jim reminded Nick that competition was usually healthy.

After graduating from high school, Nick announced, "I'm joining a group in Europe to smuggle Bibles into Eastern Europe."

Jim had stared at him. Nick had to be crazy. Off his rocker. Jim had recently read of Brother Andrew's adventures in the novel *God's Smuggler* and there was no way he could picture Nick ever doing that cloak-and-dagger type of work, let alone for God. It seemed an insane idea. And it certainly didn't fit Nick's character. He was a partier, a jock, someone who hardly had time for voluntary religious activities.

Not that the concept itself was crazy. In fact, it was one Jim had also considered. When he'd discussed the idea of becoming a Bible smuggler with a few friends, though, one buddy had stated bluntly, "Don't go looking for adventure or God may give you too much." That set Jim back initially and he'd stopped and taken stock of his motives. He needed to put God first in his life. And without a love for the people of Eastern Europe, his efforts would amount to nothing. He began to read and learn about Eastern Europeans; he began to pray for them. And he also prayed for God to change his heart.

Now, four years later, here he was. He looked up at Nick. The elders from Nick's church had seen something more in him than Jim had. And they'd been right. Nick had been on this continent now for more than four years.

Jim's thoughts turned to the nine hours spent with Kirsten on the connecting flight from New York to Frankfurt only two weeks before. It had been a rare moment alone with her, but one of excitement. When she dozed, he stayed awake, dreaming like a schoolboy and trying to muster the courage to share his feelings.

Jim's thoughts were interrupted as the van pulled off the highway into a rest stop, hitting a large pothole in the process. "Where are we?" he asked, sitting up in the seat. He leaned forward and studied himself in the rear view mirror, combing his red hair with his fingers.

Nick glanced back at Jim. "You'd better take care of that hair, what you have left of it, at least. Are you still telling people how you've always had such a high forehead?"

Jim sat back in his seat. "Hey, it's been a long night." He changed the subject quickly. "So where are we now?"

"Just north of Budapest, about fifteen miles," Nick replied. "This is probably a good spot to sleep for the night. Tomorrow we'll have a few things to do in Budapest before we head on to Romania." He opened his door. "Nature calls," he announced.

"Me too," said Kirsten.

"You always have to go. Wait your turn this time."

They exited the vehicle one at a time then dove back into the warmth of the van. Kirsten chose the back seat as usual and crawled, fully dressed, deep into her sleeping bag. Nick bedded down in the front seat and Jim between the two of them on the middle seat. They weren't as comfortable as they would be in beds, but they saved a bundle on hotel bills. In Romania, however, sleeping outside of hotels wouldn't be safe and they'd have to take time to find decent rooms.

"It's cold tonight." Jim zipped the sleeping bag over his five-foot, ten-inch frame.

Nick scratched at the dark brown stubble of his beard, two days in the making. "It could be a hard winter for a lot of people in the East."

Talk died quickly for they were tired. The meeting with Mirolek, the crossing of the border into Hungary, the many hours of driving, had all taken their toll.

Jim looked at the incandescent hands of his watch. Nearly one o'clock in the morning. Already he could hear the steady breathing of his companions, who had wasted no time falling asleep.

He turned on his side and pulled the sleeping bag over his head. *I can't believe I gave up my waterbed for a lousy seat. My back is going to be a mess in the morning.* The thought of jail bars crossed his mind and he quit grumbling, reminded of his pledge to go anywhere for the Lord's sake. He began to pray, searching for the right words, but as so often in the past, he soon fell asleep.

Nick Conrad awoke the next morning full of energy. Tonight they would enter Romania, the land he loved. He envisioned the country, one of intense passion and awe-inspiring beauty. He smiled at the thought of the breathtaking Carpathian mountain range, and the shepherds with their long woolen coats and their conical hats, strolling the slopes with their dogs and herds of sheep in a photographer's dreamland. The country was filled with people living in a nineteenth-century time warp. The insanity of life preyed unremitting upon the majority. Anger and frustration abounded, along with sadness and bewilderment.

"You can expect an exhausting time in Romania," he said to the others. "The drive itself will be an adventure."

"I thought we weren't supposed to look for adventures," Jim moaned from inside his sleeping bag.

"You won't have to," Nick said. "Get up. Let's get going."

The three took a few minutes to eat bowls of cold cereal and brush their teeth. The latter was a rule instituted by Kirsten, who complained that close quarters with two men was hard enough. Then, before going any farther, they prayed. They went nowhere without asking for the power of God through prayer. Without God's protection, their efforts would surely be in vain.

Nick stared out the front window of the van as they started out, taking in the world of glittering white. Around them lay an unflawed carpet of fresh snow, nearly an inch thick, covering the stubble of corn stalks in the nearby fields and the trash on the ground beside the road. Behind them, the driver of a diesel truck blew his horn impatiently and Nick stepped on the accelerator. He sighed. Moments of serenity in Hungary never lasted long.

At 9:30 a.m., they arrived in Budapest. It was Friday, December the ninth. Their visit to Romania couldn't have come at a better time. For many Christians, there would now be an added reason for celebration. Real food! Vitamins! Aspirin! Their own Bibles!

After parking their van next to the Roosevelt Park, they walked south past the Intercontinental Hotel. A diehard musician in a gorilla suit attempted to induce a shivering crowd to part with their coins, but his take was limited to a few Forint lying on the bottom of his guitar case. Nick shook his head. This would not be the musician's day.

For the three Bible couriers, the morning passed swiftly. At the International Bookstore on Parizsi Street, they purchased seventy-five Bibles in three languages: Romanian, Hungarian, and German. They would deliver these in neighboring Romania, where Bibles were considered illegal by the authorities. Seventy-five wouldn't be enough. It never was. But each was vital.

Once they were on the street again, Nick patted the bag of Bibles he had slung over one shoulder. "Until we get to heaven, we may never know the impact that just one of these books has. You'll rarely see it. The unfortunate part of our ministry is that we go in and out and rarely spend more than an hour with each contact. We must continue to believe, though, that we'll see the fruit of our labor someday."

"I hardly think Jim and I need extra motivation right now." Kirsten skipped a few steps to keep up with the two of them. "This is so new to us, it's almost fun."

"Yeah, but the fun side of all this is going to wear off and then you've got to keep the goal, the prize, in sight. As long as you stay in this work, don't ever reject the opportunity to go on a trip, at least not for petty or selfish reasons. You won't ever know how much good you can accomplish."

The ABC store was next. Hungary's national grocery chain couldn't compare to those in America, but it had the essentials. Its claim to fame was its bread, possibly the best in Europe. The three couriers picked up two giant loaves before filling their baskets with the basics: coffee, sugar, flour, oil, cheese, eggs, meat, oatmeal, milk, butter, fresh vegetables, fruit, and chocolate. The total came to almost three hundred dollars.

"That's an awful lot of money to be spending, Nick." Jim gripped the handle of one of the baskets.

"It's God's money, Jim, not ours." Nick accepted the change and led them outside. "As long as our supporters back home keep sending us cash, we'll keep bringing relief to these people. Sometimes it's hard to force myself to take a break."

Nick smiled and looked past Jim and Kirsten down the Walking Street—the heart of Budapest where vehicles were not allowed. "Frankly, we don't really need a vacation. This is just like being on one. How else can you see all this? Unless you've got a real good job, of course. But even then you only get two weeks a year. Maybe four. We're on the road for thirty." He pointed to a nearby coffee shop. "Hey, let's dump this food in the van and go get a cappuccino."

Jim shifted the heavy basket from one hand to the other. "How about some food, too? It's gotta be lunch time by now. Do you know a good place around here?"

"If you want to take your chances, there's always McDonald's." Nick nudged Kirsten with his elbow. "There'll be clean bathrooms there, too."

That won Kirsten over. Jim looked pleased too, which Nick understood. The desire for the luxury of an American-style toilet was always present. As much as he loved what he did, he didn't particularly enjoy using what some people called a *Turkish toilet*, little more than a hole in the ground with two wooden blocks to squat on.

By two o'clock, the van was rolling again, this time with Jim driving as they headed west on Highway 4. Nick pointed to the city of Törökszentmiklós on the map, one of those great Hungarian names that many people think they can pronounce properly until they hear a Hungarian say it.

Kirsten leaned close to him. "How do you say that? Torok… Torokezen…"

"You don't say it. You just recognize it and follow the signs for the next town."

"Why do these cities have two names?" Kirsten tapped a spot on the map. "Like this one. Oradea has Nagyvarad under it in brackets."

"It's because Hungary used to rule a big part of Romania, mostly Transylvania. At the end of the First World War, while writing up the Treaty of Trianon, the Allies divided up the land as they desired. Hungary happened to be on the losing side. And if you look," Nick gestured to the fine print in the bottom corner, "this map was made in Budapest. Hungary has her own names for those cities and I guess they just don't want to forget in case they ever take them back."

Kirsten leaned back in her seat. "Do Hungarians still live there?"

Nick wrestled with the map, trying to fold it up. "They do. That's the other main reason. Still, if you look at maps made in Romania, they'll just have the Romanian names."

Two hours later they were on the outskirts of Törökszentmiklós and Kirsten took over the wheel. Nick settled into the passenger seat beside her. Fifty weary miles later, near the town of Békés, Kirsten turned onto Highway 46a and drove another twenty miles to the outskirts of Mezösarkad. It was now after six o'clock and the city was shrouded in darkness. At Nick's direction, she parked under the shelter of a few trees on the brim of a small hill.

Over a thousand yards down the hill in a small, cold valley, Nick caught a glimpse of a brightly-lit frontier post, nestled at the foot of a range of similar hills. The Hungarian Customs and Passport Control was typical in appearance. A fence surrounded three small brick buildings, dull and lifeless. A diminutive figure standing at the gate stomped his feet in the half light, and a lookout tower loomed on either side of the buildings. Luminous halogen bulbs from the car ports silhouetted three human forms next to a vehicle.

Jim leaned forward, between the two front seats.

"See down there." Nick pointed through the front windshield. "Those guards are checking a car."

Kirsten nodded. "If the driver of that vehicle is smart, he'll stay out of the cold as long as possible."

No man's land lay before them on the face of the opposite hill. No lights. No movement. The lights from the Hungarian border carried only a short distance up the incline, the polished surface of snow accentuating its steep slope. A narrow, two-lane road wound daringly up the middle, gray and empty now as it often was.

At the top of the hill, at the Romanian border station, a single, feeble light shone. A number of low dark buildings, silhouetted against the horizon, awaited the arrival of the three Westerners. There lay their immediate goal, intimidating and terror-inspiring. Nick elbowed Jim in the shoulder. "So... how are you two feeling? A bit nervous?"

"Fine," Kirsten answered curtly. She looked straight ahead, unmoving.

Nick shifted to look back at Jim, who had sat back and pulled out his Swiss army blade to clean his fingernails. Everyone dealt with tension in his or her own way.

"Okay then," Nick said. "Let's pray."

Kirsten and Jim bowed their heads. "Protect the books, God," Jim began. "For Your sake, let the guards be distracted."

"Blind their eyes," Kirsten continued. "May they overlook the food we have. Lord, help us with our lack of trust."

Nick stared out the window at the road in front of them. With precise, chosen words, he prayed fervently. "God, we thank you that you are already there preparing the way for us. We thank you that there is nothing that the guards can do unless you allow them to. We ask for your blessing, so that your son, Jesus, may be glorified in this country of Romania. Amen."

When he finished, he climbed out of the vehicle, went around to the back of the van, and opened up the rear door. He pulled out the box of Bibles from under the seat and placed the bag of tire chains over the books. He then jammed the box back under the seat. In front of the Bibles, he positioned two boxes of food with the sleeping bags on top of them. Satisfied he'd done all he could, Nick closed and locked the back door and returned to the driver's seat. Kirsten slid over to the seat beside him.

"We can only arrange so much. You'll see that it's God who gets us in. Let's do it." He started the engine and put the van in gear; their adventure was about to begin.

Chapter Two

Romania

"Father, please hurry! We can't delay any longer." Petru Potra shifted from one foot to the other, resisting the urge to stride forward and tug on his father's arm to get him to move faster.

Yari Potra stepped out of his home. He stopped for a moment and lifted his face to the sun.

Petru's eyes met his brother Jozef's over the cab of their rusting flat-bed truck. Jozef lifted his broad shoulders. "He'll come when he's ready."

Petru's hands closed into fists. "Father, it's time to leave. There's much to do before tomorrow. Please hurry."

"Ah, Petru," Yari flicked his rough fingers through his salt and pepper hair, "you were always the impatient one. One might have hoped that after thirty-seven years you would have learned more self-control."

At the reminder that his father had been a widow that many years, since the night Petru and Jozef were born, Petru unclenched his fists and opened the truck door. "I think, Father, that my impatience comes from the Slavic side of our family. Was that our mother's or yours?"

"Okay, okay," their father held up both hands, "I will take the responsibility. But only part of it. In this country all of us must learn patience. It's not only a virtue and a command of our God, it's a necessity. I shouldn't have to keep telling you two. You hear it from me in church all the time." He opened the driver's side door and slid behind the wheel.

"But people grow tired of waiting, Father." Jozef climbed into the truck after Petru.

"I do, too." His father sighed. "But we would be foolish to believe that God has forgotten us. Enough preaching. Let's go."

Yari and Jozef slammed their doors. Together, they made a formidable-looking trio, their large muscular frames covered by numerous layers of bulky clothing.

"Where are Carl Vasilescu and his friend?" Yari asked. "Aren't they here yet?"

"They're waiting half a mile down the road," explained Jozef. "When we pass them, they'll follow us at a distance, just like last week. Carl doesn't believe it's safe that we're seen together in this village."

Yari Potra nodded. "There are many eyes in a small village."

"It would be helpful to know just how many are watching us." Petru scanned the rows of houses in front of them, each with so many windows prying eyes could, even now, be peering out of.

Jozef shook his head and smacked the palm of his hand on the dashboard. "We don't need to know because we have God who has promised to protect us."

As Yari backed the truck onto the road, he pointed his finger back at the house, to a sign still nailed over the front door: POTRA & SONS—BLACKSMITHS.

"Boys, I've told you the story before, but I remind you of it because that sign remains as a symbol of God's faithfulness to us. Before I was born, back in 1920, my father and my grandfather hung that sign there. Our country was called the Kingdom of Romania then."

"Yes, but now we have the Socialist Republic of Romania." Jozef's voice was bitter. That fact was a constant unpleasant stabbing thorn in each of their hearts.

"That's right," their father continued, "and now, under communism, our free enterprise is gone, but not our spirit. I still believe that someday we may need that sign again. Until then, God gives us grace to survive each day."

The truck rumbled and sputtered up the road, heading north into the country. A half a mile from their home, they passed a similar type of flatbed truck to theirs.

Yari lifted his chin in the direction of the other vehicle. "I see that Carl has brought Alexini Radu again. That's great. He's a good man."

Both trucks carried the same load—a collection of corroding metal pipes, a number of durable tarpaulins, and several boxes of nuts and bolts. In addition, both beds held a selection of hand tools, screwdrivers and wrenches, a sledgehammer, an axe, two shovels, and a harvest sickle.

Twenty miles north-east of the city of Cluj-Napoca, and only one mile from their home in Jablonec, they entered the village of Olcea. Olcea was little more than a collection of dirty, unpainted homes lining the sides of the road. The smell of pigs, cows, and manure used in the gardens as fertilizer hung thickly in the air.

"There is the house of Mama Angelina." Jozef pointed through the windshield. "I wonder if she's watching us again."

Petru's eyes followed his brother's finger. An old woman with a heavily wrinkled face sat in a tattered armchair on her front porch.

"Bah!" their father snorted. "She's an evil woman. An informer."

"Many say that no one's life is a secret from her." A shiver ran up and down Petru's spine. How many times had the name of his family crossed the old woman's lips?

As his father drove by her home, Petru watched the woman. Her gaze didn't leave the truck as they passed.

Petru forced himself to look away and stare straight ahead. "She is looking very old."

"Yes son, but watch out. Her eyes are still sharp and she'll see any slip you make. We must always be alert. We can never let down our guard. Throughout history, the weak often perish first and the strong remain to shape the course of the nations. God is our strength. He calls us to be alert, to be on guard at all times. Don't be fools, my sons."

For several miles, long after they had traveled beyond the old woman's view, Petru felt her eyes on them, the heat of her glare burning his back. Yes, Father was right. They needed to be very, very careful.

The two trucks made a right turn off the main road and wound their way eastward up a gentle grade. The road they now traveled was little more than two parallel tracks with a rough brown strip of grass and weeds in the middle. The men sat in silence. Adrenaline coursed through Petru, and he shook out his hands in an attempt to dissipate some of it. They had waited long enough. The time for action had arrived.

The road continued to wind uphill. Following a hairpin curve to the right, both trucks reached the top of a large knoll and began the descent into a thicker forest.

Great stands of oak had claimed victory in their battle for sunlight with the birch, maple, and hickory and now towered above them. Their greenish-yellow leaves glinted and waved in the late autumn sunlight as if to jeer at their less fortunate neighbors.

At the hint of outside interference, a ground squirrel looked up from its search for hickory nuts. Petru caught sight of the tiny animal in time to see its ears perk up as it caught the sound of the faint rumble of their engines, of skidding stones and coughing carburetors. The squirrel conducted a last, desperate search and was rewarded with a large acorn, which it jammed between its front teeth before scampering to safety. Petru smiled at the sight. What would it be like to be an animal, and to have nothing more to worry about than where your next meal would come from?

The two vehicles slowed and came to a halt. Jozef got out. Petru followed him. Leaving the door of the truck ajar, he walked quietly up the road for two hundred yards, careful not to make a sound. He scanned the hard-packed soil, searching for recent tracks in the dirt. Confident they were alone, he stepped off the road to the right and disappeared into the dense thicket of trees. His head down, he studied the ground in a wide circle around the area they had stopped. For a big man, he was light on his feet, and knew how to move through the woods quietly, avoiding any twigs or branches that might snap beneath his boots. After several minutes, he returned to the truck where his father and brother waited.

Jozef was leaning against the side of the vehicle, arms crossed. "How is it?" His voice shook a little.

"We're alone. I did see tracks from a car farther up, but they look older, at least three or four days. Might even be from our visit last week."

Their father cleared his throat. "So you think it's safe to begin?"

Petru nodded. "Yes, but as before, we must hurry." He motioned to the three sitting in the other truck to come out.

With poles and tarpaulins in hand, the six retraced Petru's steps through the woods. After about 150 yards, they came to a natural clearing. An area approximately thirty-five feet by twenty feet bore no trees whatsoever, and small shrubs had already been cleared away. Great oaks grew tall along the circumference, their branches entwined overhead providing a perfect screen from any passing aircraft.

They would not need the sickle. The grass was still pressed to the ground from their shuffling feet a week ago, and the cold weather had prevented any chance of recovery. Already, there were some patches where all grass had been kicked away, revealing the dark, acidic soil underneath.

A chattering squirrel in a nearby oak, obviously bothered by the intrusion, attracted Petru's attention. Petru stopped working and held his hands out in a gesture of helplessness. "I'm truly sorry, little one. There's nowhere else for us to go. If you promise not to tell anyone, we might make it worth your while."

They made one more trip to unload the vehicles, and then commenced construction of the tent. There was not much to be done; the poles were numbered to slide and fit together in a certain sequence, and while one man held up a section, another bolted them together.

Once the framework was erect, Petru pounded wooden stakes into the ground around the tent with the sledgehammer. To these, the others tied the tarpaulins, which they draped over the piping. In another twenty-five minutes, the edifice was completed. Petru finished snugging up the ropes and checked each one to make sure it was taut.

The five men stood back and proudly surveyed their accomplishment. The finished tent stood twenty-six feet long by fourteen feet wide by eight feet high at its lowest point. In the center of the room, a ten foot pole elevated the roof, allowing for drainage in case of rain. The results of their labor seemed worth the risks. More than seventy people would jam into the tent the next day. People would come from miles around to hear the Word of God.

Petru turned to his father. "All we need is a steeple."

Yari smiled at his son. "Our steeple to draw people here will have to be our lives. We must stand out. We have to. We don't have much choice, my son."

The others returned to the trucks, but Petru hung back, reviewing the scene in front of him. Overhead, the branches of the oaks began to sway in the brisk northern wind, separating briefly before coming together again. Another chill ran down Petru's body. Had the wind caused it, or was it a reaction to some kind of premonition, a hint of something to come?

His thoughts flashed to Mama Angelina. *What is she up to? What can she even do? Had she seen what was in the back of the trucks?*

In the distance, he heard the whine of an airplane coming closer, and his muscles tensed. After a few moments, it faded away again. *It's probably nothing. I shouldn't worry.* Petru forced himself to relax.

He turned to follow his companions, but after a few steps, stopped again and looked back. *Something is wrong.*

Petru swallowed hard. *It'll be okay. Remember what Father said. You've got to trust. The Lord is our salvation.*

Chapter Three

Securitate Colonel Cornel Mihai Popescu replaced the receiver of his brass-lined custom telephone. With a triumphant smile on his face, he leaned back into his black leather swivel chair and inhaled deeply on a Kent cigarette, spoils of a recent local house search. He looked up at his guests, Officers Douru Nuvelei and Jurri Elanului.

"You are jealous of me, yes?" Popescu asked. "You hold me in contempt because I smoke a Kent. Am I right?" He allowed two jets of smoke to escape his nostrils.

His subordinates did not answer.

Popescu clutched the cigarette between two fingers and studied it. "I enjoy this Kent for one reason today. There's good news." He raised his eyebrows and looked across his oversized, teak wood desk at his men. "We're going to have some fun to-morrow." He grinned and took another drag on the cigarette, savoring the moment.

His men shifted on their seats.

Elanului finally pleaded a question. "Will the distinguished Colonel please share his news with us?"

Colonel Popescu knew he was vain, but didn't care, much like his mentor, Nicolae Ceaușescu, the leader of the nation. Once in a while, he gave the appearance of attempting to do what seemed ethically right. But many things held him back, not the least of which were the fringe benefits like smoking and trading Kent cigarettes.

Popescu glared at Elanului. Before him was an ugly man—large lips, a bulbous nose broken too many times from fighting, dark circles under his eyes, and unkempt hair. "That was our dear old friend, Angelina Mehadiei, down in Jablonec. Do you remember her?" Without waiting for a response, he propelled his swivel chair across the tiled floor to a row of four large filing cabinets, each in great need of a fresh coat of paint. He opened a bottom drawer and searched for a file. Nuvelei and Elanului took out their own cigarettes and lit them, watching their superior through clouds of an increasingly dense haze.

Although it was not yet two o'clock, the sun neared the horizon and the light in the room was fading. Winter days were too short in Romania. Over their heads, a fly-specked light bulb hung from a wire, its light even more obscured by the billows of smoke. The office smelled stale, even nauseating, as the windows were tightly shut to hold in the heat. Nobody complained though. At least not verbally.

Popescu returned from the filing cabinets bearing a large manila envelope with the name "POTRA, Yari" printed boldly on the exterior. Sweeping the strands of gray hair away from his eyes with one hand, he opened the envelope and withdrew several dozen papers and photographs. He ignored his officers and began to review the latest developments that the Potra report offered.

Colonel Cornel Popescu was a Communist at heart. He not only conformed to the system to the letter, but believed in it also, a rare thing in present-day Romania. To him, Nicolae Ceaușescu was the valiant leader of the nation, the respected son of the Romanian people. His name was synonymous with heroism—he was a secular god. Each day Popescu read his copy of *Scinteia*, the country's national newspaper, in order to follow Ceaușescu's activities.

After a few minutes, he set down the file and centered his attention once more on his officers.

"You're well aware of my obsession to eliminate Mr. Yari Potra. I have not attempted to conceal that from you. However, I wish to be careful and not simply drag him in for no reason as my predecessors might have done. We're going to put him away this time so he'll never again see the light of day. Tomorrow at noon, we will take Mr. Yari Potra into custody. There will be no mistakes. Clear?"

His men offered him blank stares.

The colonel jumped to his feet and leaned over the desk. "How did I ever get stuck with you two?" he shouted. "You let your lazy minds become like barnyard animals. You spend all your time trying to find ways to steal money from others but you don't *think*." The colonel shook his head, disgusted at the thought. *Theft is for fools with no ingenuity. Why can't headquarters send me officers with a little more wit? Ahhh, but they have.* He sank back into his chair.

"There's a new recruit, Sergeant Andrej Mumuleanu. He has come in today from Czechoslovakia. We will have to carefully educate him in our ways, yes?" He did not wait for a response. "Yes, this one we can train easily. He is quick thinking, yet cautious. And best of all, he knows when to show respect and when to keep his mouth shut." He stopped, looking sharply at the two men in front of him.

"Furthermore, this man is intelligent. You will do well to watch how he behaves. Perhaps you will learn something from him. Keep a rein on Mumuleanu," he ordered, "but show discernment." He fingered Mumuleanu's photograph. *With such abilities in this new recruit, I've got to be sure that the young man doesn't become a threat to me.*

"And before either of you gets too arrogant, just remember that the only reason I'm placing Mumuleanu in your hands is that I don't have anyone else. Under me, you two are the senior officers. You'll have to do."

Popescu picked up the receiver of a second black telephone on his desk and, without dialing, spoke into it. "Send Officer Mumuleanu in, will you?"

Andrej Mumuleanu strode into the room. He did not wait to be acknowledged, but eased his large frame into a chair next to the other officers.

This young one can be arrogant at times. Popescu thought about sending a heated look in the direction of the newcomer, but found himself in too good a mood to antagonize the man, and smiled instead.

"The three of you will work together on this one." Ignoring the scowl of discontent on Nuvelei's face, he went on. "Find yourselves ten other officers who will be on duty tomorrow. Better, make it twenty. We will take Mr. Potra and all his followers. I want no one escaping. And I don't care if any officer claims it's his day off. Get them here." He paused to let his order sink in, then added, "Get them out of church if you have to."

Mumuleanu grinned at Popescu's attempt at a joke. Popescu, catching the movement from the corner of his eye, swung his attention to the newcomer.

"You, Mumuleanu, will find a pilot and an airplane, with fuel, and equip it with a radio set. I want it ready by tonight. If you wish to succeed in this country, you must learn quickly."

Mumuleanu's jaw dropped. Good. He was aware of the immensity of the task. And of the penalties should he fail to accomplish it. Nuvelei scowled.

Popescu tilted his head. "Why are you angry, Nuvelei?"

Nuvelei stole a glance at Popescu before looking down. "I have no complaints, Comrade Popescu." His voice rasped. "I only wish to do my best."

"I'm sure," Popescu snapped. His good mood vanished as quickly as it had appeared. He jumped to his feet again and thrust his finger at Nuvelei. "Take your ugly friend and find us enough autos for twenty men. Make sure they have fuel in them to cover one hundred miles. Also, have the armored wagon ready to go. You will drive that, and you," his finger shifted to Elanului, "will drive my car." His was a new, black, four-door Dacia, a reward from the Party.

Popescu sat down again and picked up the brass-lined telephone receiver. Ignoring the officers, he dialed a series of numbers. As the ringing sounded in his ear, he stared up at the ceiling. *This room really stinks. I must get my receptionist to take care of the problem. She always…*

"Hello?" came the voice on the other end of the line.

Popescu spoke into the mouthpiece. Threats, warnings, and cursing—a typical telephone conversation. At times Popescu shouted, heat rushing into his cheeks as his fist clenched on the desk. While valuable, informers could also be ridiculously difficult to deal with. He paced the floor as he listened to the man's pathetic pleas for a few seconds. Rather than softening his heart, the informer's attempts to cajole him infuriated Popescu. When he'd heard enough, the colonel burst into a fusillade of more cursing and obscenities.

Finally, after thirty more seconds, he declared, "That's enough. We could execute you any time. You will do this!" He slammed the receiver down on the base.

He clasped his hands on the desk and contemplated his officers. "You have help, thanks to a devoted friend from the inside." He grinned again in an attempt to keep his subordinates off-guard, as the heat in his cheeks abated. "Go now, quickly. There's much to do. I'll explain the necessary details tomorrow morning."

The three men strode from his office, closing the door behind them.

The receptionist was a comely, middle-aged woman with dark hair, brown eyes, and a good figure. Mumuleanu watched Nuvelei come from Popescu's office and stare lustfully at her. When he rounded her desk, leering as he reached for her, Mumuleanu took a step forward. The receptionist was too quick for him. She rebuffed Nuvelei with a resounding backhand across his ear. Nuvelei retreated with a wide grin of amusement, one hand pressed to his ear.

"Leave her alone, Nuvelei." Mumuleanu's hands closed into fists.

Nuvelei spun around and, grabbing Mumuleanu by the lapels of his uniform, jerked him from the office into the adjacent hallway. He slammed Mumuleanu against a wall. Mumuleanu's skull banged against the plaster with a dull, wicked thud. His vision blurred, his knees buckled, and he nearly fell, but Nuvelei held him erect.

"You will soon learn to keep your mouth shut. If you want to survive in this business, if you want to live, you will show respect to those above you. You are nothing. You are dirt. Your life is sheep's dung…"

Mumuleanu looked past the finger wagging in his face at Elanului. *He's smiling. These guys are sick.* He glanced down at the hand on his chest, holding him against the wall, then up into Nuvelei's eyes. *The man is raving mad.*

With conscious effort, Mumuleanu shut out the sounds around him. *Think. You've got to think. What did your uncle teach you? Remember the training.*

Gazing into his captor's eyes, he suddenly felt sorry for the man. He was a fool, a boor.

Slowly, he made a fist with his right hand and positioned it over the back of the hand on his chest. His left hand covered his own fist and pulled it hard into his chest. Trapping Nuvelei's hand, he dropped to the ground. A bone in Nuvelei's wrist snapped as it gave way from the force.

Nuvelei screamed and fell to his knees, his mouth agape. Mumuleanu rose, walked towards the exit, then turned around.

"Don't touch her again," he said in a now relaxed and confident voice.

His gaze shifted to the receptionist standing in the office doorway, a worried look on her face. She nodded her appreciation.

Elanului bent down next to his friend. The two of them shot dark looks in Mumuleanu's direction. An intense hatred glinted in their eyes. Before either could speak, Mumuleanu turned on his heel and stepped outside.

There is much work to do. Where do I begin?

Beside him a window opened and Colonel Popescu stepped into the light.

"So, in the space of one minute, you have made two enemies and one friend. You'd better hope the friend proves of more value than the enemies. Go to work now, Officer Mumuleanu." Popescu shut the window silently.

Mumuleanu's forehead wrinkled. *How could he have known? His office door was closed. He could have heard the commotion, but couldn't possibly have seen it.* He shook his head. The man had a sixth sense to be sure. He couldn't be a colonel without having some special talent. Mumuleanu would have to be careful. Most of all, he needed to fear Popescu, for he held the reins of power.

He started down the sidewalk leading to the street. *Two enemies now and one extra friend.* The receptionist would prove useful at some point. She'd be an excellent source of information, and information was the deciding factor in this business. If Mumuleanu stayed informed, he would do well. He smacked a hand against his forehead. *I can't believe it. I don't even know her name yet. Stupid! I spent the morning in the same room with her but didn't ask. Idiot!*

He sighed. He had made a dangerous enemy in Nuvelei. Thankfully, he hadn't told many people of his past. Nuvelei was a dangerous man, but he was no match for

Mumuleanu. Nuvelei's ignorance would cost him. Now he had only to watch out for Nuvelei's revenge. Other officers under Popescu had disappeared. Not Mumuleanu. He must not.

Mumuleanu reached the end of the sidewalk and jumped on the first streetcar heading in the direction of the airfield.

Cornel Popescu rose from his chair and headed for the door. He stopped and glanced around his office. A bizarre scene. Beautiful desk and telephone. Elegant chair. A clean flag on the wall and a picture of his esteemed leader. The rest was filth. *Things have got to change around here.*

He closed and locked the door behind him. *Trust no one.* He tapped the receptionist's desk with his knuckles. "I'll return about seven o'clock, Maria. I have to visit my family, and then Angelina Mehadiei. You can leave at four if you've finished your work. Remember to lock the door behind you."

Popescu climbed into his new Dacia and turned the ignition key, enjoying the purring of the motor. He drove from the parking lot, turned onto Calea Motilor, and wound his way through the maze of potholes and pedestrians. Like so many times in the past, his thoughts focused on Yari Potra. *Without Potra as their leader, the church will die. I'm going to enjoy watching the energy get sucked from his body. Slowly.*

He smacked the steering wheel with his hand. The church was useless. A distractive organism. What could it possibly offer that the Party couldn't? The Orthodox Church had never helped him. It was a hollow shell. It consumed peoples' energy. It gave nothing in return but false hopes. *Revenge will be mine.* Which was where Angelina Mehadiei came in.

Pulling onto Cimpului Street, Popescu evaded an open manhole, shaking his head at the workman's forgetfulness as his apartment building came into view. It was older than most in the area, and therefore in much better condition, an ironic twist.

The new apartments that had sprung up throughout Cluj-Napoca had poor insulation and less heating. The inhabitants of those buildings faced a dismal situation. One such apartment block stood farther down the road from his. Pipes jutted out of most of the windows, leading to fireplaces inside, the chimneys created by the tenants.

"Papa! Papa!"

His two youngest girls, both four years old and born only eleven months apart, ran into his arms as he stepped into his warm apartment. He thought again of the Party as he scooped up both children and carried them into the kitchen.

"How are my little girls today?"

"Fine," they answered in unison.

"What did you learn in school today?" he asked, beaming at both of them.

"We played again," his younger daughter said.

"Where are your big brothers?"

"Outside."

His wife smiled broadly. "You're home so early today." She stood on her toes and kissed him on the forehead. "Who's looking after the office?"

"I left Maria there. I told her to stay until four, but she'll probably leave early. She's always anxious to get to the food lines."

"Maria?" She frowned. "You'd leave a secretary in charge?"

He shrugged. "Don't concern yourself. That's my business."

The girls played with his hair and twisted his ears and giggled. He growled at them like a bear. They squealed with delight and twisted from his arms until he set them down and they disappeared into the living room.

Ignoring their invitation to play, Popescu moved towards his wife. She was still young, her features not yet spoiled by age. Taking her in his arms, he kissed her slowly before stepping back.

"I'm not able to stay. I still have a lot to do tonight."

Her shoulders sagged as she walked back to the counter and began to prepare his dinner. "I'd expected as much. You warned me I would pay a price for my loyalty."

"Anna, long ago you accepted your situation. I admit I'm a zealot. The Party has to come before all else, including you and the family. You know that. That's the way of things; there's no alternative." He sat down at the table. "Besides, look at all the benefits the Party gives us. You don't have to line up for food like the rest of them. I take care of you."

"Thank you, Cornel. I'm not saying I disagree." She placed a plate of bacon, potatoes, onions, bread, and cheese on the table.

They talked little as he ate. Thirty minutes later, he kissed her again and walked out. Popescu sat in his Dacia, watching his three other children playing soccer on the street with a few of their friends. It would be dark soon and, to save energy, the streetlights would remain unlit. The oldest boy glanced his way and, apparently noticing that his father was watching, stopped running and waved proudly.

Colonel Cornel Popescu admired the expression of energy on his boy's face, and the way his school uniform and red scarf adorned his young body. He noticed, too, the healthy red cheeks and the way the cold wind whipped at his short black hair. *A fine son. He'd better not get sick. Even with my influence, the hospitals couldn't help much.*

He lifted his hand to wave back and the grinning boy returned to his game.

These are exceptional children. They're going to be just like me.

Now, on to visit dear Mrs. Mehadiei. Darkness approached and he looked forward to her report. He set his jaw, determined the raid would go well. No more playing. He'd had enough of games.

Chapter Four

★

The Hungarian guard lifted the first barrier from the van's path and waved the three Bible couriers on to the border post, fifty yards down the road.

In the past three years, Nick's vehicle had been thoroughly searched only twice at the Hungarian border and on both of those trips, he was not carrying any literature. At the time of the searches, he was entering Hungary solely to gather information about new contacts—a reconnaissance trip.

Nick looked back in amusement over his past three years as a Bible courier. In an ironic way, it was a good feeling to have a guard search through the entire vehicle, believing that God would keep safe the literature inside. Those searches were a reminder that, without prayer, nothing could happen. *No one* entered a Communist country with Christian books, unless someone was interceding for them. Right now, Nick was praying fervently. This time, they really did have something to hide.

The van rolled slowly into the light like a hospital patient being wheeled into an operating room. Two Dacias waited in front of them. The cars were the combined handiwork of the Romanian auto manufacturers and their international intelligence network. The arrival of the van created a slight stir among the guards. Slush and grime from the roads could not conceal all of its glitter; dark metallic-blue would always be a stranger among the off-whites, the drabs, and the flat blacks.

A Passport Control Officer, dressed in military sheepskin, approached the driver's side window, and Nick rolled it down quickly.

"*Guten Abend. Woher kommen Sie?*"

Nick smiled. "I'm sorry. Do you speak English?"

"English. English. Where are you coming from? Austria?"

"No. We're on a transit from Czechoslovakia."

The man nodded, took the three passports, and disappeared.

Jim pulled out his knife again. "How long are we going to have to wait?"

"Probably only five minutes," Nick answered, faking a stretch and a yawn in an effort to appear nonchalant. "They seem to be quite efficient here."

In less than five minutes, the same officer returned. He handed their three passports through the window to Nick.

"Do you have anything to declare? Gold?"

"Gold? That's a new one. No. I wish." Nick grinned.

The guard smiled in return. "Thank you. Good-bye."

Nick edged the van forward under a raised gate and accelerated slowly through no man's land towards Romania. How he loved to visit the Romanian Christians, their lives sustained by the power of the Holy Spirit. How he loved to drive the back roads, observing a culture left behind in time. It was a country of adventure where the unexpected and the unwanted always seemed to happen.

What would happen this night? What events would take place in the next few hours or even days that could alter the inner state of this desperate country? How many miracles in the coming week would they actually see? Perhaps a few would appear obvious. Hundreds more would go undetected, seeming like ordinary events.

No man's land, the neutral strip between Hungary and Romania, lay engulfed in blackness. Even the silver moon had fled into the cover of clouds as if it had decided there was a better land to watch over. The Chevrolet's headlights bounced erratically on the roads, turning, weaving, then suddenly pinpointing a figure against a heavy tubular barrier.

"It's like a scene in a spy thriller movie, isn't it?" Nick said. He looked at Kirsten, who only nodded. The soldier stood rigidly, feet spaced at shoulders' width, unmoving at first, his form outlined against the white background. As the van drew nearer, his flashlight switched on, its light circling slowly to signal the vehicle to a halt.

Nick stopped the van about five yards from the barrier and whipped around to face Kirsten and Jim. "Remember," he whispered, "there's not a thing they can do unless God allows it. Be assured He's got everything under control."

The guard walked around to the passenger's side of the van, shining his light through the windows onto the floor and seats. Nick studied the AK-47 assault rifle slung across his shoulder, the knife on his belt, and the intense look on his face. The guard couldn't have been more than nineteen years old. But one didn't have to be an older man to pull a trigger.

Nick's eyes wandered past the guard. To the right, something red glowed in the guards' hut. A second guard stepped from the hut into the cold with a cigarette between his teeth and a set of night-vision binoculars hanging from his neck.

The first guard appeared at Nick's window. Nick had the passports ready and surrendered them into the outstretched hand. The second guard joined the first and together they paged through each passport, scrutinizing the visa stamps from the various countries.

The guard handed back the passports and asked for cigarettes, but Nick shook his head.

"Chewing gum?" he countered. Nick handed them each a stick; they beamed with pleasure.

"Thank you. Good time."

The barrier lifted and the van moved slowly up the incline. This would be the moment of truth. There it was! The vehicle inspection area appeared cramped, comprising a passport booth, a covered stretch of pavement, and a number of concrete tables for luggage. The van rolled under the bright lights and stopped at the white line. A rodent on a research table. A guard tower rose ominously above them on their right, as if monitoring their every movement. A plain, gray building stood directly to their left, with few lights showing. For a moment, a solemn silence soaked the van. Nothing moved. A stillness came upon them.

Then the guards appeared.

At the same time, in the small city of San Rafael, California, a middle-aged man stopped preparing his noon meal, gripped by the urge to pray for his daughter. He didn't know why God had brought Kirsten to mind, but he felt he had to pray. What was happening to his girl in Europe? What was God taking her through at this moment that prayer was of such necessity?

For five minutes he let his preparations sit, and he lifted up Kirsten before the throne of mercy. "I'm not exactly sure how to pray for my Kirsten, Lord." He voiced his prayer without embarrassment. No one would hear him anyway. "What a privilege it is to know that she's serving you and that she has dedicated her life to you. She's growing up so fast. When she wanted to go to Europe to serve you, it was so hard to let her go, because I've always been her protector. You know she is strong of will, just like her mother. And maybe just like me, too. Thank you that your voice reached her and that she has listened to your call. But I really miss her. She is such a joy to me. I don't have to remind you of these things. I'm glad that you're the one looking after her and not me. I just pray that you would bless her with strength and wisdom and health, and may she be an encouragement to everyone she meets.

"Lord, send your angels to surround and protect my girl. You know how we worry too much." He opened his eyes. "And guard her heart. Give her wisdom with those two young Canadian men, Nick and that other fellow… what's his name? O Lord, thank you that you know who they are. Protect the Bibles too, Lord. What a blessing it is that Kirsten can take your Word to all those who've never been given the chance to read their own Bibles."

He went back to his tuna salad, but his mind remained on his daughter and his prayers continued. Something was happening. Something serious.

Four men approached—a Passport Control officer in a dark blue uniform and three Customs officers in olive-brown colors. One youth wore blue pants—that one Nick recognized as a trainee. The new recruit at the border would be walked through a thorough search. There could be problems. This time it might not be so routine. He continued to pray, remembering that the guards could do nothing unless God allowed them .

The officer in blue came to the window and took the three passports from Nick. "*American. Canadian. Canadian. Wohin fahren Sie?*"

"Speak English?" Nick asked, willing his voice not to shake.

"*Nein. Wohin? Wohin?*" His voice rose.

Nick turned to Kirsten and Jim and raised both hands, palms up. "Do you understand what he's saying?"

Both Kirsten and Jim shook their heads. They watched a master at work. Nick's German was strong, but he preferred to speak only English at a border. It put the guards at an immediate disadvantage and took away the possibility of slipping up in his second language.

Nick turned back to the guard and shrugged. "English?"

The guard stomped off.

The customs officer came to the window. "*Zoll kontrolle. Baggage hier.*" He pointed to a stone table between two pillars to the right of the van.

The couriers climbed out of the van and removed their luggage. The suitcases, the sleeping bags, the boxes of food for their contacts in Romania, the coolers holding their own food, the tool kit, spare blankets, and lastly the box of Bibles with the tire chains covering them were all hauled to a stone table.

The van stood empty and the three guards swarmed around it. The trainee was shown how to check the seats, knock on the wall panels, check behind the vinyl on the roof without ripping it too much, and how to stomp on the floor. So far, the search had been quite basic.

One guard walked around the van, knocking on the side panels. At one point he stopped and his interest appeared to intensify. Clearly he thought he had discovered something out of the ordinary. The guards inside the vehicle stopped their search and began talking in hushed tones.

His stomach tight, Nick walked up to Jim and asked quietly, "Will you watch those guys inside? Make sure they don't wreck anything." He concentrated his attention on the guard inspecting the outside of the vehicle. The guard knocked on the gas cap before motioning for Nick to open it.

"Are you serious?" Nick retrieved his keys from the ignition and unlocked and took off the cap.

"Heroin? Cocaine?"

"No! No, we're tourists. What is this?"

The guard walked away from the van and into the office without acknowledging Nick's comments. *That's strange.* He went over to talk to Kirsten. She sat in the midst of the luggage, shivering.

"I don't think these guards speak English," Nick said. "I guess we lucked out. You doing okay?"

"Sure," she replied, and jerked her head in the direction of the van. "Here's your friend again."

The guard returned with a coil of spring wire. A tiny device was attached near one end. It looked somewhat like a fishing lure with diminutive metal pockets. The man stalked to the gas tank. "Cocaine?" His question was more of a statement. He smiled confidently, and inserted the wire into the tank.

Nick leaned close to Kirsten and whispered, not too softly, "Sometimes these guys irritate me so much. Try and think of a practical joke we can play on them to lighten them up a bit."

Kirsten smiled. "Do you think he has a name?"

"Ask him."

"No way. You do it."

The guard drew back the line, still smiling as though he believed he would find something. The end of the wire came out gleaming under the dim lights. Lifting it to his nose, he sniffed it carefully.

"Hmmm. Benzine."

Nick offered him a told-you-so grin.

He sobered at a loud noise from the inside of the van. The trainer was attempting to remove a panel on the driver's side, near the rear of the vehicle. The wooden panels had been riveted to the metal and would only come off with extra force. He shouted something to the men on the outside.

The guard next to Nick faced him. "My name is Officer Bulboci," he said in clear English. "Drive your auto into the first garage on the right. Now."

Nick blinked at the guard's use of English. He jumped into the driver's seat, started the engine, and followed the guard as he walked into the garage.

For nearly ninety minutes, the three guards combed every square inch of the van. They removed every visible screw. They searched behind every wooden panel. They took the seats out and checked them thoroughly. They lifted the floor mats and prodded at the carpet. They hoisted the van up and inspected the underside. They found nothing, and their frustration was evident.

"Change money and get out of here."

One of the officers gave their passports back. Nick shoved them in his jacket pocket and scooted off to buy Romanian currency as fast as he could.

As he hurried back to the van, his muscles tensed. The trainee guard had wandered over to Jim and Kirsten and was inspecting the luggage. His searches appeared cursory, but both Jim and Kirsten looked worried. *Stay cool, guys. Don't arouse their suspicions.* He made his way to them and smiled. Thankfully, their faces both cleared and they managed tentative smiles in return. Nick shifted his attention back to the guard. If the man so much as lifted the tire chains, he would discover the Bibles.

The guard gestured for Kirsten open her suitcase. Her fingers shook as she fumbled with the zipper, and Nick rested a hand on her back. After Kirsten's suitcase, there was only a gym bag and a camera case left to search before the box of Bibles. Kirsten moved forward. Nick dropped his hand. What was she doing? She went to one of their coolers and withdrew a can of cola. Nick's shoulders relaxed. *Good idea, Kirsten.* He nodded at her as she pulled the tab. The guard spun around at the hissing sound. Kirsten tossed him another can.

A shocked look came over his features. "*Nein. Nein…* " He peered around her, obviously checking to see if any of his colleagues were watching.

Kirsten moved closer to him, took the can from his hand, and opened it for him. She took a sip before handing it back to the guard. That seemed to satisfy him.

With an effort that must have nearly burned a hole in his throat, the guard downed the cola in one attempt. He grinned and burped, then smiled and walked off.

Nick grabbed Kirsten's arm. "Quick, let's get this stuff put away and get out of here."

Together they loaded the box of Bibles and the luggage into the van then piled into the front seat. One guard in front of them raised the metal gate and they cruised through. Nick stomped on the accelerator. They reached another guard post, but the soldier simply checked their passports and waved them through.

They had arrived. They had made it into Romania!

Excitement erupted inside the vehicle. "Praise God! Hallelujah!"

Back in California, Kirsten's father opened his eyes and got up from his knees. The battle had been long, two hours or more, but he sensed a victory. He smiled and returned to his workshop.

The roads were not good and the Chevrolet van had to swing wildly to miss some of the larger potholes. Jim and Kirsten stared, wide-eyed, at the houses lining the road, shrouded in darkness. Nick grew aware of a tangible sense of overpowering heaviness. This was the land where the infamous Vlad Țepeș once lived. Vlad the Impaler, known in the West as the evil Count Dracula. What surprises would Romania hold for them? What could they expect to see tomorrow? *Or even tonight?*

Both Jim and Kirsten gazed out the window, their noses nearly touching the glass. Nick smiled at their excitement. "Romania is a country of the unexpected. Things you expect to happen won't, and things you might never dream of will appear before your eyes. If you're not paying attention, they'll be gone in a flash and you'll miss out on some extraordinary experiences. You've got to keep your eyes open in this country, or strange things may happen to you."

The road came to a T-junction and Nick instinctively turned south on Highway 79 in the direction of the city of Arad. "We'll be able to make it as far as Hunedoara tonight." He stretched his arm along the back of the seat. "Tomorrow we can get up at a normal time and make it across the country to Bacau. If we make a drop tomorrow night, we'll be doing fine."

Jim rubbed his hands together. "I don't think I'll be able to sleep at all. I feel like I could keep going all night."

Kirsten nodded. "Me too."

Nick glanced back over his shoulder at Jim. "Romania has a weird effect on one's mind. It's like no other country I've visited. Tonight you're both fascinated.

That's obvious. Tomorrow will be the same. The next day, Wednesday, you'll begin to grow frustrated. That may not be caused by any one major event but by a bunch of irritating occurrences. A couple of days in that mode and your anger will begin to rise. That's when you know it's time to leave. You enter a *get-me-out-of-here-as-quick-asyou-can* stage and it's a good sign to head for the border."

Jim frowned. "Really?" He glanced out the window again. "I can't imagine feeling that way."

Nick nodded. "For the first year I went through this process every time I came here. Trust me, it will happen. After a while you anticipate it, and your mind somehow deals with it so things aren't as traumatic. I love Romania now. I'd live here if it were possible."

"Not me." From the passenger seat, Kirsten cast a sidelong glance at Nick. "There's probably no pasta salad here."

He elbowed her and laughed. "For a California girl, you have limited tastes. You'll get over it."

"It's not limited taste," Kirsten hit him back. "it's *discerning* taste. Maybe you need a little more of it."

At Arad they turned east onto Highway 7. Jim took over the driving and within two and a half hours they arrived in Hunedoara. Midnight had slipped past moments before and few cars were on the streets. The streetlamps and traffic signals had long been turned off to conserve electricity. Storefronts blended together in the dark; the drawn curtains across the display windows gave each shop a similar appearance.

A pair of policemen patrolled in the shadows and as the vehicle approached, they stopped and stared, as though the sight of the van was the highlight of their boring evening.

One took a step towards the van, but Jim drove past him deliberately, turned one corner at Nick's instruction then another, and arrived at the Hotel Dacia, named, like the country's automobile, after the barbaric Dacian tribes who had settled in Romania a few years before Jesus Christ was born in Bethlehem.

With luggage in hand they entered through the smoked-glass double doors and approached the reception desk. A woman jumped off a man's lap and hurried behind the counter, her cheeks red as she straightened her skirt and did up the top button of her blouse.

"One single room, please," Nick said, indicating Kirsten, "and one double room. If it's not too much trouble."

Chapter Five

Even through all the changes of World Wars I and II, and the restructuring of the Eastern Bloc orchestrated by the Soviet Union, peasantry had evolved little over a thousand years in this part of Europe. Communities were razed and rebuilt a dozen times and children still ran naked in the streets. The ladies in black gowns, scarves, and beige stockings still sat doing their embroidery. The men in unwashed suits, their faces unshaven, still waited at the roadside for nothing at all, but lethargically watched the days turn to years.

Through this same setting, Petru rode with his family to their church. Somehow, in the weird sense of a time warp, they escaped the lackadaisical sweep of things, even if just for a few hours.

From his vantage point in the middle of the seat, squeezed between his father and brother, he peered through the front windshield, checking to see if Mama Angelina sat in her usual chair. The chair was empty today; the wind whipped leaves crazily across her porch like tiny, brown balloons released when their knots were untied. In the ditch just past her house, Petru's attention centered on two bent old women hacking madly at a wind-fallen tree with dull-bladed machetes. One of them turned at the sound of the truck's engine, her eyes rolling and staring wildly without really appearing to see anything, her mouth agape, and her few teeth bared in a devilish grin.

Petru shuddered at the sight of her and focused his eyes back on the road. His father eventually turned right off the main road, followed the track through great stands of trees, and drew up behind a line of Dacia automobiles and horse-drawn carts. More had come this week than last. His father's face lit up, as though he was excited about the potential. No doubt he believed God would do great things today in this church.

With Bibles in hand, the three of them wound their way into the forest in the direction of the makeshift building. More leaves had fallen from the trees overnight, maybe too many, and Jozef frowned. Petru followed his gaze up to the bare branches. He could understand why his brother was concerned. Cover was scarce. None of them liked to meet in the tent. As far as they knew, they were only Christian group in the country who were forced to, but the *Securitate* had closed their previous church and left them with few options.

The Potras entered a crowded tent. Yari immediately went to the front and mounted the makeshift platform. Petru followed Jozef into a pew constructed of a plank laid across two stumps. His father liked to sing, and after a rousing hymn he led them into worship through five more songs. The Holy Spirit came in power and Yari began to preach.

"It was early morning. Jesus, battered by the palace guards, close to exhaustion from a sleepless night, and nearing a state of shock, was taken before Pilate in the Praetorium in the city of Jerusalem.

"It was here, brothers and sisters, that he was stripped of his clothing and flogged with a whip by a Roman soldier. It was here that they threw a purple robe across the ribbons of his shoulders and jammed a crown of twisted thorns into his scalp.

"It was in this state of agony that he was forced to carry that heavy wooden cross up to Golgotha. And it was on the top of that hill that nails were driven through his hands and feet and our Lord was lifted up to die."

Petru stood at the door of the tent and listened to his father preach in his authoritative voice. He scanned the room, doing a quick head count. Nearly eighty. His chest tightened. If the authorities came, there would be no way to pretend they were doing anything but gathering together to worship God.

Winter had crept upon them as it did each year. Maybe this week it would snow and the remaining leaves on the trees would drop suddenly. They had the elderly and the children to think of, and this building afforded them no heat. Would someone volunteer his home? Petru's thoughts went to some of the other churches that functioned openly in the nearby city of Cluj-Napoca. *Why did his father's church have to remain so covert?* He knew the answer, or at least part of it. It was a personal vendetta, some colonel in the *Securitate* plaguing his father. Yari would never tell them the real issue, but it certainly went deeper than he let on. Petru focused on the sermon again.

"… Who for the joy set before him endured the cross, scorning its shame, and sat down at the right hand of the throne of God. Consider him who endured such opposition from sinful men, so that you will not grow weary and lose heart." Yari looked over the faces before him. Petru followed his gaze; the people seemed alert and eager to learn.

"Turn with me now to Galatians chapter six, verses nine and ten." His father paused a moment, the silence broken by the sound of the turning of pages. "Let us not become weary in doing good, for at the proper time we will reap a harvest if we do not give up. Therefore, as we have opportunity, let us do good to all people, especially to those who..."

The drone of an airplane grew louder and louder until, with a vibrating, thunderous swoop, it forced him to stop speaking. Yuri looked up instinctively, as did others in the tent. Some cocked their ears as if to determine the purpose of the interruption. *Are they coming?* Petru slid off the end of the bench, stepped outside the door of the tent, and searched the skies, but the plane was gone.

Silence. From where he stood, Petru could see that everyone in the tent had turned to look back at him, their eyes filled with anxiety. What could he say to ease their concern? His own back muscles had tightened up and he couldn't get them to relax. He scanned the woods, searching for the unexpected. What could it be? Something was not right. Something did not fit.

With quick, quiet steps he circled the tent. He and his brother must look for a new place this week. Petru arrived back at the opening in the tent. There were just too many... He froze.

Three men stood in a gap in the brush about thirty yards away, two of them in uniform. An older man stood between them. Even at that distance, Petru could tell that one held a higher rank. He stood squarely, his feet separated at shoulders' width, his hands clasped behind his back. A gray leather trench coat was belted at his waist, but his head was bare and the gentle breezed tousled his silver-streaked hair.

The officer smiled, spoke a word, and the other two policemen started forward.

Petru spun towards the tent door, but other figures emerged from the maples on his left, then six or eight more, farther ahead and to the right. They were surrounded. He entered the tent. "The *Securitate* are here." No one responded. No doubt they had expected as much.

Pastor Potra lifted a hand. "I believe I have about ten seconds left. Remember in Ephesians it says, 'Therefore, as we have opportunity, let us do good to all people, especially to those who belong to the family of God.' We are in God's hands, my friends."

All eyes were glued to the doorway as two policemen appeared with pistols drawn. Petru tore his eyes from the intruders and scanned the body of believers. How would this day change the life of every one of them? He tried not to think of the persecution that would follow, but he could not stop his mind from contemplating it.

How many would be interrogated and beaten in the next few days? How many would lose their jobs or be demoted? How many would be forced from school?

From between the two policemen stepped the officer of higher rank. He pointed at Yari. "You! Outside now. The rest of you will wait here."

Yari Potra stepped away from the small wooden platform and walked past the officers into the cold air. Without his coat, his suit jacket flapped in the wind. "My coat. I need my coat." Someone thrust it at him and he pushed his arms into the sleeves. Two officers seized him by the elbows and shoved him around the side of the tent.

Petru followed. What would they do to him? His stomach churned. He stood to one side, watching. Recognition flashed in his father's eyes; he knew the officer in front of him. Petru studied the officer. The lines of the man's face may have been hard once, but they had softened with age and easy living. The leader had dark hair streaked with silver, and deep brown eyes, almost black.

"Popescu," Yari declared.

"Your memory serves you well, Comrade." The man nodded at the soldiers holding Yari's arms. "Beat him."

"No." Petru lunged forward, but two other soldiers grabbed his arms and yanked him back. He struggled, but they only tightened their hold. One reached for the gun strapped over his shoulder and Petru stilled.

A fist drove deep into his father's kidneys, buckling his knees. Petru felt the force of the blow as though he'd been struck himself. *Fall down and curl, Father. Protect yourself.*

His father's eyes rolled back in his head and he crashed to the ground. Petru fought a wave of nausea. Laughter resounded. An airplane buzzed. Someone cursed.

Don't open your eyes, Father. It will start again.

"Father?" Petru whipped his head sideways. Jozef. *No, stay back. Stay back.* "Jozef!" The scene played out in front of Petru like a movie in slow motion. A choking shout and the sound of running footsteps filled the air. Then a shot. The thud of a body hitting the earth. A vacuum of silence in the aftermath. The buzzing grew louder. A movement near him. A grunt of pain.

"Jozef?" Petru shook off his captors and rushed towards the prone body.

Jozef did not respond.

"Oh God. Help us!" Petru cried out.

Colonel Popescu gestured to the men holding Yari. "Bring me the other son."

They dragged Petru over to stand before the man his father had called Popescu. The men continued to hold his arms tightly, taking away any chance of retaliation.

Popescu drew his own pistol, raising it slowly until the end of the barrel touched Petru's forehead.

A surge of fear rolled over him. "But, but, you…"

Popescu pressed the cold barrel of the gun deeper into his head. "Quiet! If you interfere as your brother did, you too will be shot." He turned to one of his men. "Arrest the three of them and take them to the detention center on Highway 1. Take the names of the rest and begin the house searches as soon as possible." The eyes of all the officers were on him. "Now!" He waved an arm through the air and the soldiers scattered. "And don't forget to confiscate their Bibles."

Popescu jerked his head at one of the men who clutched Petru's arms. "Nuvelei, take another officer and the brothers with you. I'll take Elanului and Comrade Potra in my car. You will follow us."

Popescu stalked over to Petru's father, lying still in the long grass, and nudged him in the side with his boot. "Comrade Potra, I know that you're awake now. Stand on your feet or you'll be hit again."

Yari opened his eyes. Petru glared at the colonel. How did the man know his father was conscious? His shoulders slumped. It mattered little now. His body felt numb and he was near the point of not caring.

"I can't move." His father's voice rasped. "I'll need some help."

Popescu pointed to an officer next to Yari. "You. Get him into my car. Be quick about it."

But another officer came forward and reached Yari first. The man bent down and picked Yari up easily using a fireman's lift. He turned with Petru's father on his shoulders and walked past Popescu, grinning.

"No problem, boss."

"Mumuleanu. How did you get here so soon?" Popescu demanded.

"I flew," Mumuleanu said with a smile.

Jozef sat up, holding his left shoulder. His eyes met Petru's. I'm okay, he mouthed. Petru doubted it. The bullet appeared to have entered his back and come out the front, near his shoulder, judging by the blood stain spreading across his white Sunday shirt. Petru pressed his lips together to keep from retching at the sight. Jozef struggled to his feet and soldiers pushed him and Petru to a waiting militia vehicle.

The two were jammed into the back seat by a medium-built officer with a cast on his left hand. He slammed the back door, slid onto the passenger seat, and turned to point his pistol at Petru and his brother. The look in the Security officer's eyes told Petru they weren't about to escape.

The driver's door opened and the large, muscular man who had lifted their father so easily sat down heavily. He looked back at his prisoners.

"My name is Andrej Mumuleanu and I am your driver."

Smiling broadly, he started the engine and followed the black Dacia pulling away in front of them.

Petru watched the power struggle before him. Mumuleanu threw a glance at Nuvelei, the officer who had shoved Petru and Jozef into the back seat. The man's face grew red. His eyes seemed to bulge and the hand holding his trembled. The barrel of the gun waved ominously before Jozef's face and Petru tensed, ready to leap forward and knock it from the man's hand if he appeared about to squeeze the trigger.

Nuvelei's gaze dropped to the gun he held, as if contemplating a shot, then he shifted the barrel slightly towards the driver, a movement barely detectable. Nuvelei's hatred for the man who had lifted their father so easily was almost palpable. The vehicle bounced and swerved erratically on the dirt track, then made a long hard left turn back onto the main road. Nuvelei's body molded against the door. The gun swung forward. The car straightened out and increased its speed.

The driver held out a small cardboard box to the other officer. "Cigarette?"

"W-what?" Nuvelei stammered.

Mumuleanu shook the box. "Cigarette? Do you want a cigarette? It looks like the events today have played havoc with your nerves."

Nuvelei placed the gun on his lap and took a cigarette. Mumuleanu handed him a lighter. It took him three tries, but he finally lit the cigarette and drew in a long puff. He kept his eyes on the driver, appearing to study him. "There will come a time," Nuvelei said, blowing out a cloud of smoke that swirled along the roof of the vehicle, "when you will regret your actions of yesterday and today. Remember to keep your eyes open from now on."

Mumuleanu geared down as he entered the city limits and drove on the cobblestone streets of Cluj. "Yes, I'm sure I'll have to," he replied, reaching for the lighter and dropping it back into his shirt pocket. "Thanks for the warning."

Petru glanced at Jozef. The driver had an arrogance that bordered on recklessness. No wonder there was trouble between the two. Could they use that somehow? He forced himself to focus on the city. They passed the run-down Central Hotel in the city centre. He'd never been inside, but had heard tales of how disgusting it was. Cockroaches, ugh. St. Michael's Roman Catholic Church stood squarely on his left and he gazed at its closed wooden front doors. A stab of pain shot across his chest. It too, must have seen happier times. They soon left the city limits, driving north, and reached the Cluj-Napoca Military Centre a few minutes later.

The black Dacia entered the gates followed closely by the militia car. Petru stared at their new surroundings. He had been here before. Nearly twenty years ago, he and Jozef had served in the Romanian Armed Forces, and this was their base. Some new buildings had been added, but it remained largely unchanged. In the few seconds before the car ground to a halt, Petru studied the layout of the base carefully; the knowledge might come in handy.

He stared through the front windshield as two soldiers came forward, spoke briefly with Colonel Popescu, who had exited the vehicle in front of them, then dragged their father from the car and into a long, low building. "Out." The officer holding the gun waved it towards the back door of the car. Jozef shoved it open and stumbled out. Petru followed him.

Popescu rubbed his hands together in apparent glee as he approached them. "You see, the powerful arm of the *Securitate* extends even into the military. You are all my prisoners and therefore you owe your existence to me. You will live here until I decide your next course in life." He motioned to the driver, who had climbed out of the car and stood behind the two brothers.

"Bring the two this way," Popescu ordered Mumuleanu.

With the other officer, Nuvelei, behind them, the driver followed Popescu, leading Petru and Jozef past five similar low buildings, turning a corner, and mounting the steps of a large brown-bricked edifice. The bars on each of the windows meant a prison. Petru had heard stories of the atrocities behind these walls. A lifetime ago it seemed, he had even witnessed prisoners being tortured in similar buildings and now, as he climbed the steps, his heart sank. *God, how are you going to get us out of this one?* A terrible thought struck him. Would God hear him now?

The only sound that broke the ominous silence as they marched through a long dark hallway was the clicking of their heels. Flakes of plaster on the walls trembled as they passed by, and some gave up the battle to hold on and fell. The stench of mold suffocated him and it worsened as they descended a flight of stairs. Popescu selected a key from a ring, opened a cell door, and looked at Jozef. "This, Comrade Jozef Potra, is your new home. Good-bye."

The driver shoved Jozef forward. He hit the far wall only eight feet away. Petru's fists clenched, but the barrel of a gun being shoved in his back kept him from attacking the large man. The door shut in Jozef's face, the key turned in the lock, and darkness swallowed him.

Popescu faced Petru in the dim light, a smirk on his face that Petru longed to wipe off. "Come with me, please," he said.

Petru followed him up the stairs and out into the sunlight, blinding after only a few minutes in the darkness.

"You're free to go now. Thank you for your assistance. Perhaps I'll find you again in the future. Yes?"

Petru stared at him a moment. He was free to go? "My brother needs medical assistance."

Popescu's smirk widened. "We will take good care of your brother, don't worry."

Why doesn't that make me feel better? Petru waited a moment more, until the gun dug into his back again. He wouldn't help anyone by staying here. If he left, maybe he could come up with some sort of plan to break his father and brother out of this place. His shoulders slumping, Petru walked quietly through the front gate. His forceful capture at the border to freedom only three months earlier flashed through his mind. His accomplices had died; he alone had survived. Was it happening again? He was a traitor to his family and his God. Which was worse?

Barely reaching his ears came the curse of a guard and the simple but repulsive words, "There goes an informer."

Chapter Six

★

The blue Chevrolet van, its color now dulled with the grime of the roads, wound its way from Hunedoara, across the flatlands of the Transylvanian basin and through the Carpathian Mountains towards the city of Bacau, the home of Stan Dumitresti. The music from the car stereo played endlessly, this time selections of Tchaikovsky's *Swan Lake*. Jim sat quietly in the passenger seat, lost in thought.

He glanced over at Kirsten, who was driving. "Why did you come here?"

She jerked the wheel then straightened the vehicle and shot him a heated look. "Warn a girl before you spring something like that on her, will you?"

Jim grinned. "Sorry." Obviously she'd been as lost in her thoughts as he had been. "I really do want to know though."

She bit her lower lip. "I've asked myself that question a lot, actually. I mean, obviously if you and Nick were going on an adventure, I didn't want to be left out."

"Obviously." Jim chuckled. It had always been that way. If one of them had an idea, the other two had to get involved, no matter how crazy it was. *And this one has to be the craziest of all.*

"But if you two weren't here, would I want to stay and continue this type of work? Can I honestly say that God is calling me to Eastern Europe?" She pressed a hand over her chest. "Do I have a compassionate heart for Christians in the Eastern Bloc? Or do I just love the company of the two of you?"

Jim lifted his shoulders. "What's not to love?"

She offered him a wry grin. "Exactly. As to the rest, I'm still trying to figure all that out. I do know that returning to school after taking the semester off to come here will certainly seem dull. I'll miss you guys."

"What, specifically, will you miss?"

Her eyebrows rose. "In need of an ego boost today, are we?"

Jim just smiled.

Nick leaned forward from the back seat. "I'd like to hear this too."

Kirsten blew out a breath. "All right, here goes. I'd miss you, Nick, because you are philosophical and poetic, and I admire your confidence, your ability to lead, and your adventurous spirit. Enough reasons for you?"

Nick clasped his hands together between their two seats. "An adventurous, confident, philosophical poet. I can live with that, yes."

Jim laughed, but his stomach muscles had tightened. What would she say about him? He'd often wondered if she considered either of them more than just a friend. Would she share any hints of that here? They were going deeper with this conversation than they'd gone in a while, on a personal level, anyway. When Kirsten didn't speak, he cleared his throat.

She punched him lightly in the arm. "I'm getting to you. Just organizing my thoughts. She shifted a little in her seat. "Okay, got it. What I'd miss about you, Jim, is how easy-going and patient you are. I definitely need someone like that in my life. And while you might not be as intellectual as Nick ..." Nick snorted from the back seat; Kirsten ignored him, "... you are more practical and very loyal. And you have a lot of courage. All of which is going to make you an excellent—"

She slammed on the brakes and Jim pressed a hand to the dashboard to keep from flying forward. What had she been about to say? Smuggler? Boyfriend? Husband? He pressed his lips together in frustration and looked out the window. Six young children had run out to the road to wave at them. Homemade knitted stocking caps covered their heads and each child seemed to be dressed warmly. "Gummi, Gummi," came their pleas for chewing gum. Kirsten dug into the bag on the floor between their seats and pulled out a handful of Bazooka bubble-gum. After rolling down her window, she tossed the gum outside and the children scrambled frantically in the snow. Jim shifted his gaze from the children to her. A look of pure joy settled on her face as she watched the kids digging for the treats. Whether she knew it or not yet, this was where God had called her. Even if he and Nick left, this was where she needed to work, at least for the time being. So where did that leave him?

Nick squeezed her shoulder. "What a great way to breed dissension among the masses," he said with a wry smile.

Kirsten frowned. "How so?"

"You're teaching them to be unhappy with what they have. You're giving them something they can't get in this country. As they grow older, they'll learn more and more that good things come from the West and are only available in the West. I guess it's inevitable that unhappiness will come. Throwing gum may just be the first stage in that progression." Nick patted her shoulder before leaning back in his seat.

"You always have to take the intellectual approach. I think it would be wrong to deny them a moment of happiness when it's in our power to act," Kirsten replied.

Jim touched her elbow. "I agree."

Nick shrugged. "I'm not totally disagreeing with you. Here, let me have some too." He rolled down his window and pitched a few to two young boys. One of them grabbed a piece and raised it in his clenched fist in a gesture of victory.

Jim raised his fist back. Whatever the long-term implications of their simple act of kindness might be, the happiness in Kirsten's eyes and on the faces of the children made them well worth it, as far as he was concerned.

When Nick and Kirsten had rolled up their windows, they started down the road again. Should he bring it up? The moment had passed, but with a long drive ahead of them, maybe they could get it back again. It was now or never. Jim turned in his seat to face her. "So, what were you going to say?"

Her brow furrowed. "When?"

"Just before you stopped for those kids. You said all those amazing qualities of mine were going to make me an excellent ..." He held his breath.

"Oh, right. Police officer. I was about to say you are going to be an excellent police officer."

"Ah." A tinge of disappointment shot through him but he pushed it back. He did want to be a police officer, and it felt good to have that affirmation. He settled back in his seat. "Thank you." Their headlights reflected off a hand-painted red triangle on the back of yet another horse-drawn cart. Jim sighed. They had been warned about the poor driving conditions.

"Nine hours of driving." Kirsten smacked the steering wheel. "And we still have over sixty miles to go to Bacau."

Clearly the conditions were taking a toll on all of them. Jim calculated in his head. "That means that, since Hunedoara, we've only averaged about 25 miles per hour. That's ridiculous."

She whipped her head around to look at him. "Are you ready to drive?" She let go of the wheel with one hand and swept it through the air with a flourish. "Let's see what you can do."

Jim sat up, ready for the challenge, but Nick stuck a hand between their seats. "You can drive now, Jim, but take it easy. We're not in a competition. Kirsten! Look out!"

She slammed on the brakes again. Not that it would take much to slow them down, given the speed at which they were traveling. A cattle truck crawled across the road in front of them. A cow lifted its tail unceremoniously, heard the call of nature, and left watery evidence across the front of the van. Kirsten slowed to a stop. "Oh, great! Do you believe this?"

"Let Jim take a turn, Kirsten. Give yourself a rest."

Jim climbed out of the vehicle and the two of them switched seats. He wound his way along the slopes of the Carpathians and soon discovered the source of Kirsten's frustration. With half his time caught behind a number of crawling Roman diesel trucks or horse-drawn carts, his patience crumbled like a piece of cheese set upon by a bunch of mice. He gunned the engine and sped past a truck. Kirsten reached for her seatbelt.

Nick clapped a hand on Jim's shoulder. "It's getting to you, isn't it?"

Jim drew in a steadying breath. "What's that?"

"The fascination is gone already and you're getting upset. It's obvious the people on the road are getting on your nerves."

Jim nodded. "It's not just the other vehicles on the road, it's that going through village after village is maddening."

He braked suddenly as an old lady drove a large hog into his path, clearly in an attempt to protect the remnants of what had once been her vegetable garden. Farther ahead, a horse, ribs protruding from its sides, hobbled across the road, its front legs tethered together with a short length of rope. It stopped on the pavement and contemplated its descent into a ditch. To their right, a motley collection of chickens, goats, and geese paraded beside the road.

"This is like driving through a barnyard." Jim loosened his grip on the wheel as he guided the vehicle past all of those animals and down the Eastern slopes of Mount Nemira. Kirsten had called him easy-going and patient and he desperately wanted to live up to her assessment of him. Two hours later, as the sun passed its winter peak in the early afternoon, at the town of Gheorghe Gheorghiu-Dej, Nick took over the wheel and turned them northward to Bacau.

"What a name," Kirsten said. "Gheorghe Gheorghiu-Dej. Where did they ever come up with that?"

"He was the leader before Ceaușescu," Nick said. "They tell a story here that, when he was the president, a couple of Christians came up to him and told him that Jesus loved him. He had them put in prison, but on his death bed, he remembered their message and accepted Christ as his personal Saviour. Some say he was a worse dictator than Ceaușescu."

"There's hope for everyone," said Jim, staring out the window from the back seat at the bleak fields dusted with snow.

The cold, north wind thrashed about the van unmercifully while the moon and bright stars without number shone their lights from the heavens. Pine forests surrounded them, the trees cloaked in darkness as if attempting to protect some hidden secrets. They emerged from the cheerless hills three miles from Bacau and made their descent towards the city.

Nick broke a long silence. "You know, it's time to ask for the Lord's protection and guidance. Let's take a moment right now."

Jim and Kirsten bowed their heads.

"God, once again you know our situation," Nick prayed. "You know what we hope to accomplish this evening. God, you know that we're doing it for your glory, to build up your church, to encourage your people, and we ask for your blessing to be upon us. I thank you that nothing will take you by surprise tonight. I thank you that you're in control and that you already know the outcome of this evening. We ask for your protection, not only for us, but also for Stan Dumitresti when we give him the Bibles. Please protect us from the eyes of the police and from the people on the streets. We pray for victory tonight. Thank you that you're with us always."

When he finished, Jim and Kirsten both declared an enthusiastic "Amen."

Kirsten pointed towards the front of the vehicle. "Hey, you guys. Look ahead." Jim followed her finger and his chest tightened. Two militia officers stood next to a police car at the side of the road. As they drew closer, one walked to the middle of the road. He turned on his flashlight and motioned for them to halt.

Nick stopped the van next to the officer and rolled down his window. The man scrutinized him and said something in Romanian that sounded like a demand of some sort. Nick just looked at him and asked, "Do you speak English?"

"Passports!" came his stern retort.

Jim reached into his coat pocket and pulled out his Canadian passport. He gave it to Nick, who took it and added it to his and the one Kirsten had held out to him, and handed all three to the officer.

The officer did not even touch them. Kirsten's passport, with the American crest and the "United States of America" stamped on the front cover was on top of the pile and he glanced at that and waved them on. Nick pressed his foot to the gas pedal and the police control post faded quickly from view behind them.

"The power of the American passport." Kirsten took it back from Nick and dropped it into the bag at her feet.

"The power of God too," replied Nick. He made a tight turn onto a narrow and dilapidated street. Jim looked for a street sign on the corner building but found none. Ahead, the lighting was even poorer, but the headlights managed to highlight the worst potholes in enough time for Nick to avoid them. Cars lined the road, parked mostly on the sidewalks next to homes. From somewhere down the street a dog barked and another soon joined the first.

"Stan's home is two blocks farther down and another two south of here," Nick said. "I hope he's there."

Jim leaned forward. "He doesn't know we're coming?"

"No, the less communication the better." Nick pulled to the side of the street and put the van in park. "All right Kirsten. This time, if it's okay with you, Jim and I will go and make contact. Everyone takes their turn waiting on a drop, right? Will you be all right here?"

"Sure. Go for it." She crossed her arms and leaned her head against the seat, as though settling in for a nap.

"Okay then. It's now 7:30. Wait here until midnight. If we're not back by then, go to the first parking spot you find on the road to the town of Roman. Wait there until three o'clock tomorrow afternoon then leave the country if we still haven't returned. We'll find our own way home."

Jim's stomach twisted at the thought of her having to find her way across country and back home on her own, not to mention what that would say about his and Nick's fate, but Kirsten hardly blinked. He forced himself to relax. This was the way of things. They all knew what the risks were before they came to Romania. Nick looked back over his shoulder. "Have you got your passport and your emergency money, Jim?"

"Right here." Jim patted his coat pocket.

"How about a flashlight?"

"Got that too."

"Good, then let's go." They pushed open their doors and climbed out of the van. They rounded the front of the vehicle and stopped in front of Kirsten's open window. Her face shone pure like alabaster in the dim light of the street. "It's hard to leave you," Nick said. "Even for a few minutes."

"It's hard for me, too."

For a moment, Nick rested a hand on the arm she had folded on the door frame. Then he pulled away and he and Jim stepped into the street. They walked quickly, staying off the sidewalk. They would be more visible, but it was something a Romanian would do.

"I think she loves you," Jim teased as he walked beside Nick.

"Great," Nick replied, sounding definitely sarcastic. Then he whispered, cutting Jim off from further conversation, "No more talking. We can't risk being overheard."

Jim continued walking in silence. Would Nick ever open up to him, or anyone for that matter? *We've known each other for over two decades. We've been best friends for almost as long, and Nick still won't let me know what he's really feeling.*

At the second corner, they turned and strode down the road. Behind them a dog barked relentlessly from someone's front yard. Off to the right two men stood together, smoking cigarettes and talking quietly in the darkness.

One more block. A child darted out of nowhere, followed by two of his friends. All three of them ran past the two men and disappeared down an alleyway between houses. Farther up the street, on the opposite side, stood Stan's house. A man and a woman appeared at the gate and walked towards them.

Jim leaned close to Nick. "Maybe that's them," he whispered.

"Ignore them. Keep walking."

The couple passed by on the sidewalk without so much as a glance at the two young men on the street. When they were within twenty yards of the house, Nick and Jim crossed the street to the sidewalk. Were they being followed? Jim glanced back, but couldn't see anyone.

In fact, the street appeared mysteriously empty as they approached the courtyard door. Nick checked the number on the gate, nodded, and Jim rang the doorbell. *Would Stan even be home? Was that him and his wife who had just left?* It was too dark to tell. Footsteps sounded on the pavement on the other side of the gate. The door opened and a face appeared.

Nick stepped forward. "Stan Dumitresti?" he asked.

"Hello Ralph." The man inclined his head. "Come in, please."

Jim followed Nick into the courtyard where Stan held out his hand. Jim gripped it firmly. "Hi, I'm Max."

Stan was a small man with a tight, careful smile. "Max. Hmm. I've had three different men named Max visit this month. And now a fourth? Which one are you?"

"I am Ralph's good friend," Jim explained.

"That is all I need then. Please, both of you, come inside."

Nick and Jim entered a small, warm kitchen; Stan followed close behind. A robust, middle-aged lady stood in front of a tiny stove. Her rosy cheeks and smiling eyes offered a radiant greeting to their guests.

A long wooden table, covered with a simple white tablecloth, stood to the right of the door. Around it sat six children; the older three, in their early teens, smiled sheepishly at the newcomers. The younger ones appeared focused on the bread, the goat cheese, and the sliced sausage in front of them.

"Please sit here." Stan pointed to two seats at the table. "Welcome to our home."

"We have sixty Bibles for you, as well as food, vitamins, and aspirin. If it's okay with you, we'll drive our van into the courtyard and then Max and I and our other friend can spend some time talking with you."

Stan raised a hand and shook his head. "We've had some problems with police quite recently. They now know I receive Western visitors, and my house is being watched more closely. However, it will be okay for you to park at my church. Do you know where it is?"

"No, I haven't been there before," Nick replied.

Stan pulled a piece of paper and a pen from a shelf. "Here is the main street going towards the center. Here is the center of town. And here we are." He made an *X* on the sheet. "Drive back to the main road, turn right, and the church will be about five or six hundred yards down on your left. If you give me ten minutes, I'll have the gate ready to open for you. You can't miss it. It's the only building on the whole street that looks like a church."

Jim and Nick walked back to their van, around the block in the opposite direction so they could approach it from a different direction than they had headed off in. Kirsten had fallen asleep on the middle seat, but Nick's rap on the window woke her. She unlocked the doors with a sigh of relief and the two slid into the two front seats.

Nick wasted little time speaking. "We have about two or three minutes and then we're going to his church."

"Oh good. I guess I fell asleep. I'm sorry."

"Could you not watch just one hour?" Jim reached for his seatbelt.

"I already said I was sorry."

"Hey, I'm just kidding. Don't worry about it."

They waited three minutes before Nick started the engine and moved the van forward in the dark. After half a block he switched on the headlights and turned left at the first corner, then left again. At the main street they headed for the town center. Jim leaned forward to peer out the front windshield. The dim, wavering lights of the city stretched out before them.

A siren sounded in the distance. Its annoying wail broke the silence of the night, lending the small town a sudden air of chaos. They passed a factory on the left. Its gates stood wide open and workers on the late shift poured out, trudging off in all directions like tired zombies.

Under a bus shelter, three soldiers sat singing, one strumming a worn guitar. As the van passed, they all stopped and stared.

Nick pointed to the church up ahead on the left.

The siren continued in the distance. A tiny, flashing blue light cast surreal shadows on square apartments.

"I don't like this, Nick." Jim reached over and grasped his friend's forearm. "That siren makes me nervous. This whole situation feels a little off."

"You're right. But this is a dangerous country." Nick slowed the van as they approached the church.

A militia car appeared a few hundred yards in front of them, coming at them at a high rate of speed. Kirsten gripped the seat in front of her. "Oh Lord, we're goners. We've had it."

Nick's knuckles turned white as his fingers tightened around the steering wheel. "God, help us out."

Jim let go of him and stared out the front window. Only fifty yards to the church.

The militia car raced to their side, its tires screeching.

Chapter Seven

The blue light was disorienting and the noise ear-splitting. Nick yanked the wheel and pulled the van off to the side of the road. The militia car skidded to a halt behind their vehicle, then veered back onto the road and continued with a roar down the street.

Nick's heart pounded in his chest. How could that be? He had geared himself up for the worst, for disaster. He looked back over his shoulder. The police car had stopped not more than a hundred yards from them. Already, in the strange blue light, he could see two officers dragging a third person into their waiting car.

People converged on the scene of excitement. The soldier with the guitar and his two friends hurried past with the others, completely ignoring the dark blue van in plain sight. Nick glanced in the rear view mirror to check on Kirsten.

"I was sure they were after us." She pressed her palms to both cheeks. "I can't believe it. We must have guardian angels sitting on top of this van." She poked Nick in the arm with one finger. "C'mon. Let's get going before we're noticed."

Stan Dumitresti waited at the gate and he swung it open as the van approached. Nick drove the vehicle through the narrow entrance. A small, rutted narrow lane led around behind the church. The towering edifice on one side and a tall hedge on the other provided complete cover after Stan shut the gate. Nick used only the parking lights as he guided the van close to a back door. Staying out of sight was one habit Nick did not care to break, even if Stan had promised safety.

All three couriers jumped out of the van and closed the doors behind them quietly. Stan approached them and gestured towards the building. "We're safe here. We can bring the goods inside and talk there. It will be fine."

They carried the Bibles, food, and bottles of vitamins and aspirin into the church. In a small office they heaped their precious goods on a desk as Stan stood back and beamed. "Friends, this is another miracle. Three weeks ago I received a large load of food. Two weeks ago it was books. Already they have all been distributed. Thankfully, you have brought more. Come, let's sit down."

He led them from the office, locked the door behind them, and took them into a similar office across the hallway. At the door, he held a finger to his lips. Once they had all entered, he flipped a radio on, lifted a black telephone from the desk, and placed it in a nearby drawer. "Just in case," he said.

Nick glanced around the room. Was someone monitoring their conversation? He sighed. Anything was possible here.

"Please, sit." Stan gestured at three wooden chairs facing the desk. He sat down on the chair behind the oak work desk as the three of them settled themselves. When they were sitting, he looked at Kirsten. "I am glad you've all come to my town. I've met your two friends, but what is your name?"

"I'm Cathy." Kirsten reached to shake Stan's outstretched hand.

Her eyes filled with warmth. Nick wasn't surprised. With his bushy white eyebrows, his round-framed spectacles covering intense brown eyes, and his receding hairline, Stan Dumitresti bore a strong resemblance to Kirsten's father.

"It's my pleasure that I could come, believe me," she said.

Stan focused his gaze on Nick. "How are you Ralph? It's been a long time."

"Yes," Nick replied, "perhaps a year. I'm doing well, keeping very busy, of course."

"Ah. I remember the first time you came to see me. You were very nervous. Your hands were shaking. It is different for you now, yes?"

"One gets used to it. There are still times when I get really scared—like tonight."

Stan peered over the top of his glasses, his eyebrows raised. "The police can certainly be unpredictable. Tonight has been no exception."

"Your English is much better, Stan." Nick leaned forward and clasped his hands on the desk.

Stan nodded. He looked pleased at Nick's observation. "I'm glad you noticed. It was very interesting for me. I was given opportunity to study at the University of Cluj for three months last spring."

Nick's eyes widened. "How did you manage that, considering your position in the church and your age? I mean, no offense of course, but I didn't think they allowed elderly men into universities here. Especially a pastor."

"Brother, let me explain to you the way it is. My abilities in English and also in German are essential in my position. Nearly every week I receive visitors from the West who wish information on the state of our church, the political system, and the everyday needs of the people here. For me to communicate these needs effectively I had to learn English. There is no one who visits me who conscientiously learns the Romanian language so they can help me."

"In our own defense," Nick replied, "we are also working with Bulgarians, Czechs and Slovaks, and Poles. We can't learn every language sufficiently."

"I understand that and I don't condemn you for it. I am simply stating a fact. For me to enroll in the University at Cluj would normally be impossible for the reasons you stated. Why should they let me when I'm a threat to their system? Last Christmas I approached the Chief of Police in Bacau asking for permission to study in Cluj for three months. For three kilograms of coffee, he consented. For three more, the Director of the University accepted my application for enrollment."

Kirsten crossed her legs. "Is that part of the black market that we've been hearing is so prevalent here?"

"That's correct. It is sad to observe that Romania is in economic ruin. But it is my firm belief that without the unofficial economy—the *black market* as you call it—the country could not function. There would be no chance of life. People would not get enough essentials and would simply starve.

"In our province of Moldavia, it is hard for me, especially as the pastor of this church, because this region of the country is quite legalistic. I am the one who must set an example for those in my church. Many, many people believe it is a sin to have any dealings at all with the black market, or to use a bribe in any way whatsoever. In other areas of the country, it is not such a big issue among Christians. The church leaves it up to one's individual conscience. My guess is that a vast majority of Romanian Christians are involved to some extent in unofficial transactions. It is the way of life here."

"Is that an issue many Christians struggle with?" asked Jim.

"Certainly. Our standard in the church remains the same over the years; the Bible says that we must obey God rather than man."

Jim nodded. "I don't envy you the decisions you face."

Kirsten uncrossed her legs and stood up. "Excuse me, Stan. I really have to use the bathroom. Can you please show me where it is?"

Jim chuckled. "That's right. It's been almost an hour. You're overdue."

Stan led the way from the office and Kirsten followed him. At the door, she turned back and stuck her tongue out at Jim.

"I think she likes you, Max," Nick said after they had gone.

Jim frowned. "Do you think so?"

"Not really." Nick grinned and pointed to himself.

Stan returned to the room and sat down again. He had not lost his intensity as he picked up the conversation where they had left off. "Brothers, as I was saying, it is very hard for us to do anything in Romania that's not illegal. They have taken away our options."

Nick frowned. "In what way?"

"Well, it is now illegal for us to teach our children about God. This past summer a friend of mine in Bucharest led a group of over one hundred children to the mountains and conducted a week-long Bible camp, teaching them about God's Word. Mid-way through the week, they were discovered by a policeman who demanded a bribe of one kilogram of coffee. He could sell that for twelve hundred *lei* in Bucharest, or at your rate of exchange, about 130 dollars. That's ten days of wages for him. My friend gave him the coffee and the policeman never reported them.

"Now, do you understand the implication? If my friend had refused to give the bribe, he could easily have been put in jail. His family would have been persecuted. Each child would be harassed at school and maybe none of them would ever make it to the university level. Some of their homes would be monitored.

"So I ask you, was my friend right in offering the bribe? Many Christians believe that my friend did not offer a bribe, but theoretically paid a fine. Was I right in offering the bribe to the University Director? Or do I consider the coffee an extra fee that the authorities levy on Christians?"

The two Canadians were silent.

"I must tell you," Stan lifted both hands in the air, palms up. "I don't even know the answer to that question. But that is how it is done."

"Out of curiosity," Jim asked, "what else can be used to trade on the black market? Just coffee?"

"Coffee is the main item." Stan lowered his hands. "It disappeared from the shops years ago and is not officially available now. It's the same with laundry detergent, cooking oil, spray deodorants, and underwear. We can't normally buy these things, which, of course, makes them the most effective currency."

Kirsten returned at that moment and Stan leaned back in his chair, waiting for her to be seated. "What did I miss?" she asked. "What are you talking about?"

"The black market, Cathy." Nick waved a hand through the air. "We'll fill you in later. Keep going, Stan."

"Many people like American cigarettes." Stan drummed his fingers on the desk, "particularly the Kent brand. They're what you might call a… how do you say… a package deal. They're an excellent way to exchange favors and a status symbol in one. I have heard that a Romanian who smokes a Kent is like an American who lights his cigarette with a dollar bill."

Kirsten shook her head. "I guess it's hard for me to understand the workings of a black market because I've never grown up with that. In California, some are involved in it because of the money that can be made, but it's not as visible because everything essential is readily available."

"And non-essential," chipped in Nick.

Stan stopped drumming and pressed his hand flat against the desk. "Bacau is like many cities in Romania in that every person is placed on a hierarchical list. A Christian who is known by the officials as such will usually be at the bottom of the list and will be denied services like medical aid, unless he has something to trade. For example, we have a ten-year-old girl in our church who is diabetic. In the past, she has been denied insulin simply because she is a Christian. A small package of coffee given to the doctor solves that problem. She receives her insulin."

Nick sagged against the back of his chair. He knew Christians were discriminated against, but to hear a real-life example of a child being denied life-saving medication because of her faith really drove that home. His thoughts whirled. Was there more he could do to help?

Stan sighed. "Fourteen percent of Romania's population is over sixty years of age. Most of them are treated like second-class citizens. If they have to call for an ambulance, they'll need something of value so they can bribe the paramedics."

"That's absolutely ridiculous!" Kirsten smacked a hand on her knee. "It's unfair."

"Yes, it is," said Stan, "but this is an evil land we live in. The leadership is rotten. The country runs on deceit. How is a Christian supposed to live and breathe under this system?"

Kirsten shook her head.

"You have just brought us food and Bibles." Stan jerked his thumb in the direction of the room across the hall. "If I were to keep the law, I would have to go to the police, report your visit, and tell them who you are and everything we said. You would be blacklisted from Romania. People from all over are bringing us food, because without help we would die."

A knock sounded at the back door. Nick froze, but Stan stood up and whispered, "Wait here. I'll see who it is." He left the room, turning off the light and closing the door. The three were left in total darkness.

"Great," Kirsten began. "Now what are we—"

"Shhh!" Nick grabbed her shoulder. "No noise," he whispered.

He listened, muscles tensed, as Stan and another man spoke in muffled tones for a minute. Then a door closed and footsteps approached the office. The door opened and Stan flipped the light switch. "I am sorry. A friend. We get many visitors here." He held up his finger. "I have something to show you."

From his breast pocket, he pulled a small ration card. "This is what we have been able to buy this entire year. I will read it to you. Understand as you listen that this is for my family of eight." He began to list off the quantities.

"Sugar, ten kilograms…"

Kirsten held up a hand. "What's that in pounds?"

Stan offered her an indulgent smile. "For our American friend, I will translate. Sugar, twenty pounds. Cooking oil, oh… ten quarts. Flour, twenty-five pounds. Cornmeal, thirty-five pounds. Eggs, twenty-five. Sausage, four pounds. Meat, forty. The meat," he stopped and looked up from the card, "comprises no beef, just twenty pounds of pork and twenty pounds of chicken. I think that most of the chickens had died of starvation. There was little meat on the bones."

Stan handed the card to Kirsten. "That's all the government has officially allowed us."

Kirsten studied the card. "But aren't there grocery stores where you can buy other items like cheese or fruit or vegetables?"

Stan threw his arms in the air. "You can see for yourself what we have. Fruits and vegetables can only be bought from the illegal peasants' market where the prices are unreasonably high. Cheese is of low quality and only available sporadically. Listen to this, my dear sister. Three years ago, the government declared that Romanians were overweight, so they passed a law that said bread must sit on the shelves for two days before it can be sold. Crazy, no?"

Nick rubbed the side of his hand across his forehead. "I read an article in an American magazine some time ago, and it referred to a Romanian official who explained that the reason for the long lines outside the food stores is that Romanians have so much money they'll line up all day to spend it."

"Ah, you smile at that, Ralph, but it's partially true. Most of us have money to spend. But when something appears in a store, we know it won't be there long and if we don't get it then, it might not be there for another three or four months. And no one shop sells every product. One shop will sell meat. Another jams and bottled fruit. Another bread. Another flour. We must line up at each shop, sometimes all day, to buy the food we need to survive.

"Just because an item is shown in the store window, it doesn't mean they have it, or will sell it to you. The procedure must be learned. Relationships must be built. We must learn how to ask for something, or how many times we must ask, before they will sell it to us."

Jim clasped his hands behind his head. "Have you managed to learn the system?"

"Yes I have," Stan said, his breath escaping with a sigh, "but there's a dichotomy involved. On one hand I thank God for the arrangements and the contacts in the black market that I have made. On the other hand," he paused, contemplating the ration card Kirsten had handed back to him, "there is a sense of shame involved. I don't know if it's right, but there is no other way."

Nick leaned forward and spoke quietly. "Stan, it's getting late and we still need to find a hotel. Tell me what we can do for you. How can we help you further?"

Stan held up three fingers. "First, you can pray. Second, you can pray again. Third, you can bring us more food and Bibles."

Kirsten asked, "How many Bibles can you distribute? Will a hundred be enough? A thousand?"

"Two weeks ago I received five hundred Bibles. They are already gone. We could use another five thousand."

Nick closed his eyes. Five thousand Bibles. How could they possibly purchase that many? And even if they could, would they be able to smuggle them over the border? It would almost certainly take more than a can of cola to accomplish that feat.

☭

As Nick walked into the lobby of the Hotel Moldova in Bacau, he glanced around at the 1950's decor and nodded in approval. The Romanian tourist brochures had listed the hotel as first class, and it did appear to be. They were fortunate. This remained one of the nicer hotels in Romania. Hopefully, they would be given a room.

High-backed brown leather chairs graced the carpets in the lobby and Jim and Kirsten expressed their admiration for the sophisticated styling as the three of them headed for the reception desk. Nick didn't blame them. Like them, he'd heard all the stories of the dumpy hotels in the country before he'd arrived his first time, but obviously a few fine establishments still remained.

At the reception desk, a young lady with fire-red hair and horn-rimmed glasses took their passports and money and handed them each a form to fill out.

"We'd like two rooms, please. One for us," he waggled a finger between Jim and himself, "and the other for Miss Frey."

"Yes, yes, of course," the lady replied in a weary tone.

After they had filled in their home addresses, passport numbers, and other personal information, the receptionist placed two keys on the counter. "Room 611," she stated in hesitant English, passing one key to Kirsten, "and room 616 for Mr. Conrad and Mr. Barham."

Nick smiled pleasantly at her. "Thank you. Good night." He turned away and clapped his hands together. "All right! We've got us some rooms. Let's go and get our bags from the van." The three walked over the red, imitation-Persian rugs in the lobby and out through the glass doors. Close on their heels came a smartly-dressed, middle-aged man in a dark suit.

"May I help you with your luggage?" he asked, his English precise, the intonation of his speech cultured. Nick whirled around to look at him, and something immediately triggered in his mind. *Be careful. There's something suspicious about this guy.* The man was clean-shaven, even though it was midnight. And his hair was just a little too perfectly coiffed. Short, like a policeman might wear it. *Or maybe a secret policeman?*

Nick led him to the side door of the van, away from the remainder of the Bibles. "Yes, we would be glad for your help. Here, you may take this suitcase for us." He handed the man one of the suitcases and he, Jim, and Kirsten removed the two coolers of food and the rest of their luggage. The less left in their van for thieves, the better. The Bibles would have to remain, however. It was too much of a risk to carry them openly.

When they returned to the steps of the hotel, a policeman stood guard. That was to be expected. All of the major hotels typically had one, day and night. But where had he been five minutes ago? The hair on the back of Nick's neck prickled. *Something's not right.*

They crossed the lobby to the elevators and entered one. The man in the dark suit went before them and stood farthest from the door. As soon as the door shut, he leaned close to Nick and whispered, "You came to Romania as tourists? You have just arrived?"

"Yes, that's right." Nick pushed back his shoulders. Why was this man so interested? The stranger leaned closer. "Do you have Bibles?"

Nick blinked. His immediate thought was, *Of course! What do you think I'm here for?* He kept his mouth shut. Fortunately, so did Jim and Kirsten. Clearly they were letting him take the lead in this bizarre encounter.

The man glanced around, as though someone else might have entered the elevator as they talked. "You see, I am a Christian. Do you have some Bibles for me?"

He sounded so hopeful, Nick was tempted to give in. He waited a second before answering. "Of course not. We are just tourists."

The door opened. Nick grabbed the suitcase the man had been carrying and gave him a one-dollar bill for his help. "Thank you. I can manage it." The three of them stepped out with their luggage and the door closed behind them on the man in the dark suit. As they walked down the hallway, Nick spoke again, his voice low, "The rooms will be bugged. Count on it."

They stopped at room 611 and carried Kirsten's luggage inside. The room appeared comfortable and clean, with two single beds and a small bathroom. The walls were covered with a felt paper, gray like much of the country; the thick, red, floor-to-ceiling curtains showed a hint of color coordination. "Lock your door," Nick advised, "and leave the key turned in the lock. That should prevent anyone from using their key or breaking in. We're going to stay in hotels as much as we can because it's safer than the van. In Czechoslovakia, there weren't many criminals running around on the streets but here there are."

"Also it's cold out there," Jim added.

"We'll see how long our money allows us this luxury." Nick set Kirsten's bag down on the bed. "When there's no more money, we'll sleep in the van for the night."

He lingered for a moment, not wishing to leave her. Finally, Jim walked out, but Nick hung back. From his gym bag he pulled a small, canister-like object. "This is an air horn," he explained to Kirsten. "If you have any troubles at all, give it a blast and we'll come running. It can be heard a mile away, so don't worry." He grinned. "See ya' in the morning. We need to be on the road by 9:30. Can you be ready by nine o'clock?"

His question was rhetorical and Kirsten smiled her reply. Nick leaned close, drawn to the longing in her blue eyes and struggling to control his emotions. He rested his hand on her arm and whispered, "You did great today. I'm proud of you. And I'm glad you're here. Maybe someday I won't have to leave you."

Kirsten blushed and pushed him through the doorway. "What do you think you're saying to me, young man? You'd better get out of here. I'll be fine."

Nick retreated, picked up his suitcase, and winked.

"Nick," Kirsten said in a soft voice.

"Yeah?" He swung around to face her.

Her eyes peered out from a crack in the door. "I'm glad you're glad I'm here. Good night."

The door shut and Nick meandered down the hall to his room. Jim waited by the door, shifting his weight from one foot to the other.

"What was that all about?" Jim cocked his head. "Is there something going on I should know about?"

Nick tried helplessly to stifle a grin. "Uh uh." He slid the key in the lock and opened the door. "I hate to leave her, Jim," he said, the grin fading.

"Me, too." Jim followed him into the room.

"No, tonight was especially difficult. I have a bad feeling about this place."

"Really? Are you sure you aren't just tired? It's been a long day." He threw his suitcase on one of the beds and wasted no time heading for the shower. Nick *was* tired, but still, sitting on his bed, he could not resist. With a mischievous gleam in his eyes, he leaned close to the telephone. "Red dog Rover. Red dog Rover. We have a situation alert. The chicken is plucked. I repeat, the chicken is plucked. The camels have left the Alfa Romeo." He grinned at his own sense of humor. "Let's see if that brings them running."

Nick entered the shower soon after Jim finished and within twenty minutes they lay on their beds with the lights extinguished. For a while, Nick tossed and turned, his eyes open, staring at nothing, his mind slow to relax. He needed sleep. Already he could hear the even breathing of Jim in the other bed.

For a long time he lay there, disquieted, staring at the ceiling. *So much happened today, and not the kinds of experiences they prepare you for in the average Canadian high school.*

He turned again then bolted upright as a noise shattered the silence in the room. "The air horn, Jim!" He leapt from the bed and tugged on the jeans and T-shirt he'd tossed over a chair. "The air horn." *Oh Kirsten, we're coming.* He sprinted for the door. *God, let her be all right.*

Chapter Eight

★

Nick darted out of the room in time to see an immense man dressed all in black shove his shoulder against Kirsten's hotel room door. The wood cracked on its hinges, but failed to give way, even under the intense strain. The air horn continued to split the air. *How is that not driving him away?* Nick's chest squeezed. He must really want to get to Kirsten for some reason. "Hey!" He bellowed the word in an attempt to be heard over the ear-splitting racket. Other doors along the hallway cracked open as he sped by, but he didn't slow down.

The figure glanced in his direction before fleeing towards the stairs, reaching his hand up twice to shatter two uncovered light bulbs. He hit the stairs in darkness and was gone.

Nick raced to Kirsten's doorway, Jim on his heels. He stopped and rapped on the door, resisting the urge to pound on it in case he scared her even more. "Kirsten?" The air horn continued, becoming almost unbearable. Jim raced off in the direction the man had fled. Nick covered his ears, waiting, and soon the blasting ceased, leaving in its wake a frightening hush.

"Kirsten?" Nick rapped again. "Kirsten, it's me. Open the door."

After a short pause, the door opened a crack. Terrified blue eyes peered into Nick's. "It's okay, he's gone," he said.

Kirsten flung open the door and rushed into Nick's arms. Her body trembled. Nick held her tightly and stroked her hair, trying to calm her. "It's okay. It's okay. It's all over. Tell me what happened."

"It was awful. I had just finished praying and was dozing off to sleep when I heard something at the door. I thought maybe it was you or Jim, and I asked who it was, but no one answered." She stopped for a moment to catch her breath, wiping the tears from her eyes.

"I was terrified and I prayed, 'Dear God, please protect me' and... and I saw the door handle rattle back and forth, but the key was in the lock like you told me, and then I remembered the air horn. I was so scared and confused. I just didn't want him to get in. Why would anyone want to come in here? Why would anyone want to hurt me? Oh Nick, I can't stay in here by myself tonight. This place is just evil. I want to stay with you and Jim."

Nick wiped the tears off her cheeks and pulled her close again. "That's okay. You can stay in our room. Everything's going to be okay. Hey, you wanted adventure. Put that in your journal," he said, trying to ease her tension.

Jim walked into the room, followed closely by the receptionist and the man in the dark suit. "What kind of place is this anyway?" Jim thrust his arm in Kirsten's direction. "Look at her."

The receptionist shook her head. "Oh, we are sorry. We are sorry."

The other man examined the door and stepped forward. "What did this person look like, young lady? Did you see him?"

Jim spun around and flung his hands in the air. "What do you mean? You were the one I met on the stairs when I was going down. You had to see him. You can't tell me you didn't see anyone coming down the stairs."

"I saw no one. I think you are making this up. She must have had a nightmare. Now look, the other guests are awake."

"A nightmare?" Jim shouted. "Look at this! Does this look like a nightmare to you?" He dragged the man by the lapel of his jacket to the door and pointed to the shattered wood. "Call the police. We're going to report this."

Nick walked over to Jim. "Jim, relax. The police won't do anything. They're a joke. Leave it be. This isn't Canada."

"Are you serious?"

"Yes. Let's call it a night. Grab a mattress and pull it into our room."

"You can't do that," protested the receptionist.

Jim glared at her. "Watch me." He picked up a mattress and shoved by her and the man, bumping the man into the doorway of the bathroom.

In room 616, the three bedded down for the second time that night. Nick spoke into the darkness, "Forget our schedule. Sleep as long as you like. There's no point in us going out without rest."

For hours after he'd made the pronouncement, he stared up at the ceiling, too much adrenaline coursing through him to sleep. From the sounds of creaking springs and light breathing, his two roommates were having a hard time settling too.

Finally, just as a dull light petered into the room between the heavy red curtains, Nick finally drifted off into a fitful sleep.

After a late breakfast the next morning, they prayed and resumed their journey through the rugged Moldavian Carpathians, this time more to the north through Piatra-Neamt and Gheorgheni. It was high noon and the cold mists still hung in the mountains, unbothered by the winds and the hint of more snow. In places, the road wound through colossal splits in the rock and the blue van was dwarfed on either side by hundreds of feet of sheer cliff. Occasionally, a narrow river appeared close to the road, running more slowly than in the summer, its edges already covered in a thin veil of ice. Several times, without warning, the river broke away from the road, only to appear a few miles farther upstream.

"In Cluj-Napoca this evening," Nick rested his arm on the steering wheel as he drove, "you'll hopefully meet a young woman named Cristea Greceanu. Her father is a widower and was recently sentenced to eleven years in prison, likely for his involvement with the Christian church. There are a lot of details we need to find out."

Jim had been staring out the passenger side window, but he shifted now to face Nick. "This woman lives alone?"

"Yes," Nick replied, elbowing Jim in the arm, "and she's very good looking. I want you to control yourself."

"Thanks for your concern." Jim laughed. "You, too."

Nick raised his eyebrows. *I've only got eyes for one woman.* "That won't be a problem."

At the Hotel Central in Piatra-Neamt they purchased large quantities of sugar, flour, coffee, and other basics in the *Comturist* store, a shop where only foreigners could buy goods with Western currency. The clerk gave them no problems and asked no questions. Nick tipped her with a half-pound of coffee and she remained happy and quiet.

The roads became increasingly treacherous near Gheorgheni, and Nick slowed the van to a crawl. He glanced down at his watch. It was nearly two o'clock and they would be fortunate to arrive in Cluj by seven that evening. No matter, they weren't in a big hurry. Experience had taught him the hard way that it was better to arrive late and safe, than not at all.

He searched in his rear view mirror for Kirsten, but didn't see her. "You back there, Kirsten? I've hardly heard from you all day."

She sat up and folded her arms on the back of the seat in front of her. "Sorry guys, I don't mean to be unsociable. I guess I just have a lot on my mind."

"Are you thinking about what happened last night at the hotel? Anything we can help you with?"

"No. Actually it's about something Stan Dumitresti mentioned. I'm conflicted about some of the issues he talked about."

Nick met her eyes in the mirror. "Such as?"

"I was thinking primarily about his offering of bribes to the officials to go to school. Something tells me it's wrong and another part of me tells me it's necessary. My mind can't sort it out."

Jim looked up from his Robert Ludlum novel and focused his full attention on Nick. Nick grimaced. This was a complicated issue. He took a moment longer to choose his words carefully, searching for a way to help Kirsten without telling her what she should think. "That, my dear friend, is something which I forever ponder. It's not that I don't have peace about the way I act. I just like to keep a constant check on my motives. Whatever stand I take, at least a third of the people in my home church will disagree with me."

"Why is that?" Kirsten asked.

"Because they're complex matters that aren't necessarily black and white. If each person is looking to God as his final authority, and God is unchanging, yet Christians still disagree with each other, then it's clear that we see things through different eyes. You grew up in California, went to one type of church all your life and were taught by a multitude of different men and women, both in church and in school. I grew up in a small Canadian city, I was taught by a completely different set of men and women and lived through completely different experiences. I see the world differently than you do, but that doesn't mean any of us is wrong."

"Well, except maybe for Jim," Kirsten joked. Jim reached back over the seat and gave her a playful slap on the knee.

Nick blew out a breath. "We may never achieve perfect unity on a lot of ethical issues. I think, though, as long as we continue to search for answers and try to view situations from others' perspectives, it'll give us a greater sense of confidence in the decisions we make."

"Confidence would be good." Kirsten offered him a wry smile.

Nick nodded. "To take it a step further, what happens when Ceaușescu creates laws specifically to frustrate the Great Commission? What must our response be? How do the Christians in Romania respond to laws like those?"

Jim stretched an arm along the window frame. "The Bible says that we must obey God rather than men."

"There's where the problem lies." Nick stepped on the brake as he approached a slow-moving truck in front of them. "If we're going to fulfill the Great Commission, that includes coming to Romania. But in doing so we place ourselves in extremely tough ethical situations. Is it ever right to tell a lie, for example?"

Kirsten shifted to the front of her seat. "What's the difference between telling a lie and acting out a lie?"

"Good question," Nick said. "Is there any?"

No one answered.

"When we write on our visa applications that we're coming to Romania as tourists, we're deceiving them. We're not tourists. We're missionaries bringing in Bibles. If we tell them that, though, we'll never get in. If they asked me at the border, 'Do you have Bibles?' and I said 'Yes', they would confiscate them, ask me who I was going to see, then turn me around and point me in the direction of home."

"It's important to interpret the question then, isn't it?" Kirsten pursed her lips. "Do I have Bibles? or Do I have Bibles that I am free to tell you about if I want to obey Christ's command to take the gospel into all the world?"

"Exactly. If you tell them the names of the people you're going to see, can you honestly expect God to intervene with a miracle so the police don't go to them, when you know that Scripture teaches that miracles are exceptional occurrences? Can you or I ask God to supernaturally intervene each time, including in situations where we have knowingly put others in danger?"

"So," Kirsten clasped her hands together and tapped them against her chin, "what you're saying is that it's possible the motivation and circumstances behind me deceiving the Romanian border guard justifies that deception."

"I guess I am." Nick nodded. "Hey, look!" He jerked his chin to the left where an obese Babushka prodded a monstrous sow, nearly as big as she was. "Have you ever seen anything like that?"

"Where's my camera?" Jim searched under the front seat.

Nick caught Jim's arm. "Can't do that, Jim. Remember? No photographs until we've seen our last contact. The police are skittish here about cameras. We can't chance them pulling us in for taking a picture of something they think could be important when it really isn't."

"You're right." Jim straightened up. They drove slowly past the interesting pair before speeding up and continuing their drive towards Cluj.

Jim leaned forward to stretch his back. "Are you saying that saving a life creates a higher moral obligation and makes it okay to tell a lie?"

"In most instances I'd say so."

"Any exceptions?"

Nick thought about it a moment. "From my perspective, martyrdom, for one."

"Good point," said Kirsten.

"Thanks." Nick grinned.

"I think the most important focus should be to understand the heart of God," said Jim. "What would God do in that certain circumstance?"

"So what process do I have to take to help me arrive at my own stand?" Kirsten asked.

Nick pursed his lips. "I think the first step goes along with what Jim just said. You have to understand the heart of God. From there you're faced with two levels of decisions.

"As it says at the end of Hebrews chapter five, you must decide as mature Christian what is right and what is wrong. Dealing with Romania, it becomes very complex because there seems to be a variety of conflicting rules of action that must be considered when deciding on what is right. It's clear to me, though, that your decision is an individual one, but you must keep in mind that you're a Christian and there are basic principles that you must follow.

"Knowing what's right to do is most important. That's where the spiritual battle is. Satan's job is to confuse us about what is right and wrong, at the same time drawing our focus away from actually doing what's right. Your moral decision comes when you decide if you're going to follow through on what you know is the right thing to do. If your conscience isn't genuinely clear before God, you're going to go through some serious emotional and spiritual stress."

The three sat in silence for a full minute and Nick sensed that the conversation was over. He reached into the pocket of the car door, pulled out a Phil Collins cassette tape, and plugged it in. *Something's coming in the air tonight, that's for sure.*

They approached Cluj-Napoca in silence. Jim was occupied with thoughts of the past twenty-four hours. The cold wind blew stronger about the van, as though angry it was denied entrance. It played out its wrath on the primitive cottages, the occasional gypsy wagons, and the trees that lined the road, their trunks painted white to mark the way, but it did not enter the van. For that, Jim was thankful. His thoughts turned to the task ahead, and to Cristea Greceanu, whom they would be visiting shortly, Lord willing.

Three miles from Cluj, they rounded a corner and were confronted by a Militia Post Control. The officer appeared busy with another truck driver and only looked their way for a few seconds. Hopefully they would be forgotten.

At the center plaza, under the great stone Catholic church, they parked and silently observed the throngs of people waiting for a tram a short distance away. The statue of the great Hungarian King Matyas stood boldly in front of them, a convenient resting place for hungry pigeons.

Jim contemplated the people walking past the van. Nick tapped the dashboard. "All right, hardly anyone is paying attention to us. We're not as unusual a phenomenon here as we were in the smaller towns or villages. Look, there goes a German car."

"Probably posing as tourists, just like us." Jim watched a Mercedes with a German license plate disappear around a corner.

Nick nodded. "Except there aren't a lot of tourists here at this time of year."

"So you're saying that we should still be careful." Kirsten tugged on her coat.

Nick reached back to pull out the hood that had gotten caught in the back of the jacket. "That's right. There could be secret policemen or informers anywhere and a mistake on our part might change the course of someone's life. You guys can't afford to be followed."

Jim's eyes widened. "What do you mean, 'you guys'?" Was Nick sending the two of them out alone? Were they ready for that?

"That's right. We should pray before you two go." Each took their turn and prayed for God's wisdom and protection.

His stomach tight, Jim turned to Nick. "What are we supposed to do?"

His friend gestured to the station down the street. "Tram number four goes from this point straight up Calea Motilor. When the street changes to Calea Manastur, that's where you'll want to get off. Cristea's house should be directly on the left, number 157."

Jim took a deep breath and tapped Kirsten's arm. "You ready for this?"

She looked as uncertain as he felt, but she nodded.

"Good." Nick clapped a hand on Jim's shoulder. "I'll be right here until one in the morning. If you don't come back by then, I'll drive south the way we came in and wait at the first rest stop on the right. It's about five miles from here. I'll stay there until six tomorrow evening, then I'm going home. Try and come back, okay?"

"Sure, Nick." Jim injected as much confidence into his voice as he could muster. "Just don't hide on us like you used to do in high school. It wasn't funny then and it certainly wouldn't be funny now."

Nick snorted. "Don't worry. I want you back here as much as you do."

"Is there anything you specifically want us to find out from her?"

"Just the details of her father's imprisonment. And ask if there is anything else they need. Oh, also, tram number four doesn't come back this way." He grinned. "Try number 11. If, for some reason, it's not running, you'll have to walk."

He squeezed Jim's shoulder and let him go. Jim clambered out of the van and he and Kirsten joined a queue of people boarding the nearest tram. They expected to buy tickets from the conductor, but he was at the front and they had mistakenly boarded from the rear door. There were too many people to make their way to the front. Jim looked around him at the full seats and the crammed aisles. *We aren't going anywhere.*

More people jammed into the streetcar and Jim suddenly found himself pressed uncomfortably into the armpit of the woman next to him. He turned his head in disgust; the stench of the entire car was nauseating. *Don't these people ever shower?*

He leaned down to whisper in Kirsten's ear. "This is *unreal*. I can see why Nick sent us."

Kirsten jabbed him in the ribs with an elbow. "Shh."

Jim clamped his lips together. If the people around them had heard him, they would know he was a foreigner, and suspicions would be raised. His cheeks warm, he glanced around the car. No one seemed to have noticed.

They exited at the fifth stop and Jim let out a long breath. They walked back towards the city center for a block and crossed the street, watching for signs of anyone following them. He didn't see anything out of the ordinary. On the far side of the street they reversed direction again and strode towards the home of Cristea Greceanu. The night air was bitter and they didn't want to waste any time.

The main gate stood open and Jim slowed and held out a hand for Kirsten to go ahead. When she reached the door, she rang the bell. A young brunette woman pulled open the heavy wooden door. After glancing up and down the street, she stepped back. "Please, come in."

Some of the tension left Jim's shoulders. The woman spoke English, and she clearly recognized them as Westerners. They followed her into the living room, removed their coats, and seated themselves on a worn sofa covered in sheepskins.

The woman took the armchair across from them and crossed her ankles gracefully. Jim swallowed. If this was Cristea, she was every bit as attractive as Nick had said. Their eyes met and she smiled. "My name is Cristea Greceanu."

"I'm Max." Jim's voice came out a little husky and he cleared his throat. "And this is Cathy."

"You are welcome here; I've been waiting for someone to come."

"We have food and Bibles we can bring you." Jim propped an elbow on the arm of the couch. "We heard that your father was in prison and thought you might need the food. Do you want the Bibles, though? Is it safe for you to distribute them?"

"The Bibles? Yes, I will… take them." She nodded. "My father has friends who will… know what to do with them. There is a great need."

Jim studied her. Was the hesitancy in her voice the result of fear or simply a lack of confidence in her English?

"There is also a great need for the food." She folded her hands in her lap. "But not only for myself. I am young and I can work, but there are others in the church, older people, who are not so able… capable. For all the presents, I am very thankful."

A smile broke across her face, which answered Jim's question. Clearly she was proud that she'd been able to make that speech in a language that wasn't her own. Jim returned her smile, his heart rate picking up. She looked young, perhaps twenty or twenty-one, and she held herself with dignity and an inner assurance that sent a distinct message. She did not seem like one who would be easily intimidated, either by two Westerners or the *Securitate*. Her skin was clear and beautiful like Kirsten's, her cheekbones were high, enhancing her beauty, and her rich brown hair was pulled back and braided perfectly.

"It gives us great joy to help you," Jim said.

She tilted her head. "You two are married?"

Jim and Kirsten looked at one another and laughed.

"No," Jim said, "but her boyfriend is in our van waiting for us."

"He's *not* my boyfriend," Kirsten exclaimed through gritted teeth, punching Jim on the arm. Jim grinned and looked across at Cristea, who was smiling. "We are all single," he explained, holding his left hand in the air to show her. "And you?"

"I am not married." She raised her hand as well. "I am a student at the Cluj University studying English, French, and music. I am sorry, that is not correct. I *was* a student at the university. When my father was taken into prison, I had to leave the classes so I could work. Now," she said, "I sell bread rolls in the city square. It pays me a little."

Kirsten slid to the edge of the couch. "How is your father doing?"

"Yes." Jim gripped the arm of the couch. "Can you tell us what happened?"

"I am surprised that you now… know… is that correct?" They nodded. "I am surprised that you know about my father. It only happened a short time ago," Cristea replied.

"There are ways that this type of information reaches the Christian organizations in the West who are particularly interested in the Christians in Romania," Kirsten told her. "Your father's story was even mentioned briefly in Radio Free Europe's reports. They said there was suspected injustice."

"My father is innocent, culturally speaking." Cristea gripped her brown wool skirt in her hands and the material bunched beneath her fingers. "But technically he is guilty. Perhaps it will be difficult for you to understand."

Kirsten reached over and rested a hand on her knee. "Please try to explain."

Cristea drew in a shuddering breath. "My father was the foreman of one of the metal shops here in Cluj. Years ago he had been a loyal Communist, but he became a Christian. He abandoned Communism and left the Party. It was a hard decision for him because a Communist can get paid up to three times more for the same job than someone who is not in the Party. At his work they began to persecute him. They reduced his wages and threatened him. They looked for ways to make him disappear without... how do you say it... raising the alarm."

Kirsten pressed her free hand to her mouth. "That's awful."

"Yes. Because of the way his bosses had organized the system, much of the material they used at work was wasted. It was thrown in the garbage. The same things that went in the garbage were impossible to buy in the stores so the material was often taken. The idea of all the workers was that the garbage belonged to no one. It was an accepted fact. How could they be stealing if they only took from the garbage?"

Cristea leaned forward, tears forming in her eyes, desperation in her voice. "My father took one bolt from the garbage to fix his car, and for this he was caught. At the trial, his bosses claimed that he stole many things, but they did not have any proof. They also claimed that he encouraged the other workers to steal. Finally, they blamed him for carrying out the plan poorly, which caused all the waste. It is not so." She lifted both hands in the air. "My father was wrong for what he did, but he is not a criminal. He does not deserve eleven years in prison."

Kirsten squeezed Cristea's knee. "We're so sorry." Kirsten pulled back her hand. "Will he actually spend that long in prison, or is there a chance of him being released early?"

"It is not possible. In Romania, much depends on the officer in charge of the case. The officer who arrested my father is very loyal to the Communist Party. He was once my father's good friend, but I think he feels betrayed. In America it is your culture to try to have more than your neighbor. Here we have a different mentality. If a person sees that his neighbor has something that is very nice, he will find a way to have it taken from him. Here the people think, 'What information about my neighbor can I tell the police that will make me a big man in their eyes?'"

"It is said in the West that one of every three people in Romania is an informer," Jim said.

"No. One in two people," Cristea declared. "Many times I think there are even more. My father was told after the trial that seventeen of the twenty-one people who worked with him had informed the *Securitate* of his theft. Seventeen! He told me this before he was taken away.

"Can you understand that? Seventeen separate reports to the *Securitate*. If they had been working together against my father, only one report would have been enough. Each informer did not know that the other workers were also informers. It is unthinkable…" She pounded her knee with her fist. "But this situation will not last. It cannot go on."

"What will you do now that you are on your own? You have this house to look after and that costs money. How will you survive?" Jim leaned forward on the sofa and looked into her eyes. "Cristea, how can we help you? What can we do for you?"

"I may try to sell the house."

"You own this house?" Jim's eyebrows rose. "I thought that private ownership was nonexistent in Romania."

"No, this house belongs to my father. He bought it years ago and he pays taxes on it. Of course, today that means nothing because the government can pass a decree at any time to take it away from us. I suspect that this is what will be done, now that he is in prison, so if I am going to sell it, I should try soon. If I can get enough money for it, I will rent a small apartment. Perhaps I will have enough so I can finish school. I would like to work as a translator. Doina Cornea taught me French at the university. Have you heard of her?" They shook their heads. Her shoulders slumped. "It is not important."

"How is your church handling your father's imprisonment? Are they doing much to help him?"

"There is nothing that we can do except pray. We don't know where he is being kept."

Silence descended on the room. Jim's mind whirled. If her father's own church couldn't do anything, what could they possibly do?

"Do you still go to church?" Kirsten asked.

"Of course," said Cristea. "We can't live our lives in fear. It would destroy us. We are not… paranoid. We don't go to church each week looking over our shoulders. It is not possible to live like that." She paused for a minute, then said, "I would like to know how you came to Romania. I see very few Americans in our country."

Kirsten sat back on the couch, "We have heard about the situation in Romania and how hard it is for believers. It has always been important for me and I wanted to help any way I could. Our friend, Ralph, who is waiting for us in the van, came first about three years ago. He kept sharing the need with us then God showed us also that we should take some time to work with him."

Jim looked at Kirsten. "Speaking of Ralph, we should return to him now or he will wonder what has happened to us. Cristea, how would you like us to give you the books and the food?"

"How long will it take us to carry it from your car if you bring it here?"

"Less than one minute."

"You may pull into my driveway then. I will close the gate behind you."

"Okay. We brought the tram here, so it will be a little while before we are back."

"That's fine; I'll watch for you."

"May we pray with you before we leave?"

Cristea nodded and rose to her feet. Jim and Kirsten followed her example. They uttered quiet, simple prayers of thanksgiving for God's protection on their lives. And they prayed for Cristea's father, that God's will would be done.

Kirsten pulled on her coat. Jim held out his hand. "Thank you Cristea."

She slid her hand, small and warm, in his. When Jim let go, a little reluctantly, Kirsten held out her hand, but Cristea stepped closer and they embraced instead. When Cristea moved back, her eyes shimmered with tears. "Please keep praying for me. And for my father," she whispered. "We do need your help."

His throat tight, Jim nodded and he and Kirsten left the house and entered the street. Jim glanced back, but Cristea had disappeared inside. He and Kirsten rode tram number 11 directly to the city square. This time Jim was silent all the way.

The tram deposited them within a few yards of their van. Instead of approaching it, they turned in the opposite direction and walked around the square. Nick sat in the front seat, a street light shining clearly on his face. He nodded to his companions walking in front of the van and they entered the side door.

"We're dropping at her house." Jim sat down and did up his seat belt.

"Great. Let's go." Nick drove swiftly over the cobblestone streets to Cristea's home and pulled carefully through the narrow gate. Cristea waited at the side of the driveway. When Nick stepped out of the van, she smiled her recognition and said in a quiet voice, "Hello, Ralph."

"Hello, Cristea. We pray for you." He pulled her into a quick embrace.

"Thank you so much. But quickly, there is little time." The four of them un-loaded her boxes then carried the books and the food into her kitchen and set them down on the counter. When they'd finished, Cristea opened the gate for them and waved as they reversed onto the street.

Jim watched her as she closed the gate. She looked up one final time and their gazes met for a brief second. Tiny wisps of frosted breath curled around her features; she smiled quickly and was gone. Jim shook his head. That was an interesting eve-ning. Would he ever see that girl again? *It might be better if I don't.* She was wonder-fully attractive, strong, and determined at the same time. It would be too easy to fall in love with her.

At Nick's direction, Jim drove west on Calea Manastur. The long rows of apart-ment buildings ended suddenly, replaced by an open field and a snaking pipeline running parallel to the road. As they passed the city limits, the sparse lights of the city faded quickly behind them.

A flicker of movement up ahead to the left caught Jim's attention and he leaned forward to see more clearly. "Hey, Nick, what do you think that is?"

"No idea."

"Could it be an animal?" Kirsten grasped the back of his seat.

"No." Jim slammed on the brakes. The van fish-tailed and slid sideways on the snow-packed road. "It's a person."

The figure lurched onto the road, fell once to his knees and struggled up, then fell again. In the glow of the headlights, the man turned in their direction and strug-gled to rise again.

"Oh my goodness. Look at him," Kirsten exclaimed as the van came to a stop at the side of the road. "I wonder what happened."

The man stumbled towards them, swaying briefly in the glaring headlights, before falling to his knees again. Blood was splattered across his face. Nick and Jim leaped from their seats and ran to him. Nick crouched down and grabbed the man's legs. "Jim, get his arms." The two of them carried the man to the side door.

"Put him inside, quickly," Nick ordered. The two of them laid the broken man across the middle seat. "Drive Kirsten. Let's get out of here."

Nick turned to the man. "Who are you? Do you speak English? *Sprechen sie Deutsch?*"

"*Ja, Deutsch. Oh, preisen Gott! Mein Name ist Jozef Potra. Bitte, helfen mir!*"

Chapter Nine

Nick's mind spun. Where could they take this man? "Turn the van around. Quickly!"

"Are you serious?" Kirsten threw a look back over her shoulder, her eyes wide. "The militia will stop us if we try to go past them now."

"Yeah, and we're sitting ducks out here in the country." Nick tugged the scarf loose from around his neck and used it to wipe blood off the man's face. "We've got to get him out of sight where he can get help. He needs medical attention. We're not going to be able to help him out here. We can go back to Cristea's. This man said 'Praise God'. He could be a Christian."

"And he could get us in a whole lot of trouble, too," protested Jim as Kirsten completed a three-point turn on the road and headed back towards Cluj.

"What are we here for?" Nick met his friend's gaze steadily. "Are we going to help these people or not? If this guy's a Christian, then he's your brother. Are we going to neglect him?"

"That's not the point, Nick," replied Jim.

"Actually, it is. These Christians put their lives on the line every day. Maybe it's time for us to do the same. What would you suggest, that we leave him on the side of the road?"

Jim exhaled loudly. "No, you're right. Keep driving, Kirsten."

"What if we come up on a police check?" Even from the back seat, Nick could see that she had a white-knuckled grip on the steering wheel.

"I'll roll him onto the floor and put my feet on him."

"You'd better not." Jim lifted the man's shirt. "This guy's pretty messed up. Wow, look at this." He lifted the shirt higher so Nick could see his chest. "Aw, man, he's getting blood all over the seat."

"Don't worry about that, we can clean it later. The important thing is to get him help."

"Yeah, but how?""

"Let's get him to Cristea's and figure it out from there. Grab a blanket from behind you."

Nick leaned over to get a closer look at the man, who had lost consciousness. His fingers trembling slightly, he undid the buttons on Jozef's shirt and spread it open. Then he tugged the flashlight from his pocket and shone it on the blood-stained upper body. Large bruises covered his chest and abdomen, intermingled with cigarette burns. Higher up, deep lacerations had been carved on his neck and throat, the skin literally peeled away. Nick pushed back a surge of nausea.

Jim pushed the shirt off the man's left shoulder and drew in a sharp breath. "Looks like a gunshot wound." His fingers slid around to the back of the shoulder. "Yep, it goes right through." In the dim light, his face went ghostly pale.

"We've gotta get this guy to a doctor, quick." Nick pressed the scarf to the shoulder wound that oozed with pus. "Cristea will know who can help. There might be a doctor in the church."

"I hope so, for his sake."

"We're coming up to the military barracks guys," warned Kirsten. A pale blue iron fence appeared on their right, stretching before them for several hundred yards. They glided by it. Nick strained to catch a glimpse of any activity in the compound through the back window. None. A guard stood coldly by the main gate, smoking a cigarette. Not surprisingly, his gaze followed them for a time—a Western van would always be a novelty—but he made no move to stop them or raise an alarm.

They passed no post controls as they entered Cluj from the north side. For this, Nick was thankful and he silently praised God for allowing them to re-enter the city undetected by the police. Cristea's house was only a few blocks farther down the main road. When they were a block away, Nick reached over the seat and clasped Kirsten's shoulder. "Park here." She pulled over and turned off the engine.

"Wait here," he said. "I'll be back soon." He hopped out of the vehicle and moved quickly like a shadow among the lifeless buildings to Cristea's back door. Her hair was tousled when she opened it, as though he'd pulled her from bed, but she didn't hesitate once he'd explained what was going on. "Of course, bring him in. I'll phone the doctor and see if he can come."

He was back at the van in less than five minutes. "Cristea's waiting for us. She's phoning a doctor who will hopefully come shortly. C'mon. Let's get him in there."

Kirsten eased the van between the gates of Cristea's driveway; once again, the young Romanian woman was waiting to swing them shut. Jim and Nick jumped out. They lifted Jozef from the vehicle and carried him gingerly into the house.

"Bring him in here." She led them to a sparsely-furnished bedroom. "This is where my father slept. It is sufficient, yes?"

Nick looked around the large, clean room. "It's fine. Is the doctor coming?"

"Yes. He should be here in about ten minutes." She began removing Jozef's shirt to get a closer look at his wounds. In the light, they looked even more pronounced, even uglier. "Come with me. We can talk as I boil some water." She led them from the room into the kitchen. "Where did you find this man? The story of his family is well known among the churches in Cluj. We knew they were put into prison about one month ago, but we were not sure where. The authorities like to keep these things a secret."

Nick dropped onto a kitchen chair. "He came stumbling out onto the road just after the military compound on the way to Oradea. At first we weren't sure what we should do, but then we agreed that you might be able to help him. You have heard of him then?"

"If he truly is Jozef Potra, he was arrested with his father and brother when the police discovered their secret meeting in the forest last month. They are a branch of the Lord's Army, an underground church movement that broke away from the Romanian Orthodox Church." Cristea filled a large pot with water and set it on the stove. "No one among us knows for sure all the details, but I believe that Jozef's father Yari decided he could not live with some of the principles that the elders in the Lord's Army followed. He left the Movement and apparently some of the others joined him. There was a lot of bitterness."

"That's strange." Jim leaned back against the counter and crossed his arms. "In North America we hear so many good things about the Christians in Romania and the revival that is happening, but we don't hear much about strife."

"It is very common here, Max. As in America, the devil seeks to interrupt a revival with disharmony in the churches. The issues are small, but the consequences are usually quite large. Why can't we understand that it is God-honoring to work together, even when we don't believe exactly the same way as other brothers?"

The large pot of water came to a boil and she turned the flame lower and left the pot on the stove. "It will not be good for you to stay too long. There may be people who watch."

"We have to leave the country tomorrow," Nick said. "Our visas will have expired. Would you like us to come back after that, though?"

"I was just going to ask you that. Perhaps the doctor will need you to bring medicines to help Jozef."

A knock sounded on the door and a gray-haired man who looked to be in his fifties entered before anyone could open the door for him. He nodded to all of them, shook their hands, and disappeared into the bedroom. Cristea followed him, the two of them speaking in Romanian. Kirsten sat down across from Nick and rested her head on one hand. Fatigue had drawn circles under her eyes and Nick's chest tightened. If he hadn't forced them to come back here, she might be sleeping somewhere safe and warm by now. She met his eyes and, as though she could read his thoughts, managed a wan smile.

Jim settled on the chair beside her. "Cristea's right, we probably shouldn't stay too long."

Nick traced the outline of a flower on the tablecloth with one finger. "No, we shouldn't. As soon as we know if Jozef will be all right, we'll head out."

Cristea stuck her head back into the kitchen. "The doctor asks you to wait for a few minutes. Now he is examining Jozef and he will tell you soon what he needs. He also says that Jozef is hurt badly but will be all right. Most of his injuries are superficial and will heal quickly. However, the wound from the bullet must be cleansed and cared for properly. It's possible he doesn't have the right medication."

A cry drifted from the bedroom, sharp at first, then tailing off into a long, low moan. Cristea stepped back into the hallway. "Wait here for a moment, please. I will see how he is."

She returned after five minutes. "He is awake and wants to talk to you." The three of them followed her into the bedroom. Jozef lay on the bed, talking haltingly with the doctor.

Nick approached them, leaving Kirsten, Jim, and Cristea standing by the door. "*Guten Abend, mein Bruder. Was ist mit dir passiert?*"

"One month ago," Jozef began, speaking in German, "my father and my brother and I were taken captive by the *Securitate* for holding a religious meeting in the forest. From the start there was more to the situation than I could perceive." He struggled to sit up, then winced and sagged back into the pillow.

The doctor stepped forward. "I think you should tell them later, Jozef."

"No. There is little time. I must continue."

The doctor nodded. "Just one minute, then."

Nick quickly translated what he had said for his friends, who moved closer to the bed to hear.

"The colonel who arrested us is named Cornel Mihai Popescu. He has a personal vendetta against my father that I don't fully understand. It goes back a long time to when my father and Popescu were young men. Along with my father and my brother, I'm sure, I've suffered much. They haven't given us a trial. They have not even made charges against us. They just keep us for their pleasure. Someday soon, I'm sure, they would have become bored with us and we would disappear."

"How are your father and your brother?" Nick rested a hand on the headboard of the bed.

"I haven't seen them since I was arrested. I assume they are both being treated as badly as I was. I don't know."

"What can my friends and I do to help you and your family?"

Jozef Potra stared blankly into space. "If we stay in Romania, we will be killed. Please help us escape to the West."

The *Suicide Strip* in Yugoslavia was appropriately named for its danger, its insane driving conditions, and the deaths that frequently occurred on it. It was a two-lane, one hundred-mile extension of the German-built Autobahn that stretched from the city of Belgrade in the south to Zagreb in the north. Police speed traps often slowed traffic to the unbearable rate of thirty or forty miles per hour. The Germans, Austrians, and Italians in their Mercedes, Audis, and high-powered Renaults threw caution to the wind, as did the impatient drivers of the immense eighteen-wheelers. Everyone had a goal to attain and a schedule to keep. Unnecessary competition was commonplace. How close could one come to an oncoming vehicle when passing another? How many cars could fit abreast on a two-lane road? The stakes of the game were high. There were many losers and many more who wished they hadn't played.

Jim had been forewarned of potentially slippery roads and the surprises that could be waiting around the next corner. Still, tension was building, the muscles in his shoulder and neck tightening. Beside the highway, numerous workers labored to extend the Autobahn. As was the universal practice, however, there were more kings than peasants; Nick had told them it would likely be years before they completed anything.

All three sat in the front seat, with Kirsten securing the warmest spot, in the middle, in front of the heater. Nick huddled in the depths of his winter coat, a book open in front of him. He'd either been absorbed in the words, or in his thoughts, for the past hour as he hadn't spoken, but he closed the book now and looked over at Jim. "Tell me what you're thinking, Jim."

"I'm excited. I really want to help those people. How soon can we get back into Romania?"

"We'll probably need three or four days in Vienna to clean up and rest, and to purchase the medicine. I know of a drugstore that will sell it to me without a prescription. They don't ask a lot of questions."

"We could get our visas while we're there. That might save time at the border."

"Sounds good."

"Wait a minute, guys." Kirsten held up a mittened hand. "This isn't unanimous yet. We can't just go back in there like some kind of Indiana Jones crew and bust a pastor and his son out of prison. No way. You're crazy."

Nick leaned forward and flashed Jim a smile. "That's not what we're proposing, Kirsten. We're simply going back to take Jozef medicine and help Cristea's church any way we can. We'll work with them. They'll know what can be done and what's not safe. Hey, I don't want to be sneaking around some prison any more than you do. I want to live, too."

"That's right." Jim guided the van around a curve. "You go looking for adventure and God may give you more than you bargained for. Yikes!" He swerved suddenly. "Like that stupid truck there that almost killed us."

Nick didn't flinch. "You're doing fine, Jim. Just keep it slow. Kirsten, God never promised that front-line warfare would be easy. I can think of a thousand things that would be more fun to do than smuggle Bibles into Romania. We promise you we won't do anything without your approval. Right, Jim?"

"Right."

"I'm still worried." Kirsten frowned. "We were in Romania for three days and look at all that's happened. What's going to be waiting for us this time if we purposely go looking for trouble? The militia will be on full alert, searching for Jozef."

"We'll be looking for a *solution* to the trouble." Nick covered her hand with his. "Look, whatever we face, we know God will be with us, right? He's proven that over and over. Why don't we pray that if God doesn't want us to go back in to help Jozef and Cristea, He'll make it abundantly clear to us. How does that sound?"

"Are you thinking of trying to smuggle them out of Romania?"

Nick shrugged. "If that's what God leads us to do. Wouldn't that add to your journal?"

Kirsten gulped. "Why do I feel like I'm getting more than I bargained for? I sure hope my dad is praying right now."

Jim tightened his grip on the wheel, his shoulders cramping up now from more than just the traffic. He hoped Kirsten's dad was praying too; they needed all the help they could get.

Chapter Ten

"**M**aria? Why aren't my phones working?" Colonel Cornel Popescu leapt to his feet and kicked his swivel chair across the room. Where was that woman? Why was everyone so unreliable? "Maria, get in here right now!"

His secretary rushed into the room, wisps of hair flying from her usually tidy bun. Popescu glared at her from behind his desk until she stopped all movement. When he spoke, his voice was low and stern. "Get Colonel General Iulian Vlad on the phone this minute or your job is finished. And I will make sure that you don't get another. Now!" Maria rushed from the room and Popescu paced the floor. "*Idiots! Jozef Potra is gone because I have* fools *working for me.*"

His thoughts raced. *I will find him. I always do. I have informers everywhere. Nothing passes through my district that I am not made aware of.* He sat down and slammed his fist on the desk. Petru Potra! That man had to be found and questioned immediately. Perhaps he'd had a hand in his brother's escape. Popescu shook his head. How could a person work for two sides at the same time? Petru was an informer, but could the man also be working against him? If so, he must be crushed.

Popescu jumped up again and stalked to his filing cabinets. He withdrew a folder containing the names and particulars of all the people who had been present at the secret church meeting. Two names had an extra asterisk beside them; Carl Vasilescu and Alexini Radu had been given special attention because of their role in helping to build the church. At the formal questioning, they had seemed like loyal, stalwart men, but who could tell the heart of a man and how easily he could be broken? Or tricked. He must recruit one of them to help track down Petru and Jozef Potra. Once he had all the Potras in his custody, there would be no more time for games. They needed to disappear.

Patrick D. Bell

He closed the filing cabinet drawer as Maria walked into his office. "The Colonel General is on the telephone. He doesn't sound too happy."

"No one is. Close the door as you leave." Popescu picked up the receiver. "Greetings, most austere Colonel General. It is a sincere privilege to speak with you."

The voice on the line from the *Securitate* headquarters in Bucharest exploded. "How could you possibly let a man escape? You are an imbecile!"

Heat flooded Popescu's face. "Sir, you know this already? It only happened last night, not many hours ago. There are but a few who are aware of what happened."

"You fool! You forget I'm the head of the nation's security. Nothing escapes me. I'll expect you in Bucharest tomorrow morning for a full report. Make sure that you're not late."

"Yes sir. Of course."

"And Colonel Popescu, let me warn you that if this man is not caught, you, too, will vanish. It would not look good for our country if he reports to Westerners how you have made him suffer. I hope it will not be necessary for me to remind you of this."

"I shall be there." Popescu slammed the receiver down.

The tables had turned. He was losing control. There was a great element of pressure on him now—something he had experienced only a few other times. But he would overcome it. Was he not the one who, last summer, had personally uncovered a plot by a party of dissidents in Cluj to assassinate the president? The Colonel General had taken the credit for that one, even though it did not belong to him. Was he not the one who put Nicolae Greceanu, that old colleague of his, in prison for eleven years, and probably much longer? Was he not the man who had thousands of informants reporting both directly and indirectly to him? Could he not command many to go out and locate one man?

He looked at his watch. It was exactly ten o'clock in the morning. A five-hour drive to Bucharest meant he should leave sometime in the early afternoon. That would leave him time to find a room in a good hotel and get plenty of rest. It wasn't often he visited Bucharest. How had it changed in the past year? Would there be any improvement? He smiled at the thought. It could only be worse.

A Communist he was, and a loyal one at that. However, experience had taught him to be a skeptic.

He had three or four hours remaining to work. In that time he must alert his people of the problem, organize his men to begin the search, and write his report. Knowing something of Colonel General Vlad's propensity for exactness, it would have to be concise and letter-perfect. There could be no mistakes.

He lifted his special brass-lined telephone receiver again and dialed the number for old Mama Angelina Mehadiei. She was always the first one he called in that Northern district. If Petru was there, she would know it. If Jozef Potra appeared, she would know it, too.

The phone rang and rang. Popescu slammed the receiver down. Where was she?

He picked up the receiver of the other phone and waited for his secretary to answer. When she came on the line, he barked, "Find Officer Mumuleanu and have him report to me immediately." He dropped the receiver back on its cradle, not even waiting to hear her reply.

The report. He should begin it. He reached for a pad of paper and a Bic pen stolen from one of the professors at the university, and began to write down ideas and statements.

One man had guarded Jozef Potra. He would report that there were four. Twist the facts slightly. Cover what must be covered. Shift the burden of fault to another. Protect his friends. Tear down someone else's private kingdom.

That was just the way things worked.

Popescu looked up and scowled as Sergeant Andrej Mumuleanu walked into his office without knocking. His recent promotion after the big arrest in the forests had left him even cockier. That would need to be dealt with.

The colonel tossed his pen on the desk. "I must leave in three hours for Bucharest. You will oversee the search for Jozef Potra while I am away. I should not be gone longer than two days. Get in touch with our main network and have them contact their informers to locate this man. This is top priority."

"What you ask has already been done, sir. I've informed each of our officers to begin working on their people. I've also passed on the word in the small towns farther north on Highway 1."

Popescu stood so abruptly his chair crashed against the wall behind him. "You did that without my orders?" he bellowed.

Mumuleanu hardly blinked. "You have been teaching me how to anticipate, sir. Even now there are many with their ears and eyes open, many on the lookout for this man. They expect a reward. I was hoping you would be pleased."

Popescu sank back down. "Yes, I am pleased." He smiled briefly. "Some of course we may have to reward. Most we will threaten." He leaned back in his chair. *How had this happened, anyway?* He glared at Mumuleanu who stood at ease in front of his desk. "How was it possible, this escape? You were on duty last night. What is your hypothesis?"

"I was not there myself, sir. I was visiting Father Radescu of the Catholic Church. Officer Elanului was at the compound, though not directly guarding the prisoner. The regular military guard was in the building and two of our officers, also. I thought it to be enough security."

"You were wrong. Obviously your training in Czechoslovakia was not as sufficient as you reported. Your bosses acted so incompetently, they lost complete control of the country."

Mumuleanu shifted his weight from one foot to the other. "Yes, sir. You're correct. But this morning I looked into Jozef Potra's background and discovered that he had done service for a number of months at the same military compound. He must have known something to aid his escape."

"What of the guard he overpowered?"

"He says he was taken completely by surprise. He's being interrogated even now."

"What do you think our chances are of apprehending Mr. Potra?"

"Assuming there are no outside forces involved, we should—"

"Outside forces?" Popescu almost choked over the words. "What do you mean by that?"

"Help from the West." Mumuleanu lifted both hands. "The CIA perhaps."

"It's unlikely."

Sergeant Mumuleanu shrugged. "Who knows? Otherwise, I think we can have him within two to three days. It should not be that difficult."

Colonel Cornel Popescu shouldered his way through a food line and strolled up the newly-completed Boulevard of the Socialist Revolution in the core of Bucharest. Before him loomed the immense Palace of the People, the headquarters of the *Securitate* and the various branches of the Romanian government.

The front of the building was designed to impress and overwhelm in an instant. White marble and stucco covered twelve stories of intricately-designed concrete forms. Thirty-foot-high pillars of marble rose from the steps, greeting the thousands of top Communist bureaucrats who came to work each day.

The Palace was 250 yards wide and 300 yards long, a behemoth, a pale symbol of power and terror. Unseen to the public were seven underground floors of offices and living areas. From here, the Communist Parliament of Romania could rule in safety, surviving even the devastation of a cruise missile attack. It was from here that the Ceaușescu dynasty and its puppets stretched out their tentacles of control.

People would come and go, powers would shift, but the Palace of the People was built to remain. And in its shadow, the fear and resentment in the hearts of the people multiplied.

Popescu mounted the steps, impressed at the enormity of the edifice. Turning to look down the Boulevard of the Socialist Revolution, he suddenly became very aware of his own insignificance. Before him was an awesome sight. The Boulevard stretched for three miles, perfectly straight and symmetrical. Trees lined the pavement, obstructing the view of the lower half of precision-built apartment blocks. Here lived many of the top officials, though no one from the *Securitate*. Many believed that every room in each apartment was monitored with sophisticated bugging devices. Nothing could be spoken that was not overheard. A family would have to walk a knife's edge to live here. Popescu pursed his lips. *My family could do it.* The Party had been very good to him and none of them would complain.

Along the center strip of the Boulevard, planners had placed identically-shaped ponds, surrounded by carefully-trimmed lawns. Hundreds of gardeners would labor here in the summer months, but now only a few dozen worked, clearing remnants of slush from the edges of the curbs.

In spite of the magnificent appearance, the everlasting Bucharest smog hung in the air, settling upon the Palace and its boulevard. The raw beauty could not last. *How beautiful will it be in five years, when the white has faded to a vile gray?*

He turned and bounded up the steps. He must not be late. The office he entered was relatively spacious despite numerous desks, each occupied by a plain-clothed officer. Directly facing him sat a male secretary dressed in a charcoal suit. Popescu greeted him cordially. The man's quick, intelligent eyes and compact frame were quite obvious, even under layers of clothing. Perhaps he was more than a secretary? Another colonel, possibly.

The secretary stood to greet him, using Popescu's name even before he presented himself. "The Colonel General is expecting you, Colonel Popescu." The secretary wasted no time in leading him to their superior's office. After he had knocked, they entered and the secretary introduced Popescu. "Colonel Popescu of Cluj to see you, sir."

"Thank you Lieutenant," the Colonel General replied quietly, without looking up from his papers. "You may leave us."

Popescu stared at the man seated in front of him. His voice had been relaxed and unassuming, even gentle, as if his present position left no strain upon him. A dark blue suit formed perfectly to a frame that showed that food in his later years had not been in short supply—he was not obese, but solid. His graying hair was combed back, revealing a receding hairline. Steel-framed glasses were centered over heavy-set eyelids.

"Take a seat. That one." Vlad indicated one of the chairs in front of his desk.

Popescu obeyed.

"Cigarette, Colonel? It's a Kent."

Popescu blinked rapidly. He had braced himself for as harsh a rebuke as he had heard the previous day on the phone, but received the opposite. He pushed back his shoulders. "Yes, of course. Thank you."

"I am a very busy man and have much work to do, so let's make this experience as brief and as pleasant as possible. You brought your report, did you? I should read it first."

The colonel pulled a small folder from his briefcase and handed it to Colonel General Vlad. Vlad opened it and scanned it quickly. Even so, those keen eyes likely retained everything.

"Good," he declared simply when he finished. "You understand that if Jozef Potra comes in contact with any Western visitors, his story will be told around the world. That means bad publicity for Romania and," he leaned closer to Popescu, lowering his voice and slashing the side of one hand across the palm of the other, "old Nic puts my head on the chopping block. And if I suffer, you will suffer even more. Is that understood?"

Popescu swallowed and nodded.

"Discipline Officer Elanului as you see proper. Make sure it is adequate enough that he doesn't forget his mistakes. Send the four officers who guarded Potra to me and I'll put them to work in one of our factories here in Bucharest. Perhaps in two years they will be fit to serve Romania properly."

The colonel cringed. Vlad wanted four officers to punish. Popescu would have to come up with three more.

"Increase the search for Potra in the Cluj District and notify our colleagues in each city within a 150-mile radius to put pressure on their people. Begin to interrogate the church leaders in Cluj. Your man was a Christian, yes? Then use your contacts in the churches. You must have enough of them.

"If you have no clues within forty-eight hours, begin a thorough house search of every Christian family in Cluj. That would be the logical place for him to hide."

Vlad settled back into his chair, fully concentrating his gaze on Popescu. "Today I must report this to our most esteemed President. Your future will be directly affected by his response to my report. Let us both hope that his honored wife has not been tormenting him today."

It took everything Popescu had to remain erect, despite the sudden, shooting pain that gripped his stomach.

"Return to Cluj now and I will inform you if storm clouds are building on your horizon."

When the secretary ushered Colonel General Iulian Vlad into the expansive office, President Nicolae Ceaușescu turned from the potted Birds of Paradise flowers in the corner and smiled his welcome. "Do you like my new plant, General?" he asked.

Vlad bristled at the lowered rank, but schooled his features to remain even as the president waved his hand in the direction of the pots. "I just had them imported from Zimbabwe. Robert Mugabe is a personal friend of mine. Did you know that?"

"I believe you mentioned it once, sir."

The president shot Vlad a suspicious look. "All those problems he had back in '78 with Ian Smith—he was lucky I was there with my influence or he still might be a dirty *Kaffir*."

"Yes, sir." Vlad knew that Ceaușescu's relationship with Mugabe had been non-existent at the time. He wouldn't disagree though. "Sir, I have come to…"

The door burst open. "Why is this man in your office again?"

The shrill, squeaking voice of Elena Ceaușescu, wife of Nicolae and Deputy Prime Minister of Romania, sent chills ripping through Vlad's body, but again he kept his features carefully neutral. She studied Vlad, circling him once like a buzzard. "Look at him Nicolae, he can't even dress himself. His trousers are wrinkled."

"I only have so many suits to wear," commented Vlad. Unlike the President, who wore a brand new suit each day for fear of an enemy poisoning his clothes, his wardrobe was limited.

The remark was a mistake. "You will guard your tongue when speaking about me," the president shouted, shaking his fist as a purple flush spread up his neck and across his cheeks. His eyes bulged in their sockets. "I put you in that office only last year. I can take you out again today!"

Vlad clamped his mouth shut. The president's demonic rages were legendary. One more word from him and he could end up on the chopping block, as he had suggested to Popescu.

The silent aftermath of his outburst was broken by Elena. "I think you should, dear. He hasn't done a thing since you gave him a desk here."

The president spun his chair to the window and stared out over his Victory of Socialism Boulevard.

Vlad held himself perfectly still. The president was clearly having a bad day and someone was going to pay for it. *Please, don't let it be me.* He had no interest or belief in a greater being, but on the off chance the fates were out there somewhere, listening…

"You're ignoring me, aren't you Nicolae?" Elena turned and blazed out of the room, likely looking for another victim to terrorize.

"You were going to tell me something new, weren't you General?" Ceauşescu spun his chair back around. "It's my birthday soon. I dare you to spoil it."

"I'm afraid I must report a prison escape, sir. Colonel Cornel Popescu from my division had a Christian church leader and his son in custody at Cluj. The son escaped."

Flames ignited in Ceauşescu's eyes, giving him a maniacal look. Still, when he spoke, the words were matter of fact. "Find the son and kill him then."

It was as he had expected. "We are doing our best, sir."

"But he's not in custody yet," Ceauşescu stated, his voice still eerily calm. "No one escapes and gets away with it."

"No, sir."

Ceauşescu's open palm came down hard on the desk. Vlad forced himself not to jump. "Then do your job! Find him or your grandchildren will end up in an orphanage."

The president rose from his chair. "And remove the father of this man from Colonel Popescu's little jail and take him to Brasov to our training grounds. Let him suffer for a few weeks then…" He waved a hand through the air dismissively. "You understand, of course."

He turned to his Birds of Paradise, signaling that the meeting was over. Vlad walked quietly from the office. Whether they were building on his horizon or Popescu's, the storm clouds had indeed begun to turn black.

☭

Popescu replaced the receiver of the telephone on his desk and contemplated the three officers standing in front of him. He had called Andrej Mumuleanu, Jurri Elanului, and Douru Nuvelei in from searching the streets.

"Sergeant Mumuleanu, you and Nuvelei will escort our friend Yari Potra down to the stockade at the training centre south of Brasov. Have him there by eight o'clock tonight. Make sure you handcuff him from behind and put him in leg irons.

If he escapes, put those military daggers of yours into your own hearts and drive your car into the Black Sea. I won't want to see you again."

Nuvelei flinched, but the other two remained impassive.

"Elanului, my orders are to discipline you for your negligence at the prison. I can't demote you much lower or you'll disappear, and you are still of some use to us. You will continue to walk the streets on this case, only this time you will bring all of your spoils to me. If you find coffee in a house, I want it. If you find Western cigarettes or too much sugar or flour, bring them to me. If I learn that you have kept anything for yourself, you will be sent to Bucharest to visit the Colonel General. And that will not be pleasant, believe me."

Elanului paled. "Yes, sir."

"Leave me now. I have phone calls to make." He dialed the number for *Potra and Sons—Blacksmiths* as his officers filed out of his office. To his surprise, someone answered the phone; he was speaking with Petru Potra, as he had hoped.

Popescu did not waste time with small talk. "Do you love your father, Petru?"

After a brief pause, Petru blurted, "Who is this?"

Popescu gave him a moment. When Petru spoke again, the anger in his voice had given way to resignation. "I think I know."

"If you are thinking that it's your good friend Colonel Popescu, you are correct. We are still friends, aren't we Petru?"

"How is my father? You haven't hurt him, have you? And my brother? What are you doing to them?"

"It's your brother that I want to talk to you about. Have you seen him lately?"

"No." Had there been a slight hesitation in his voice? Did he know something that he was hiding? "I haven't seen him since that final day at the church in the forest. What have you done with him?"

"Dear Petru, he has simply disappeared."

"You killed him?" Petru exclaimed.

"Petru, Petru. Such thoughts. Of course not. He has escaped from prison and I think that you know something about it."

"Escaped?"

Popescu chewed his bottom lip. The man sounded relieved. Maybe he didn't know anything after all. "Yes."

"I know nothing."

"Then you will find him for us, of course."

"I don't wish to work for you any longer. How many times have I supplied you with information? Is it not enough?"

"It's never enough," Popescu said harshly. "I will tell you when you are finished. Find your brother for us or your father will die before the new year." He slammed the phone down. He'd get results now.

He wheeled his chair to the filing cabinets and pulled out the folder of those caught at the secret church meeting. Two of them worked with the Potras: Vasilescu and Radu. Which one would be most vulnerable for a setup? They were Christians, but even the Christians had faults and weaknesses. He must uncover those weaknesses and use them.

Carl Vasilescu—he was a single man. Popescu could get at him through his parents. *No, wait.* Alexini Radu, age 27 years. Wife, Margaret, age 24 years. Daughter, Natasha, age 6 years. The daughter. Radu would do anything to keep his only child safe. And Popescu must do everything to keep his job.

What time was it? He checked his watch. Nearly four o'clock. The schools would be out. Tomorrow morning then, he would pay a visit to the Jablonec District Primary School and see little Natasha Radu. Drastic changes would come to the Radu family.

Popescu jumped to his feet. Maybe he could see his own wife and children now for a few hours. It had been a week since he had spent any time with them. Just a short while, then there would be lots of work to do.

"Miss Pall, may I speak with you?" The sun had shone upon his face that morning and Popescu was feeling content. It was a fine day, a bit milder than the previous ones, though he still needed his overcoat. Perhaps today he would find Jozef Potra. He rubbed his hands together so vigorously at the thought that his palms grew warm.

Miss Pall stepped from her classroom of first graders into the hallway. She glanced down at his highly-polished dress shoes and her cheeks blanched. She obviously recognized him as an officer from the State Security Department, the *Securitate*. The quality of his suit and shoes gave him away. "What can I do for you, sir?"

Popescu wasted no time. "Natasha Radu is in your class and she is a Christian. You are to make an example of her. You must encourage the other children to tease her, and you must be relentless. Send her out to me now and I will have a talk with her. And Miss Pall, you will remember nothing of my visit. Is that clear?"

Something flared in her eyes he couldn't quite identify. Hatred, maybe. Or fear. Either way it didn't matter. She knew what would happen if she defied his orders. She would obey. The young teacher lifted her chin. "Yes sir. I will do my best."

The girl came from her classroom, petite for her age, but cheeks full with a healthy color that showed proper nourishment. She wouldn't meet his eyes, but stared at the floor, her long, curly brown hair covering her dainty features.

"Look at me," Popescu ordered. She didn't move. He gripped her chin with his left hand and forced her to look up. "You are a Christian," he said, and slapped her. A red welt rose on her cheek. Within seconds, her left eye began to swell and turn a deep red.

Natasha Radu stared at him in shock. Tears filled her eyes and spilled down her face. He turned her around and pushed her back into the classroom.

Later that afternoon, Popescu drove his black Dacia slowly through the village of Schitu Tansa, looking for house number 14, the home of Alexini Radu. Schitu Tansa could have been any village in Romania; the sights, smells, and sounds all blended together to produce the same repugnant compound.

The road through the village had been rebuilt not more than a few months ago. Concrete had been poured into forms at the rate of twenty feet per day, the effect being a rhythmical bumpy ride in any automobile. The shoulders were not quite finished and incautious drivers faced a drop-off high enough to destroy a small tire. The village was comprised of forty-two cottages, twenty-one on each side of the road, facing each other. Each cottage had its own fence, gate, and bench in the front—a perfect setting for the older people to watch the cars and horse-drawn carts go by, and to gossip about their neighbors. Most families had chickens, ducks, or geese that wandered freely on and off the road, and a cow or pig was tethered to a stake in front of several of the homes.

Popescu passed a small group of children playing soccer in the snow, but they all ignored him, likely because he was riding in a Dacia and not a Western vehicle. He had seen before how the children would run out to the road as a Western car approached, pleading for *gummi*, or chewing gum.

The afternoon was overcast and the temperature had dropped, cutting away at the pollution and mists. The clouds had descended now, bringing the habitual depression upon the countryside.

Popescu saw the number 14, barely visible on the wall of the house, and swung his car into the driveway, stopping just short of the gate. Wrapping his coat about him, he stalked up the path to the front door.

Alexini answered his knock. The man was tall and Popescu drew himself up to his full height. "I have come to talk about the problems your daughter had at school earlier today. Will you let me come in?"

Alexini didn't budge.

Popescu's jaw tightened. "If I were in your shoes, Mr. Radu, I would be most anxious to help a man in my position. I have much influence in high places."

Alexini paused a moment then stood back from the door and let Colonel Popescu step past him into the living area. The colonel frowned as the warmth of the room enveloped him. He whirled towards Alexini. "It's quite warm in here. Do you know the penalty for turning your heat too high in the winter?"

"My daughter will get sick if I turn it any lower."

"And you will be moved to one of the new complexes in Cluj if you don't. Forty-five degrees is all we can allow. There is a budget in this country that must be adhered to, you know."

"Yes."

Popescu cleared his throat. "But, Mr. Radu, I don't come here to give you trouble about your heating; I simply want you to do a small favor for me. One small favor, that's all, and you won't hear from me again."

The man's eyes narrowed. "And if I refuse?"

"Then your daughter will have a very tough childhood."

A wild look came into Alexini's eyes. He lunged at Popescu with a raised fist. "You're the one who hit my little girl," he cried, grabbing Popescu's coat lapel with his free hand. "How dare you use an innocent child to—"

"Stop!" Popescu commanded. "It was not I, but her teacher. Your daughter had been disobedient and needed to be punished. One small favor, Mr. Radu, and your daughter will resume a normal life. Her teacher will be nice to her again and will encourage her classmates to be as well. No one has to know about it except you and me. If you agree right now, I'll drive by the school on my way back to Cluj."

Alexini let go of his coat and stepped back. "What is it?"

Popescu smiled briefly; he had gained the first victory. "Jozef Potra has escaped from prison. Find out where he is hidden and report his whereabouts to me. For your own benefit as well as mine, no one will know about my visit." He reached into the inside pocket of his jacket and withdrew a small white card. "Here is my telephone number. You will use it, yes?"

Alexini Radu stared at the card in Popescu's outstretched hand. He hesitated. Popescu knew exactly what he was thinking. To take it meant to betray his Christian friends. To refuse it could cost him his daughter. He would take it.

Alexini snatched the card from the colonel. "You leave me no choice. Now get out."

Popescu laughed, wrapped his coat around himself again, and walked out the front door, leaving it open to the cold and the wind.

Chapter Eleven

The ascent of the winding road was steep. Tall, dark firs lined the sides like astute sentries. The car that carried Pastor Yari Potra did not slow as it plateaued near a barbed-wire fence and high iron gate. The car's horn sounded and two guards rushed to swing the gate open. The prisoner made no effort to conceal his interest; his eyes ranged freely as he made note of the layout of the encampment.

The two guards at the first gate will be a constant. Each guard carried a Russian-made AK-47 assault rifle, the standard issue for Romanian forces. They were an excellent short-range weapon and he would avoid those at all costs. He would need to learn the pattern for the shift change of the guards, too. *Who can I trust? Who can I confide in? Will any guards become my friends?*

The gates clanged shut behind him. *So this is it. This could be my final stop in life.* Yari grimaced at the thought. Perhaps God would still intervene.

Scanning the compound, Yari observed army barracks, two buildings on each side, all long, low to the ground with few windows. Fifty yards from the first gate stood another, identical gate, this one flanked by a ten-foot fence. No doubt there would be an electric current running through it and guards patrolling its perimeters.

A guard came over from the second gate to check their papers then waved to his colleague, who promptly swung the gate open. They drove northward into the inner compound. Yari's eyes remained active. The area was about 150 yards across and perhaps 300 yards long. The east end was squared off and the west end came to a point, like a row boat. Directly in front of him was a parade square and behind that a two-story building with two flags at the entrance—probably the administration building for the officers.

The plateau ended abruptly on the north side with a natural rock wall, perhaps forty feet high. For the majority of the compound, the wall provided a perfect shelter from the cold north winds.

The officer who had brought him here drove the vehicle to the west side, stopping in front of a one-story red-brick building with a brown-tiled roof and barred windows. The guards dragged him from the car into the prisoners' building and stopped at the first metal door. One guard inserted the key into the lock and turned it.

When the door to his cell opened, a thick stench of unwashed bodies, urine, and human excrement billowed out, taking Yari's breath and nearly knocking him back. *Was he to live in this? No, God. It can't be possible.*

The guard shoved him through the opening. The stares of seven men seated on the bench greeted him. Their eyes were empty and hard, their thoughts unexposed. Did they think he was a criminal, or possibly a *Securitate* informant? Would these men ever confide in him? How could he possibly gain their trust? *Oh Lord, even worse, how can I bear this smell?*

The cell was only twenty feet long by twelve feet wide. A wooden bench lined one wall, rows of narrow, shelf-like bunks the other. At the far end sat a metal toilet. Given the stench, the hole it flushed into was rarely emptied.

The guard who had shoved him through the door gestured to a bunk, then to the bench. Yari sat down with the others and imitated their lack of movement. The prisoners continued to stare straight ahead, as though they had learned the hard way what happened when they moved in the presence of the guards.

A death-like silence hung in the cell, until one of the guards jerked his chin in Yari's direction. "His name is Yari Potra. He is a Christian and an enemy of the State." With those words, he and his colleague turned on their heels, marched out, and slammed the door shut.

The atmosphere of the cell immediately changed. Three of the prisoners stood and headed for their bunks. Yari followed them, curious to inspect the quality of his new accommodations. The mattress was four inches thick, stuffed with ancient straw. It reeked of urine and vomit. Yari flipped it over; the reverse side was little better. The mattress was held up by thin, wooden slats spaced an inch apart. Perhaps he could sleep on the wood. He certainly would never get used to the mattress; steam rose from it in certain places.

One man, not quite as filthy as the rest, but still dirtier than a human should ever become, shuffled over to him. "My name is Greceanu. I, too, am a Christian. I come from Cluj. I was thrown in here two weeks ago by the authorities on a contrived charge. I will stay here for eleven years. Perhaps we can become friends."

Yari shook the man's hand. Warmth spread across his chest; he had already made a friend. Maybe it would not be so bad here. "I don't know how long I will be here. It could be just a few short days. They want to get rid of me because I'm an embarrassment to their system. I am a pastor." He propped an elbow on the bed frame. "I had the charge of a church that met in a forest for fear of the police. One month ago we were caught by the *Securitate*, headed by Colonel Popescu. Perhaps you have heard of him if you come from Cluj."

"Colonel Popescu?" Greceanu's face darkened. "He was the officer in charge of my case."

Yari shook his head. "Something has to be done about that man."

"I heard about what happened to you," Greceanu said, "as did all the churches in the Cluj area and perhaps across the country. There was much talk of informants among the congregation. Perhaps those were just rumors."

Yari's shoulders sagged. "I admit I've thought about that. Our church had new people joining us all the time, so it's quite possible that someone was present who shouldn't have been."

"Pastor," Greceanu shot a quick look towards the cell door and lowered his voice "there are a few things you must know before we go on. There are different routines in this prison that you must learn. The quicker you do, the longer you will survive. You saw how we all sat on the bench when you entered. It is a ritual the guards like to make us perform. As soon as you hear the door opening, get in your place. If you move too slowly, they take you down to the guard house where they will torture you."

Yari's stomach lurched. So the stories he had heard were actually true.

"It is unbelievable what they do." Greceanu drove his fingers through greasy, matted hair. "They continually dream up new methods to torture a person. Sometimes the prisoners who come back are never the same. Look at Rantiu over on the corner bunk." He inclined his head towards a man with long, white hair, stretched out on his bed. "He was a gypsy who spent his days in a covered wagon on the south side of Bucharest. Look at his eyes. There is a vacancy in them that wasn't there even three weeks ago. The man does not have all his senses now. Maybe it's all a part of his defense mechanism."

Yari shot a look at the old gypsy. "What did he do to deserve that?"

"He won't tell us, but it's certain to be something quite severe. Maybe he was an important figure among the gypsies. Usually they just disappear if they cause any problems, so they must be keeping him for a reason."

Yari pressed a hand to his stomach. Would he suffer the same treatment? How much could he bear before he, too, retreated inside himself? "Do they beat him often?"

"Once every two days. Sometimes more often." Greceanu's hands had clenched into fists. He glanced at them and then, as if surprised to see them that way, straightened his fingers. "He always comes back a broken man, bleeding in more than a few places. Sometimes he manages to collect his senses together, but never enough."

Greceanu took Yari by the elbow and drew him to the bench. They sat down together. "There are other things, too, that you must realize. You notice that throughout this room we have five different nationalities. You are Slavic Romanian, yes? I am ethnic Romanian, along with two others. There are two Hungarians, a German, and the gypsy. Sometimes, there might be flare ups, but we do get along sometimes. We like to cooperate when we can because it makes it easier on all of us. But the tension can grow high in here. Maybe one day they won't give us food. Without food, tempers become very short."

"What's the food like here? It's not the Inter-Continental, I suppose."

Greceanu barked a laugh that sounded a little rusty. "Keep your sense of humor. It will be useful. The food will become a major concern for you, which you will find out very quickly. Twice a day they'll bring each person a plate of food. If you're not fast enough, things may get stolen off your plate. If you are sick and you have no friends, it's almost impossible to survive because your food will be taken."

Yari leaned back against the damp stone wall. "Do you mean that other prisoners in this cell would steal my food?"

"Brother, listen to me. When I first came here, there was a man among us who was very sick. When the guards came into the cell, others here would prop this man up between them on the bench so that he would not fall forward. No one told the guards that he was sick and every day his food was stolen. He was unconscious almost the entire time I was here, and only this week he died."

Yari fought back nausea. They forced men to become like animals in this place. *God, keep me from becoming like that. Fill me with compassion for these desperate, suffering men.*

Greceanu nudged him with his elbow. "We're Christian brothers and for this reason we must care for each other. It's not the same with the rest of them. They only look after themselves. I believe, even among us, there are those who work for the guards and receive special privileges."

Potra leaned closer and spoke into Greceanu's ear. "If I stay here, I'm sure I'll be killed soon. Is it possible that there's a way out?"

Greceanu pulled back and studied his face. "If you are caught outside of the building, you will be shot instantly. We never leave except to go the guardhouse. I think your chances are very slim."

"But perhaps they are even smaller if I stay."

"Perhaps so." Greceanu lowered his voice until it was barely audible to Yari. "Brother, there may be a way, if you are brave enough. Consider it thoroughly, for it will not come without pain. Still, I hesitate to tell you for I can see that you aren't a man to sit still. I think you may easily die if you try."

"And I will certainly die if I stay. Please tell me brother." Yari gripped the arm of the man's worn shirt. "Give me the chance."

"Okay, then." Greceanu shrugged. "But I can take no responsibility for your actions."

Yari tightened his hold on the arm of his new friend. "And I leave you no responsibility."

"Of course not." Again he leaned very close to Yari's ear. "In this same block, there is a single cell that they use for solitary confinement. It's in a small room, perhaps half the size of this one, and in the center is a cage with bars on every side.

"The only way to get into that cage is misbehaving in an extreme way. But, before you are taken to solitary, you will be beaten and tortured. When I first arrived here I went berserk. I could not stand the thought of being imprisoned like some animal. My first twenty-four hours were spent in that solitary cell."

Yari winced. Did he want to get out badly enough to go through all that? "And you think it will be easier to escape from there?"

"I believe so. When I was strong enough to stand, I noticed that one of the top bars is slightly loose in its fitting. You are a very large man. Perhaps you may regain enough energy in time to break out from the cage."

"But the walls and the ceiling here are made of concrete. There would be no place to go."

"In this cell, the ceiling is made of concrete. In solitary, there are only wooden ceiling beams and roof tiles. They believe the cage to be secure enough. Besides, no one is ever left in it for very long. Once out of the cage, however, you could be under the stars within minutes."

A pang of sorrow shot across Yari's chest. Would he ever see the stars again? "And if I did get out? What about the guards in the compound?"

Greceanu stood. "Come, look at this." He slid an arm around Yari's shoulder and led him to the window. Yari tried to ignore the odor wafting from him. "Notice the guards," he whispered. Yari stared out the grime-smeared glass, a tiny pane fitted into a hole two feet long and only a few inches high, not nearly big enough for a body to squeeze through. Four or five guards had gathered near the corner of another building. "They are lazy and often sleep at night when on duty; usually only one or two cover for them."

Interesting. Yari scanned the compound. What would be the best path for him to take once he was out of the building?

As if he could read Yari's thoughts, Greceanu jabbed a finger against the glass. "Over there. The trees near the face of the cliff are close to the fence. That whole west side is covered with pines and firs."

"What if I get to the fence and no trees are close enough? I'll be stuck. I'll have no other place to go."

Greceanu shrugged. "I told you it wouldn't be easy. Remember, too, that you won't be in much shape to travel far. And if the weather is as cold as usual, you could easily die from exposure. Try the cliff as your last resort. They tell us it is too sheer to climb, but who knows? Maybe after scaling that wall, there will be no other fence. It might be the easiest way."

"I could take my coat."

"It's unlikely you would have that with you in solitary. They might even strip you naked. Who can tell the mind of these people?"

Yari shoved back his shoulders. "I will go this week."

"This week?" Greceanu pursed his lips. "Then this week you may die. We must pray about it."

Yari turned from the window. "Yes, and I must also sleep now. Please pray for me. It's been a long day and I have nothing left." Sleep he did, for it came easily, but his dreams were restless, repetitive, and frightening. He woke with a start once in the middle of the night, drenched with sweat, but he managed to pray himself back to sleep.

In the morning he woke to the sound of a key in the lock and a hand on his shoulder, and he rolled from his mattress to the floor, then to the bench on the other side of the room. He was slow, but the guard was struggling with the tray of food and did not step through the doorway for an extra couple of seconds. *Thank you, Lord.*

The guard placed the food on the center of the floor and retreated from the cell, clearly wishing no part in the sulfuric stench of the prisoners or the ensuing melee the arrival of the food would precipitate. The moment the door clicked shut, the prisoners scrambled for the food. Yari wasn't slow, but as he reached for a plate it was snatched unceremoniously from under his hands. He succeeded in grabbing hold of the next closest one and withdrew to his bunk with it, only to find that the bread had already been stolen. Now he had seen the process. Next time he would be quicker.

Breakfast that day was comprised of one scrambled egg, one thick slice of stale bread, and a hot drink they called tea. Although Yari detected a hint of lemon juice, he doubted any tea had been added. Greceanu, who had sunk down on the thin mattress next to him to eat, elbowed him in the ribs. "We'll get pretty much the same around four o'clock in the afternoon. Be ready."

Yari pressed a finger to the plate to pick up the last crumbs, barely resisting the urge to lift the dish to his mouth and lick it.

"They don't feed us much," Greceanu said, "which serves many purposes for them. We are easier to control if we are weak, and our spirit is partially broken, so our body lets our mind play tricks on it. Our stomachs get confused and that upsets our mind."

Yari tipped back his glass to drain the last drops of hot liquid. "Two meals a day doesn't seem too bad."

"It wouldn't be, except that it isn't always that way. One day they may feed us nothing, the next day more than we need. Some days they leave only five or six plates of food in the cell and they watch us through that narrow window to see what happens." He held out half his piece of bread.

Yari had already been here long enough to know what a gift that was. "Thank you, my friend." He took it and chewed on it thoughtfully. "How then do we keep our sanity and a sharp mind through these tortures?" he asked, his mouth half full.

"Have you ever fasted?"

Yari nodded. "Yes. Many times."

"Then you understand," Greceanu tapped his empty plate with a dirty fingernail, "that there is a struggle between mind and flesh. As a Christian, this should be obvious. In the case of fasting, your stomach tells your mind that you have skipped a meal and something must be done about it. Your victory comes when you inform your stomach that you are taking control and it cannot order you around."

"So it's all about being in control of ourselves, a fruit of the Spirit."

"Exactly. Let them take your body. Let's face it, in reality it already belongs to them because they may do with it as they please." Greceanu set his empty plate down on the bed. "Yari, they will punish your body. They may even take your life. But don't let them steal your spirit. If you can beat them in this area, in a sense you will have gained your victory."

Yari leaned back against the wall. Scrutinizing the cell, he took in the filth of the bunks, walls, and floor, the toilet at the end of the room that made the word *privacy* a fantasy, and the other men who wore their misery like another set of clothes. A sigh escaped him as he turned his head to look at Greceanu.

"I would find it very difficult to sense a victory here, Brother Greceanu." *I don't even know his first name.* He set his dishes down on the dirty mattress and clasped his hands between his knees. "My victory comes in walking through the villages among the common people, telling them about Christ and listening as they respond with repentant hearts. My victory comes as I stand up on a Sunday morning in front of my congregation and preach to them the truth of what the Bible teaches, even when I know that some are offended by what I say."

Greceanu waved a hand around the room. "You can treat this cell as a mission field. You'll have a congregation who can't leave the room if they wanted to."

Yari smiled grimly. "Brother, perhaps God has given you a gift for prison ministry. At least you'll have eleven years to develop it. I am sorry to say that I won't be here to help you. Either I leave this week or I'll be killed in short time. Of this I am sure."

"If you escape, please don't be like the cupbearer in Genesis chapter forty who forgot his friends."

Yari reached out and clasped his friend's forearm. "Rest assured, brother. If I make it, you won't be forgotten."

On the fifth morning, Yari woke early to pray. After some time, his soul at peace, he looked out the window at the lightening sky. It must be nearly seven o'clock. The guards would arrive soon with food.

He began to dress, which didn't take long as he only had one set of clothing. He pulled on a second shirt and then his wool sweater; the cell was cool in the early mornings.

The day before, guards had come and taken his overcoat. Just like that. They had walked in about noon and taken it without a word. Would it be his sweater tomorrow? He could delay no longer. Today he would go to the cage.

Twenty minutes later, Yari sat on the bench, waiting for the others to join him. In another three minutes, everyone was in his place, since the guards would enter any minute with their meal. When the key turned in the lock a few seconds later, Yari shifted to the end of the bench nearest the door, nodding solemnly at Greceanu as he passed him. The peace he'd experienced that morning slipped from him as his stomach tightened into knots. What terrors awaited him? Would they put him in solitary or just kill him?

The cell door swung open and the sullen stares of the two guards turned to shock as they saw an empty place in line. They scanned the bunks but swung their attention back to the prisoners as a roar, like that of a madman, came from behind the door.

The first guard dropped the tray of food as Yari's large frame drove into his. The guard doubled over and flailed with his fists as Yari embedded his shoulder into the man's midriff. The momentum of their bodies carried them into the second guard. The three of them surged back into the hallway, a wild mass of clawing arms and driving knees.

The second guard fought desperately to disentangle himself and, and at the last second, managed to sidestep Yari's sweeping arm.

It didn't matter. Yari was not trying to win. Not this battle, anyway. He rolled around with his man on the floor. He was vaguely aware of the piercing shriek of a whistle. Then something heavy crashed into the back of his skull and knocked all consciousness from him.

Chapter Twelve

Jim walked out of an OAMTC travel office, paused to straighten the sheep-skin hat resting on his red curls, then dashed through the heavy traffic on the *Schubertring*, slowing only as he entered the old district of Vienna.

In his hand he held Romanian hotel coupons, enough for the three of them for ten days. Ten days? It was not an appealing thought. What new challenges could they be presented with in those ten days when so much had happened in just three? A gentle voice inside rebuked him and Jim hung his head. "Forgive me, Lord," he whispered. "We will meet and accept any challenges you allow into our lives, knowing you are with us and that you fight on our behalf." He quickened his pace, anxious to be back with his friends. *Thank you for keeping us safe so far, and for meeting all our needs. Please heal Jozef, and help Cristea as she endures the hardships of life without her father. And please watch over Jozef's father and brother, wherever they are. May they feel your presence with them, giving them strength.*

Jim followed the *Schubertring* until it joined with the *Kärntner Ring*. Three hundred yards ahead stood the magnificent *Staats Oper* or State Opera House as the English-speaking called it. Nick and Kirsten should be there waiting for him. The travel office had been crowded and they had decided only one of them needed to endure the Christmas-time hordes when the city of romance and magic waited to charm and to please.

Up ahead, Nick leaned against the concrete edge of a fountain, its waters at rest for the winter. Kirsten stood in front of him. Jim's forehead wrinkled. Had Nick won Kirsten's heart? From what he'd observed, it seemed as though he had. Jim came within a hundred feet of the two and stopped. They did not appear to have seen him approaching.

Kirsten and Nick faced each other, holding hands, their faces inches apart. They were talking, probably sharing secrets and dreams and silly ideas for the future. Jim's chest tightened. Part of him was jealous of their relationship, yet happy for them at the same time. *His* turn would come someday, as God saw fit. He nodded curtly. He would be content with his singleness. He pressed a hand to his still-tight chest. Of course, contentment would not be achieved without a battle.

His mind strayed to Cristea Greceanu. What was she doing right now? Selling bread? Perhaps thinking of him? His brow furrowed. Why would she be thinking of him? He straightened. Why not? Hadn't he sensed those beautiful eyes on him when he was in her home? Did she not hold his hand a little longer than necessary at the door? Or was he just dreaming?

A movement in front of him pulled him out of his musing. Nick and Kirsten were waving to get his attention. Jim joined them under the eaves of the great Opera House.

"Quite the incredible structure, isn't it?" He focused his gaze on the giant building. Were his cheeks as red as they felt? Could his friends guess who he had been thinking about?

"That's what Kirsten and I were just discussing." Nick grinned. "This building has quite a history behind it. In World War II, American bombers smashed it up, but the Viennese rebuilt it. If you ever have time, you should take the tour."

"Can we go to an opera or ballet sometime, Nick?" Kirsten said, tugging on Nick's arm where her hand had remained.

Nick faked a horrendous moan. "Oh, let's see an opera please. Tell me, who in their right mind would want to see a guy in tight pants jumping around on stage?"

Jim shook his head. "You know all about the history and culture of this place, yet you think anyone who participates in it is out to lunch. Sometimes you amaze me, you know that?"

"What I find amazing is the differing attitudes of the Russians and the Americans." Nick made no attempt to free himself from Kirsten's hold. "Did you ever read about the 1956 Hungarian Revolution when the Russians came in and practically destroyed the entire city of Budapest?"

Jim and Kirsten both nodded. "The Russians call that the *liberation* of Budapest from those who revolted. Then they turn around and say that the Americans destroyed Vienna in the Second World War."

Jim rolled his eyes. "And I suppose Americans hold the exact opposite viewpoint."

"Not quite," said Kirsten. "I thought the Russians liberated Vienna from the Nazis and then later destroyed Budapest in the face of the freedom fighters."

"So your view then depends on whether you're a Russian or American supporter," returned Jim.

Nick shook his head. "I think it depends on if you have enough common sense to look at the facts."

"What facts?" Jim threw his hands into the air. "Both the U.S. and Russia distort them. Look at the various American newspapers. They send over reporters who put their own impressions together with the word of a few locals and they report these as facts. We see it all the time."

Kirsten gaped at him. "You're exaggerating."

"No, I think American reporters are actually worse than those in the USSR."

"How so?"

"Because they've given themselves a moral obligation that they don't keep. The world believes much of what the U.S. reports, but who believes what's printed in Russia?"

Silence fell between them, until Kirsten broke it. "I guess that's a Canadian point of view. Can we go now? I'm cold. By the way, we need to stop at the post office so I can mail this letter to my dad." Without waiting for a response, she let go of Nick and crossed the street to the van.

Jim and Nick meandered across the street behind her. "If we drive into Hungary tonight," Nick ventured, "we can do our shopping in Budapest tomorrow morning before we go to Romania."

"Sounds good," Jim said.

"Hey Jim." Nick grabbed Jim's elbow. "No hard feelings, right?"

Jim met his friend's gaze. "Of course not. Don't flaunt it though. We never did let a girl come between us. Let's not start now."

The next morning, they hit a cold front on the far side of Budapest, sending fingers to the heater controls and hands to the scarves and coats. Before they left the capital of Hungary, they stopped to buy food for Cristea and Jozef Potra and to eat at McDonald's, but Nick had a hard time sitting still. He shoved his hash browns into his mouth and glanced out the window at the car. "We should keep moving, guys."

They were on the road again before eleven o'clock. This time, they took no Bibles, as their chances of being able to help their fellow believers there were better if the border patrols found none on them. The decision came after a slightly heated debate. Jim had argued that, since God was so great, He would take them through.

Nick countered that Bible couriers do get caught on occasion, and always had to weigh the benefits against the risks. As leader of the team, Nick's decision held.

To make the most of their time, they agreed to deviate from the plan of going through their regular border entrance, and instead attempt the one at Nadlac, the Romanian town across from its Hungarian counterpart, Nagylak. That would save at least one hour on the road.

At two o'clock in the afternoon and only twenty miles from the border, they passed the last vestiges of the Soviet army in Hungary, more than a dozen soldiers lined up in a field, relieving themselves. "Don't look, Kirsten." Both guys laughed. One soldier isolated himself from the others behind a tree and a few of his mates pointed, likely laughing at his bashful bladder syndrome.

Five miles from the border, they stopped to pray. To somehow think that God could be left out had become an absurd idea to the three couriers long ago. Prayers *must* be made. God *had* to be with them. His mercy and grace and love and presence *had* to be upon them at the border as they would seldom make it across on luck alone.

Nick prayed last, lifting up Cristea and her father, Jozef and his family, and agreeing with Jim and Kirsten's requests for safety on the road, a smooth-running vehicle, and victory at the border.

The Hungarian border control posed little problem. One of the guards asked Nick where he was going and why, and Nick told him that they were going to Romania to tour around. The guard just shook his head as though unable to understand why anyone would willingly do that, stamped their passports, and waved them through.

Nick drove slowly towards the Romanian side. "Remember," he said, "anything you say could be picked up on a microphone. Be very careful what you talk about. No names at all."

They came up behind three German cars waiting to be processed. One guard was walking away with a bottle of whiskey, the result of either a bribe or his thieving fingers. His smile showed that he didn't care which it was. He would have a warm night, as long as he made it home.

Posters overhead displayed advertisements for vacation spots such as the ski resort at Poiana Brasov and the spas at Baile Felix. One sign read, *Probil-Forte: A Romanian Drug Highly Effective in the Treatment of Gastro-Duodenal Ulcer.* Another, more obscure one, spelled out, *Authenticity Oneness Universality: Features of the Romanian All Along Your Routes.*

An officer in darker grays approached their van. He was about forty-five years of age, his hair immaculately combed, his eyes dark and scowling. Nick rolled down his window and handed the man their passports. *Please just let us through this time.*

The officer held them to the light, examining their covers. "American, Canadian, Canadian. A likely combination." His face peered through the rear windows of the van, his flashlight piercing the shadows in the far corners. "I suppose all this food is for you?"

"Yes, of course."

"Yes, of course," the officer imitated Nick's voice. He left with the passports.

"Whew." Jim let out a breath. "That one doesn't like us at all."

"Take it easy." Nick stretched an arm along the back of the seat. "It's all an act. He's paid to be that way. It'll be okay." *God, let me be right about that.*

They waited for forty-five minutes before the cars in front of them had left and they were allowed to move up. Nick rolled the van gently under the bright lights, next to the stone tables.

The same officer approached them. "Put everything on the tables. Customs control." He stood back and watched as Nick, Jim, and Kirsten unloaded all their personal luggage, plus four boxes of food for Cristea. They carried twenty pounds of flour, twenty of sugar, and twenty of coffee. They also had five gallons of oil, and large quantities of chocolate, milk, bread, cheese, butter, and meats. Dispersed among them were four types of medicine, intended for Jozef Potra.

"This is all for you?" The officer's scowl deepened.

"Yes." Nick patted his stomach. "We eat a lot."

"Your visa says you are here for ten days. This is a lot of food."

"But we are traveling other places too. Maybe we will go to Yugoslavia or Greece after."

"Are you coming back out this way?"

"Yes, I think so. We want to spend some time in Budapest as well." The guard gave Nick a disgusted look, reminding Nick about the hatred that existed between some Romanians and Hungarians.

Jim moved to Nick's side. "Have you ever been to Budapest? It's really beautiful, especially at night."

"No," said the officer curtly.

"What about Vienna?"

"No, I have not been there."

"Vienna is very pretty also. We were just there." His lips twitched. "Nick told me the Americans destroyed it during World War II, but already it has been rebuilt and it's much nicer."

"You said you are going to Greece after?" The officer straightened, clearly trying to regain control of the conversation.

"Yes, perhaps we will." Jim leaned a hip against the table. Nick shot him a look. What happened to saying as little as possible? Jim either didn't see him, or ignored Nick's attempts to get him to stop talking. "Parts of Greece are very beautiful, though Thessaloniki is a garbage dump. Have you traveled to Greece yet?"

"No. I have not seen all of my country yet. I will do that first before I travel to other places."

In spite of his concern over the lengthy conversation, Nick felt for the man. Was that the truth, or had he never been allowed to leave Romania? If so, that would be a tragedy. What kind of prison was this? He cleared his throat. "You speak English well."

"Yes, I speak eight languages. Let me see your car papers, please." Nick retrieved them from the glove compartment of the van and handed them to the officer. He disappeared into a booth.

A female guard came out of the building and began going through their vehicle, slowly and meticulously in spite of the cold. She knocked on all the wall panels inside and out, obviously listening for a discrepancy in the sounds. She rolled down the windows and shone her flashlight into the gap held open by her screwdriver. She looked through all the maps in the glove compartment, studying each one carefully. Was she looking for circled towns, cities, or streets?

The first officer came out and stared at the three of them. Beside Nick, Kirsten shifted, as though the man's stern eyes frightened her. Nick moved a little to his left, until his arm pressed against hers, and she stilled. After what felt like an interminably long time, the officer left them and joined the woman in the van. She was groping under a seat, and suddenly let out a shout.

What did she find? Nick's throat tightened as he peered through the window of the van. A book. *Oh God, help us out of this one.* Was it a Bible from a previous trip? Or another type of Christian literature?

The officer showed the book to Nick. "What is this?" he demanded.

Nick took the book and read the title. "*Death at Chappaquiddick.* This is Kirsten Frey's book," he said to the guard. "Here's the book you lost, Kirsten."

"You." The guard snatched the book from Nick's hand and smacked it on his palm. "Look at me. I have questions for you."

God help me. Give me the right answers. "Yes?" In spite of feeling like a kid caught running in the halls, he forced himself to speak as calmly as possible.

"Do you have drugs?"

Would anyone be foolish enough to answer yes? Or to try and smuggle drugs past a command post? "No."

"Do you have guns or ammunition?"

"No."

The guard shifted his gaze to Jim. "Do you have Bibles?"

"No," Jim said. Nick watched him from the corner of his eye. Good. His friend was looking the guard directly in the eyes, just as Nick had told him to do.

"No Bibles?" The man continued to look at Jim.

"No," Jim said, a little louder this time.

The officer's eyes narrowed as he contemplated Jim, but Jim didn't move. The guard turned to Nick and Kirsten.

"Do you have Bibles or any Christian literature?"

"No," they both said.

"Do you have any books or magazines or newspapers with articles on Romania?"

"We have a *Time* and a *Life*," said Nick.

"And I have a volume of an Encyclopedia," added Jim.

"Show me."

They went to their suitcases and withdrew the magazines and the Encyclopedia. The guard confiscated the magazines then took the Encyclopedia and flipped through the pages. "This is a book about war?"

"No." Jim sounded slightly incredulous, as though the answer should be obvious. "It's a book about the world."

Nick shot him another warning look.

The officer spun around and circled the van. Nick watched him warily. Was he that determined to find something to hold against them? Finally the man stopped in front of Nick. "Whose van is this?"

"It's mine. I showed you the papers."

"Yes, of course. I have seen the papers."

"Look," said Nick, opening and closing his fists in an attempt to tamp down his impatience. "Is there a problem?"

The man's jaw worked. "Something is not right here. I expect you are up to no good."

Nick gave the officer his best *this-is-frustrating-I-don't-believe-it* look and turned away.

The officer disappeared again and was gone for more than half an hour. The three waited in the van to warm themselves, none of them speaking as there wasn't much they could say. At least nothing they wanted recorded.

The officer came out with the female guard and rapped his knuckles on the glass. "Wake up! This is not a hotel. Leave your van and come inside."

Kirsten gave Nick a weary look as they climbed out of the van. He squeezed her fingers quickly and let her go as they followed the two guards into the administration building.

"This way." The officer pointed to a door directly in front of them. A long, empty table took up most of the space, and the three of them stopped in front of it.

"We must search you, you understand. It is part of our job."

Nick started to take off his coat. He had been through this whole routine many times before. The guard would protest and simply search his pockets.

"No, no, please. Leave your coat on. Just empty your pockets onto the table."

They did so, removing their keys, coins, tissues, and hard candies. The male officer ran his hands over Jim and Nick's bodies. The female guard did likewise with Kirsten.

When they finished, both guards stood back. The officer handed Nick the three passports, slapped him on the back, and said, "Pay for your visas and leave."

Then to the female guard, he issued an order in Romanian and she swiftly left the room.

They soon had the van loaded and were back on the road. They passed the first outpost after only a brief stop by the guard then they drove into the open.

Nick breathed a heavy sigh of relief. That had been more intense than most crossings. What if they had decided to bring the Bibles? They certainly would have been found, and that guard would not have been inclined to let them off lightly. He briefly contemplated throwing that in Jim's face, but managed to hold his tongue. It wouldn't be helpful for them to turn on each other at this point.

Kirsten smacked the back of Nick's seat. "I did *not* like that, guys. That was not fun at all."

"It's called warfare, Kirsten." Nick gripped the steering wheel. "God never promised us an easy trip. I'm afraid it's only the beginning. Thank you Lord for getting us through!"

"Amen," the others agreed.

From the passenger seat, Jim tapped his arm. "Where to now?"

"It's five-thirty, Romanian time. We lost an hour coming in because of the difference in time zones. It's about two and a half hours to Oradea and another three to Cluj. We can be at Cristea's by eleven tonight, but probably closer to midnight, depending on how long it takes us to eat and refuel."

Kirsten poked her head over the front seat. "There's a car coming up fast behind us."

Jim whipped around to look. "They let us go; would they send someone to follow us?"

"Anything is possible." Nick tightened his hold on the wheel. "Let's wait and see who's in the car. One of you write down the license plate number if you can. If it looks like they're tailing us, we'll have to find an alternate route. If we stay on this road, they'll likely pick us up in Arad."

The car gained on them quickly. Nick studied it in the rear view mirror. It was a standard, four-door Dacia, that ugly Renault copy that Romania was famous for. It pulled abreast of their van and Nick glanced over.

The driver was a woman, but he couldn't see her face. Nick swung the van a little closer to the shoulder to try and get a better look into the car. The driver looked sideways at him. Through the glass and the frosted ice, he could make out the face of the female border guard. She did not look the least bit happy.

Chapter Thirteen

The car shot past the van. Nick's forehead wrinkled. *What was that about?* The Dacia veered into the lane in front of them and raced ahead. In minutes it was nearly out of sight.

"I wonder where she's going in such a hurry." Kirsten sat back in her seat.

"I don't know." Nick bit his lower lip. "Maybe she's planning to set up surveillance on us. We're only about twenty miles from Arad. If we could get off this road, we could detour around the city and head north to Oradea." He gestured to the glove compartment. "Look at the map, Jim. Is there a turnoff before Arad that takes us north?"

Jim opened the compartment and pulled out a map. Nick tapped his fingers on the steering wheel as Jim studied the paper. *Come on, come on.*

Jim pressed a finger to a spot on the map. "There are three roads that lead north of the city, but those are dead ends. It looks like there's no other way around Arad."

Nick gritted his teeth and stepped down harder on the accelerator. "I know a way. If we can make it to Arad before she sets up surveillance, there's a detour that takes us north of the city center and leaves us two miles outside the city limits on the Oradea side. From there, it's just over 150 miles to Cluj."

"Let's do it." Jim wrestled with the large, unwieldy map, trying to fold it back up.

They arrived in Arad in exactly thirty minutes, thanks to the Chevrolet's powerful engine. Nick turned left onto an industrial street, just inside the city limits.

Kirsten prayed aloud. "God, you see what our plans are, but we want to know your mind in this matter. I pray that you'll show us in the next few minutes whether you want us to go to Cluj tonight on this route, or perhaps alter our plans. God, give us protection from their watchful eyes. Give us a way out of this situation. Frustrate their plans. Create confusion, Lord."

"Amen." Nick maneuvered the van down the industrial road and onto the main highway from Arad to Oradea. Although he watched carefully, he didn't see any sign of the Dacia that had passed them. It was 6:20 in the evening, dark and bitterly cold. The road was straight for the most part and not too uneven, definitely one of the better ones in the country. Numerous villages dotted the sides of the road, but Nick tried to keep the van at a constant fifty miles per hour. Some of the larger towns were shrouded in darkness and full of pedestrians, and he was forced to go slower through their streets.

They reached Oradea shortly before eight o'clock. "I've been watching," Kirsten said, "and we haven't been followed. Should we continue on to Cluj?"

"Yeah," Nick said, "but we should get gas first. There's a station on the right just before we leave the city. We've tons of gas coupons, so let's get it now."

Hopefully they could get enough to take them all the way to Cluj, as every stop along the way increased the chances they would get stopped and held for questioning.

After a cursory police check at the outskirts, Jim took over driving and guided the van through the city. After filling the gas tank, they continued on to Cluj. Conversation slowly died as the weariness of the day overcame them. Nick stretched out on the middle seat; Jim and Kirsten listened to the soft sounds of instrumental classics on the radio. After two hours they stopped and switched places without waking Nick, whose even breathing revealed that he remained asleep even after a bumpy ride.

Kirsten reached back and shook him awake as the van rolled quietly through the outskirts of Cluj-Napoca. Calea Manastur Street was dark as usual. To conserve energy, no street lights were allowed to burn, and few windows reflected interior lighting. Many people, however, walked the streets. Had a factory just completed its nightly shift change? Anything seemed possible and Jim stirred in his seat.

Nick pointed ahead as they approached a street corner. "Jim, why don't you pull over here and walk ahead to Cristea's house. Let her know that we've come to help her and ask if we can bring our van into her courtyard. I'll park the van about three blocks past her house, facing you. Come back as soon as you can."

Jim's eyes narrowed. Had his friend noticed his attraction to Cristea and decided to help him out? He shrugged. If so, who was he to argue? "I will." He stopped the van and hopped out. "See ya." He strode along the street, a few yards behind a small group of youths. Impatient to see Cristea, he crossed the street, looking both ways as if to check for traffic, but instead scanning the sidewalks for potential followers.

Hopefully his dark clothing and boots allowed him to blend into the dullness of the street. No one appeared to be paying him any attention, which was good. The young people, now on the opposite side of the street far ahead of him, seemed to be minding their own business.

Jim reached the Greceanu gate within minutes, rang the doorbell, and slipped past the gate without waiting for an answer. Cristea waited at the door for him and Jim's breath caught. She was as beautiful as he remembered. She wore a clean, blue dress with a simple flower print. Her rich, brown hair glowed as it fell about her shoulders. The light shining from the kitchen behind her outlined her figure, and as Jim came closer to her, her magnetism began to kindle a fire somewhere deep within him.

Was she expecting him? Did she know he was coming this evening and therefore put in an extra effort to look her best? Jim tugged on his mustache as he approached. Voices drifted out from inside the house and his thoughts, galloping off in a wild direction, screeched to a halt. What had he been thinking? She had guests, male ones at least, and he was interrupting. His shoulders relaxed. Whoever it was, they would likely be happy to see him. Happy to see the supplies he'd brought, anyway. And, whatever the reason, Cristea really did look good.

"Hello Cristea. You're up late."

"Max, I'm so happy to see you." She gave him a quick hug. Was that a Romanian custom or something more? "Please come inside." She stepped back so he could pass. "I have some friends I wish for you to meet."

"Wait. Ralph and Cathy are parked just up the street. Can we pull our van into the courtyard here? Will it be safe for you?"

"Yes, of course. I will be waiting to open the gate for you. Will the three of you be staying the night with us?"

"Umm, I hope so. I'll have to ask." He met her eyes. "I, uhh, I'll be right back." He headed back down the sidewalk before he embarrassed himself further, and jogged to the van.

"It's okay, guys. Hey, she called me Max. She remembered."

Kirsten looked sideways at Jim. "Of course she did. You're a Westerner and you're single and that fascinates her. Don't read too much into it."

Her words doused the flame that seeing Cristea had ignited and he frowned. "I appreciate your concern, but I think I can handle this." He slid onto the back seat and slammed the door behind him, a little harder than necessary.

"I'm sorry, Jim." Kirsten reached back from the passenger seat and rested a hand on his arm. "I don't mean to be negative. Just be careful, okay?"

Jim let out a breath and mumbled, "Yeah. Sure."

"Let's go." Nick started the vehicle and drove to Cristea's house. "We all need to remember to use our code names. We still have to protect ourselves. And her."

"That's right. So you know, there are other people in the house. She has friends there that she wants us to meet."

"Let's just hope they're on our side."

"And she wants us to stay the night."

"We'll have to see. Maybe it would be okay."

Nick swung the van through the narrow courtyard gate and Cristea shut it behind them. After they had parked and climbed out of the vehicle, Cristea shook Nick and Kirsten's hands warmly, flashed a quick smile at Jim, and led the three of them into her house. Four young men sat in the living room. One of them was Jozef Potra. Nick, Jim, and Kirsten embraced him as a close brother.

"You're looking much better, Jozef," Nick said in precise German. "How do you feel?"

"I improve quickly, with much thanks for your help."

Cristea spoke Romanian to the other men, apparently introducing the three Westerners. Likely for his and Kirsten's benefit, she repeated the words in English, which Jim appreciated. "This is Ralph," she said, pointing to Nick. "And Cathy, and Max."

Jim looked into the eyes of a tall man, not too handsome, yet with strong features. He sported a large nose, an even row of yellow teeth, and a shock of brown hair that continually fell into his eyes. The man shook his hand firmly. "My name is Petru Potra. I am Jozef's brother." Jim gulped at the uncommon power rippling through the big man's forearms. "I do not speak good English, but perhaps better than my friends here. Except for Cristea." He offered her a smile. "We have all studied English in the school, but I think I have remembered more. Jozef learned German instead. It is a long time since we practice."

"Your English is very good." Jim pulled back his hand. *Wouldn't want to take that guy on in a fight.* Good thing they were on the same side. He almost smiled at the thought.

"You remember my brother, of course?" Petru motioned towards Jozef. "We are the same. How do you say it? Twin?"

"Twins." Nick clapped Petru on the shoulder. "Good to meet you."

"Yes, and these are our good friends, Alexini Radu and Carl Vasilescu. They are brothers in the church." They shook hands all around before settling on the chairs and couches in a rough circle.

Kirsten sat between Jim and Nick on the couch. While Cristea asked the other men in the room what they would like to drink, Kirsten whispered to Nick and Jim so no one but the two of them could hear her. "Something's not right with Petru."

Nick cast her a quick sidelong glance. "What makes you say that? You don't even know him."

"Call it a woman's intuition."

"You aren't old enough to have that yet," he whispered into her ear.

She gave him a quick elbow in the ribs. "Call it the Holy Spirit's voice, then. Keep it in mind, both of you."

Jim studied Jozef's brother as he accepted a cup of tea from Cristea and thanked her. Something had struck him a little funny when he'd shook the man's hand, now that Kirsten mentioned it. He'd chalked it up to the man being an alpha male, but maybe it was something more than that.

As Cristea served the three of them hot drinks, she inclined her head to the two friends of the Potras. "They are farmers," she stated. "I have only met them twice before this week, but Jozef says that they are good brothers and can be trusted. He had me call them to come to see if they could help. They, too, were at the church when it was disrupted by the police."

Jim contemplated the two farmers. They looked to be in their late twenties, but could be younger. He'd met a lot of people who looked older than they were because of a harsh lifestyle. Both men seemed to have a small paunch, although that was likely from an unbalanced diet rather than a lack of exercise. Their faces were hard and tanned from years spent in the fields, but they also suggested a gentleness of character.

The one Petru had introduced as Carl set his mug down on a small table. "My English not so good, but I understand a little. I think is better than Alexini." His friend must have caught the mention of his name as he looked questioningly at Carl. Carl laughed softly. "You no speak English." Alexini grinned widely and shook his head.

Jim smiled. They seemed like they would be good people to have as friends. Kirsten was right, though. There was something about Petru that put him a little bit on edge. And if he was going to be spending time with Cristea … Jim's fingers tightened around his mug. While he was here, he planned to keep a very close eye on Jozef Potra's brother.

Nick tipped his head to drain the last of his coffee and set down his mug. "Petru, your brother told us you were there when the church service was disrupted by the police.

He said that he didn't see you or your father after the three of you were taken to the military compound. Can you tell us what happened to you? Were you arrested?"

"Yes, I was captured also, but was held only for a short time. I did not know the condition of my father or my brother, but just this week, Cristea telephoned our house and I was home. I was very worried for my brother, but she said that he was here. It wasn't until I came here that I found that he had been beaten."

Petru didn't quite meet Nick's eyes as he spoke. Was Kirsten right? Was something not quite right here? He wouldn't be lying about what happened to him, would he? "Why do you think you were released when your brother was tortured and your father has disappeared?"

"But we know where my father is being held now." Petru lifted one finger. "There is a small military training base in the mountains south of Brasov where the *Securitate* keep certain prisoners. I discovered that our father is being kept in this place."

Cristea shifted her attention from Petru to the three couriers. "Petru said that he has an old friend from his military days who is now an officer in the army. This person agreed to share the location of their father for only two kilograms of coffee. It was a great risk for this officer."

Nick had a lot of questions for Petru, but he pressed his lips together. Maybe now was not the time.

"What are the plans now, Ralph?" Jim hissed from the corner of his mouth. "Are we going to bust their father out of prison?"

"A little sarcasm there? No, it's not likely that we'll bust anyone out of prison. Perhaps though, we can take a drive down to Brasov and have a look around the area."

"What will that accomplish?" asked Kirsten.

"Maybe nothing. Maybe something will come up though. It's doubtful we'll be able to do anything from here in Cluj. What do you think, Cristea?"

"I think that we will all think better with food in our stomachs. You are hungry, yes? I have prepared something to eat."

"Oh, something small please, Cristea," Kirsten said. "It's very late."

Nick shot Kirsten a look. He hadn't eaten much that day, only a few small snacks, and he was hungry.

Jim apparently felt the same way. He patted his stomach. "I'm ready, Cristea."

The eight of them sat down to a meal of bread warmed slightly to detract from its staleness, goat's head cheese, eggs cooked heavily with oil, and a stew with sizeable chunks of meat and a few vegetables.

"My friends," Cristea said, indicating Carl and Alexini, "were very kind to bring me supplies from their home. It is difficult for me to look for food when I must work all day."

Nick choked down a bite of goat's head cheese. "We've brought you a few supplies too," he said. "It's not much, but maybe it will keep you for a while. We also have medicine for Jozef. There's penicillin and something else for infection."

Cristea translated what Nick had said and Jozef smiled and nodded. He said something in Romanian to Cristea. "Jozef is very grateful," she said. "Our doctor friend from church works at the Second Department of Obstetrics and Gynecology here in Cluj. He told us that he gets only two new syringes each month and now the medicine shelves are empty. They have no penicillin and only small amounts of other antibiotics."

Petru looked up from his meal. "What plans will we make? Will we go to Brasov now?"

"What would we do there?" Cristea asked. "Even if your father is being held there, it will be impossible to get him out."

Jozef pointed to his brother and said something quickly in Romanian. Petru answered him before glancing over at Nick and the others. "He asked if I could go to the prison and plead with the officials to release our father. He thinks that might have worked sometimes in the past. I told him we could only try. If we have coffee or something to trade then anything could happen."

"And if that doesn't work," Kirsten waved her fork through the air, "we may have to leave Romania and try to get him out using diplomatic channels. Perhaps the American government could put pressure on the Romanians."

Nick swirled the traces of tea in his cup. "You forget what just happened recently, Kirsten. When Romania finally paid off its twenty-four billion dollar foreign debt, it rejected America's offer of a Most-Favored-Nations trading status."

Kirsten blinked. "You're kidding."

"No. America had accused Romania of human rights violations and Romania wouldn't admit it. I highly doubt that Romania would care what America thinks."

Carl said something to Cristea, who translated for the Westerners. "Romania does care, Carl thinks. But Ceauşescu is the leader." She passed the plate of bread to Nick. "He wants to go to Brasov in the morning to see what can be done."

The Romanians began speaking among themselves while the three couriers waited patiently.

Finally, they fell silent and Cristea said, "We are all coming with you. Except for Alexini. He said he must stay home to look after his wife and girl. But the rest of us can come. Carl has two days off work, and if he is gone longer, no one will care. It is not unusual for someone to miss work."

"We have friends in a house near Brasov, in a small town named Vulcan." Nick sopped up the gravy on his plate with the last bit of his bread and popped it into his mouth. "I'm sure they would be glad to see us. Perhaps some of you could stay with them. Max and Cathy and I will check into one of the hotels in Brasov. We have coupons we can use and it will be safer for all of us."

Petru picked up Carl's empty plate and stacked it on top of his. "I would like to stay with you also. Maybe I can be of help."

Nick bit his lip. Could they trust the man enough to let him stay with them? If he did, it would be easier to keep an eye on him. He nodded. "That would be great." He handed his plate to Petru. "We'll need all the help we can get. But what happens if we get your father released? Won't the colonel who put him in prison just do it again?"

Petru took his plate and added it to the pile. "Yes. My father would have to leave the country. As a pastor, his work is finished. The others in the church have found other churches farther away to worship in. Another man would need to bring them together again."

"Are you that man?" Kirsten asked.

"No, my sister, I am not that man. It is not possible."

Jozef gathered up cutlery and carried it to the sink. He turned and leaned back against the counter and spoke to Cristea. She translated when he was finished. "He says that if you help his father leave the country, he would like to go also. I think Carl and Alexini might want to escape too."

Nick sighed. "We'll have to decide on that later. What time will we leave tomorrow? We can all go in our van. There's enough room."

"What about the post controls?" Petru set the stack of plates down on the counter.

"We will tell them that Ralph was kind enough to stop and give us a ride to Brasov," Cristea replied. "It is the truth."

She walked over to the sink and turned on the water. "We can leave at eight o'clock. Now I must wash these dishes. Max and Ralph can sleep in the living room. The couch pulls out into a bed. I hope it will be okay." She spoke in Romanian to the others and the men moved off to a different part of the house. "Cathy, you can sleep in my bed, if you don't mind. It is quite large."

"That sounds fine. But I'll help you with the dishes first." Kirsten carried glasses over to the sink.

"We'll help too." Nick grabbed two dish towels from the handle of the stove and tossed one to Jim.

"Cristea," Kirsten ran water over the dish cloth and wiped down the table. "I don't mean to be rude, but we aren't sure we can trust Petru. There's something about him that just doesn't seem right."

Cristea sighed. "I know. I believe I am suspicious also. Why do you think Jozef would be taken and beaten and their father put in prison, but Petru let go without a penalty?" She ran a plate under the hot water and handed it to Nick.

Nick took it and swiped the dish towel over it. "That's a very good question."

"So why did you agree to take him to Brasov?"

"If Petru is with us in Brasov, we can keep our eyes on him. If he turns out to be loyal to us, then we're fortunate. However, if he is working for someone else, we may be able to catch him and confront him."

"I have an idea." Cristea set the last plate in the rack. "After you drop us off at your friend's house in Vulcan and go with Petru to Brasov, I will take the others to a town called Codlea. It is only a short walk farther south. I have friends there also who will welcome us to stay with them. Then, if Petru does inform on us to the *Securitate*, they will look for us in the wrong town."

Nick hung the dish towel over the handle of the stove. "I have been to Codlea. I've dropped books there more than once. If you give us the address, we'll know where to find you. But don't tell the others until after you arrive in Vulcan. If we hope to help Yari Potra, we can't make any mistakes."

Colonel General Popescu stood in front of his window, staring out at the dreary day. Tiny rays of sun struggled to force their way through the smog. Lost in thought, he jumped at the shrill ringing of the telephone. With a heavy exhalation of breath, he made his way over to the front of the desk, leaned over, and picked up the receiver. "Yes?"

"Colonel Popescu?"

Popescu frowned. "Who is this?"

"It's Alexini Radu."

Popescu straightened abruptly. "Do you have something for me?"

"I have information, but I need you to promise that my daughter won't be harmed at school."

"Of course. I promise."

"Jozef Potra is staying down near Brasov, in a small village named Vulcan. That's all I know."

The line went dead.

Chapter Fourteen

The next day, Popescu lifted the brass-lined receiver of his telephone again. He drew in a deep breath and dialed the number. Colonel General Vlad's secretary put him right through.

"Comrade Popescu, you are having problems with Jozef Potra." The colonel general nearly shouted the words and Popescu had to force himself not to move the receiver away from his ear. "I was quite sure that you would have everything under control by now. You are disappointing me."

"I am terribly sorry, sir. But there has been—"

"You cannot allow this to turn into an incident of international exposure. You must remember the time in Brasov only two years ago when a man of similar position to yours showed terrible judgment. That situation developed into riots for food and soon the whole world knew about it."

"Yes, sir, I remember. But—"

"Colonel," Vlad was clearly in no mood to listen and Popescu's fingers tightened around the receiver. "I flew up from Bucharest in November of 1987 to oversee the control of that revolt in Brasov. You can be certain that I have no desire to fly to Cluj to discuss the Potra situation with you."

"No need, Colonel General. I have good news to report."

"Then you are fortunate. Our most esteemed president is preparing for his visit to Libya to spend time with his good friend, Mu'ammar Qadhafi. He will leave his stupid wife in charge. Fortunately, I'll be with the president on this visit. If reports are bad, Elena will wipe the floor with your head. I repeat, we can't let Brasov happen again."

"Colonel General, is it safe for you to speak of our gracious Deputy Prime Minister with such disrespect?"

"You imbecile! I'm the head of the *Securitate*. I'm the one who installs the listening devices. Do you think for a moment that I would put one on my own private telephone? Do you think I would allow my own office to be monitored? You're an idiot."

Not your phone, but what about mine? Did you think of that? "I'm sorry, sir. I certainly meant no offense. As I said, I do have good news."

"It had better be good, Colonel. The church can be very difficult for us. They are a major dissenting group in this country."

"We should exterminate them all, sir."

"Your good news, Colonel." The colonel general sounded weary. "What is it? Have you located Potra?"

"There's been a great breakthrough, sir. An informer called yesterday to say that Jozef is in a town southwest of Brasov. We should be able to round him up shortly."

"Why didn't you do that yesterday when the news came through? He could be gone by now."

"My men were in Brasov, sir, delivering Yari Potra to the stockade. They didn't return until late. We'll have Jozef Potra within hours, I assure you."

"There must be no mistake. Once you find him, eliminate the man and his father. While you're at it, get rid of Petru Potra. Let the entire family disappear. They have caused us enough worries."

"Sir, I was hoping to use Petru Potra to my advantage. I have that man tied around my finger. He's very valuable to me."

"Colonel, I only give orders once. By Monday, the whole family will disappear. Or you will. That's only four days away. You had better get moving, Colonel Popescu."

"Yes sir. It will be done as you wish."

Colonel Popescu contemplated the three men sitting quietly in front of him. Nuvelei, Elanului, and Mumuleanu had to have picked up on a great deal of what the Colonel General was saying, as he had spoken so loudly. They had likely even heard his superior call him an imbecile and an idiot. His cheeks warmed slightly as he slammed the receiver down and rose to his full height.

"Pack your things and be ready to leave in one hour," Popescu ordered. "We are going to Vulcan to pick up Jozef Potra."

The Parc Hotel in central Brasov was a six-story dilapidated affair, not quite meeting the standards of its two modern competitors down the street. Its walls were beige, darkened slightly from the smog; recent efforts to repaint its white trim had failed to enhance it. Nick had attempted to find them a room in the other two hotels, but they were booked up. He stepped through the Parc's huge wooden front doors and looked around. *I don't envy anyone who extracts a meager existence from working in this shell.* It was warmer inside, not as it should be, but still much better than spending another night in the van.

There was no elevator so, after checking in at the reception desk, the three young Westerners and Petru Potra climbed two flights of stairs with their luggage and deposited them in two separate rooms. Petru took a room across the hall from the three couriers. For him to join them would be too obvious.

Nick stood at the window of their room, gazing out over the parking lot of the hotel. It was still early in the afternoon. The sun, eclipsed by the smog and overcast skies, appeared to accelerate towards the horizon as if in search of a more cheering land upon which to shine its rays. The temperature had plummeted in the last hour, and people hurried about their business on the streets, some stomping their feet and banging their hands together in an effort to keep their blood circulating.

"Where do we start?" Kirsten asked the others after Petru joined them in their room.

"Wait a minute." Nick held up a hand. "Remember to keep your voice low. In fact, we should turn on our cassette player whenever we're in the room. The walls may have ears."

"Good idea." Kirsten turned on the small cassette player she had brought up to the room with her.

"I have a plan," declared Petru, not too loudly. "I can talk to people in the city. I have friends here who served with me in the army many years ago. Perhaps some of them may have heard news of my father. There is always talk if one goes to the right places."

Jim came out from examining the bathroom, a look of disgust on his face. "The water coming out of the tap is red. What's the deal?"

"Let it run for a few minutes," Nick suggested. "It should clear up. I wouldn't drink it, though."

"Oh, glad you mentioned that." Jim popped back into the washroom and a second later the sound of water splashing into the sink drifted from the small room. When he came back out, he held up a plastic cup filled with red liquid. "I was just about to have a big drink."

Nick punched him in the arm and Jim spun around and dumped the cup into the washroom sink before any of it hit the floor. He came back out drying his hands on a small towel. "What would you like us to do, Petru? Can we help you in any way?"

"You must all rest. It would not be good for us if we are seen too much together. Stay here, or go shopping, or eat in a restaurant. Maybe God will bless us and give us a lead to go on." He flashed a grin of yellowing teeth and walked to the door. Just before walking into the hall, he looked back at the others. "It might be good for us if I had some American dollars to use as a ... how do you say ... lever?"

Nick pulled his wallet from his hip pocket. "How much do you think is enough?"

"Twenty dollars will be very good, I think."

As soon as he was gone, Kirsten whirled around to face Nick. "Aren't we going to follow him?"

Nick flung himself down on the gaudy floral bedspread on one of the beds. "No way, Kirsten. You keep forgetting we're foreigners. We stand out too much in this country, remember?"

"But if Petru is an informer, he could set us up. How can we trust him if we don't know which side he's on?"

"We agree that we don't trust him. However, we can watch him and listen to what he has to say and then do our best to evaluate his words and body language. In the meantime, we'll sit and wait and try to get some rest."

☭

Petru straightened up from the other side of the doorway where he had been listening and strode down the hallway to the stairs. So they were on to him. How could they even begin to think he was an informer when he had given them no clues? Or had he? Had he said or done anything that had given him away? He exhaled heavily as he bounded down the stairs. It mattered little now. From this point on, he must be extra careful.

He stepped into the hotel lobby, looking for a telephone. He was in a tough situation. How was he to help his father and brother yet remain in good standing with Colonel Popescu?

The colonel had given him the choice just over three months ago: be executed for attempting to escape Romania or work for him as an informer. That tragic day at the border when the guards appeared with machine guns blazing would haunt him for many years. But what now was life when it was spent betraying his family, his own Christian brethren? *Maybe I should try to escape again.* Once he was out of the country, he could attempt to help his family. That had been his plan from the beginning. He made his way over to the reception desk. First he must focus on the problem at hand. He had a very important decision to make. He could be used in a powerful way for evil or he could channel his potential to help his family. There was no middle ground. He could think of no other alternative.

He slipped the hotel clerk a Kent cigarette from his hidden stash and asked to use the telephone. The man behind the counter pushed the phone towards Petru and turned his back, offering a spurious privacy. Petru dialed six numbers and asked for Sergeant Branicevo.

"Where are you?" boomed a robust voice. "Have you more coffee for me?" Branicevo's laugh churned Petru's insides.

"How is my father?"

"Mr. Potra, I'm surprised." The laughter had vanished from his voice. "Not on the phone, you dimwit."

"Forgive me, Sergeant. Can we meet today?"

"Certainly, if it's worth my while. I finish my shift at six o'clock. Where are you calling from?"

"I just stepped into the lobby of the Hotel Parc in Brasov. I have no transportation; I'm sorry."

"I'll be there shortly after seven. Do you mind if I bring a couple of old friends? They've just arrived from your very own city. Maybe you are acquainted with each other."

"Who are they? What are their names?"

"Now, now, Petru," Branicevo chuckled. "Are there no more secrets in the army these days? We'll see you around seven."

The dining room of the Hotel Parc was neatly decorated and basically clean, but still an ugly sight. Only a few lights were left on this Saturday evening in order to conserve electricity. The music was loud, however. Together, with billows of cigarette smoke and the heat exuding from a mass of predominantly male bodies, it could have represented a scene from a discotheque in hell.

Petru Potra waited at a table in the extreme back corner, his back to the wall. He wanted no surprises. It was shortly after seven o'clock and he expected Sergeant Branicevo to appear with his two acquaintances at any moment. He could barely see for more than fifteen feet because of the density of the smoke and the weaving of too many drunken bodies.

Petru hated this place. His father would not approve of him being in the restaurant at this time. He knew of few Christians who would even dare to enter such a place, for it was practically forbidden. The environment was a far cry from the simplicity and cleanliness of church. There, at least, he had been able to breathe.

Sergeant Branicevo appeared as if by magic at the edge of the table, taking a seat without waiting for an invitation. The men who sat down on either side of him were completely dissimilar in appearance. The first was short and stocky, with a flat, ugly face that told of a cold, cruel spirit. The second was taller and much better looking. He had school-boy features that suggested an innocence that probably did not exist. "These are the good friends I wish for you to meet, Comrade Potra. This is Nuvelei," he inclined his head towards the ugly man. "A very beautiful suit, is it not?"

Petru nodded his greeting. Where had he seen that one before? His forehead wrinkled. Actually, he'd seen both of them together recently. The memory struck him with the force of a fist to his gut. The church in the forest. That was it.

"And this is Mr. Mumuleanu." Branicevo nudged the taller man with his shoulder. "We all have much in common."

Petru attempted to gain control of the meeting. "Shall I order drinks for us? They're on me tonight."

"Well, well, Mr. Potra." Branicevo laughed. "You're truly seeking privileged information to be so generous, are you not?" He waved a hand dismissively. "No drinks. Let's get to the point. I have many things to take care of this evening. First of all, what do you have for me?" He held out a hairy hand, palm up.

This was not as Petru had hoped. He tugged the twenty dollar bill from his pocket and set it on Branicevo's palm. "That's all I have." He had hoped to reach this stage gradually, allowing time for the alcohol to loosen their minds and their tongues. "I want to know about my father." He pulled back his hand and clasped both of his in his lap. "How is he keeping? What will they do to him?"

"For twenty dollars, I can tell you certain things." Branicevo shoved the money into the inside pocket of his jacket. "Your father is doing fine. He is being treated the same as the rest of the prisoners. If he behaves himself, he does okay. If he gets out of line, they punish him. It's all normal."

Petru leaned across the table, desperate for further information. "Is he being tortured?"

"Come now, Mr. Potra." Branicevo drew back as though the very idea offended him. "That is something of the past. We are much more civilized these days. We aren't like the one the Americans call Dracula, impaling offenders on stakes."

"Can I see my father?"

"It's not possible at this time," Branicevo retorted sharply. Then, in a softer voice, he said, "Much of our force has been called away. We are not in a position to handle visitors right now. You would have to come back in a week. Perhaps longer."

A waitress arrived and Branicevo stood up. "I have things to do. My friends will stay and talk with you if you wish." He gave his friends a wink that Petru did not fail to notice, then turned and disappeared into the smoke. Petru ordered two beers for the officers and a cola for himself.

Nuvelei said to the waitress, "Keep track of our bill. Our friend here," he jerked his head towards Petru, "will take care of it later."

"Bring us many beers." Mumuleanu grinned. "We might be here a long time."

They drank into the night, talking mostly of women caught and lost, great deals each had made over the less fortunate, and dreams of grandeur for the future. Petru consumed only colas, staying sober and waiting for his chance to glean another piece of knowledge regarding his father.

"You come from a good family?" he asked Mumuleanu.

"Nah. My father was a drunk and so was my mother. They abandoned me when I was a baby. I grew up in an orphanage until I was sixteen and then spent two years with my uncle. He was a mean one, that man. We never did get along well. Taught me a lot though."

"Do you know what became of your father and mother?"

"I heard when I was about seven that my father had been sent to work in one of the factories in Bucharest. He was dead within weeks. My mother?" Mumuleanu stared into his beer. "My mother killed herself. They told me she jumped in front of a police car."

"Do you really believe that, Comrade?" his friend, Nuvelei asked.

"They had witnesses."

"Of course," Nuvelei said. "We… they will have witnesses when they want them. I think my father died like that too."

Petru caught Nuvelei's slip of the tongue. How many times had Nuvelei run over an innocent with his police car? He cleared his throat. "And what of my father? How will he die?"

"Your father does not die so easily." As Petru had hoped, the beers appeared to have loosened Nuvelei's tongue. Would he even remember telling him so much by tomorrow morning? "But on Monday, we will show him another option."

Chapter Fifteen

The knock on the door came too early. Jim's eyes flew open. *What is that noise?* "Wake up," Petru hissed through the door of the hotel room where his three companions had been sleeping.

"Hang on." Dressed in a pair of pants, a shirt, and two sweaters, Jim reluctantly tossed back the covers and climbed out of bed before stumbling to the door and flinging it open. "Isn't it a bit early, Petru?" he asked, walking back to his bed.

"It's past nine o'clock. You must not sleep all day. There are many things we must try to do." Petru closed the door and crossed the room to turn on the cassette player. "Your room is very cold. Don't you have any heat in here?"

Nick appeared from his refuge under the covers. "No. We phoned down to the desk last night and they said there would be heat by morning. It's typical if you ask me. You should know these things. Why do you think we're wearing all these extra clothes?"

"Where's Cathy?" Petru asked.

Kirsten peered out from the many layers of blankets on her bed. "I'm alive. I'm still here."

Jim looked closer at Petru. There was a distinct redness around his eyes and an intense lingering stench of smoke on his clothing. "What time did you get in last night?"

"It was very late. I think two o'clock in the morning."

Nick sat up in bed. "Did you find out anything new about your father? Is he okay?"

"Yes, my father is good. For now, he is good." Petru sank down on a chair in the corner. "I learn that tomorrow, he might be killed."

Jim looked up from tying the laces on his shoe. "How did you find that out?"

"I speak with soldiers last night who work at the compound where he is kept. They tell me this. They said also that Colonel Popescu is in Brasov right now."

"Who's Colonel Popescu?" Nick climbed out of bed and stretched. "Where have I heard that name before?"

"He is well known in the Cluj area," Petru said. "He is a member of the *Securitate*, the secret police force, and is a very important man in this organization. Thousands of people in Cluj inform for him. It is difficult for a man like him to be a secret."

"Ah, yes." Nick lowered his arms. "That's where I've heard the name."

"Colonel Popescu is the man who put my father and my brother into prison. Now he will kill my father tomorrow. I think it is because Jozef has escaped. He must have his revenge. Maybe he is looking for me as well."

"Then he could find you here." Jim finished tying his shoes and stood up. "Didn't you register your name last night?"

Petru shook his head. "You were not watching. I used a different name and paid immediately with *lei*. They asked me no questions."

Jim ducked into the washroom. He combed his hair and tugged on his mustache, smoothing it into order before going back out into the room. "We can't just sit here all day, guys. Let's see if we can find Yari Potra."

"Wait a minute, Max." Kirsten sat up, clutching the blankets to her chest. "There'll be soldiers guarding him. Remember? I've seen those machine guns work before. My cousins used to fire them in the gravel pits down near Houston. You don't fool around with them."

Petru shook his head. "I think it might not be a problem. One of the men last night told me that most of the soldiers were called away to a different part of the country. Only a few are left. I do not believe they will be the type who are all good workers. I think maybe they get drunk and don't worry too much about the prisoners. If there is a time to reach my father, it is now."

Jim held his arms out to both sides. "What's it going to be, Ralph? I'm willing to get a closer look at the compound if you think now is the time."

"Let's pray about it first." Nick sat down on the edge of the bed. "Then, unless God gives us a clear indication that we shouldn't try it, we'll keep moving ahead. How does that sound?"

The others agreed that it was a good idea. They bowed their heads and their hearts to seek the mind of the eternal Father. Even Petru prayed, speaking in Romanian.

Jim shivered, loving the reminder that the Church of Christ was global. When they finished, he looked over at Nick. "What do you want to do now?"

"Shower first and then breakfast. Later this afternoon, when it is starting to get dark, we'll get Petru to show us where this compound is and we'll see what we can do about getting Yari out. It will be better for whoever we decide will go to approach the compound at night."

"We can eat breakfast in the restaurant downstairs," Petru suggested.

"No way." Nick shuddered. "I stayed in this hotel two years ago and the food here was terrible. Petru, we'll show you how to put together an American-style breakfast." He rose from the bed and crossed the room to where he had hung his overcoat and pulled a set of keys from the pocket. Returning to the others, he tossed the set to Petru. "Why don't you go down with Cathy and help her bring up some food? You can scare away the people who come begging for presents."

Kirsten looked as though she was about to protest, but Nick nodded and she got up and pulled on her coat and boots. "C'mon Petru, let's see what we can find."

When they had left the room, Jim looked over at Nick. "What are you thinking?"

"Let's get Petru to show us the location of the compound. Since you're a more experienced outdoorsman, hopefully you'll be able to tell if there's anything you can do to get in and out of it. It might be worth a shot. If you're gone too long, we'll come back to town here and wait."

Jim's stomach twisted. "You'll leave me there by myself? Why don't you just wait for me where you drop me off?"

"That'll be fine for a short while, but if a lot of time passes, it'll be too risky. Even if you don't run into trouble, we'll be sitting there for any patrols to find. After you've left us, we can pressure Petru to tell us what he's really up to. Whatever he says, we won't let him out of our sight."

Jim blew out a breath. "If you do come back to the hotel, I can't bring the pastor here if there's any chance Petru is an informer. We'll have to set up a signal."

"Yeah, I guess so."

Jim contemplated various options then smacked his fist on his palm. "I know. Across the street from the hotel, where the van is parked, there's a *P* sign. Do you remember it?"

Nick nodded.

"Bend it over to a forty-five degree angle and I'll know as I approach that you won't be here but you'll be waiting for me in Codlea."

"Have you got the address?" asked Nick.

"You'll have to write it out for me. I'll memorize it before we go then flush it down the toilet."

"What if you don't show up say, within three days?"

Jim shrugged. "Leave the country. I'll find my own way out."

"We could wait for you at the Central Hotel in Belgrade. If you don't show up in another two or three days, we'll go to the embassy. They might be able to help."

"Okay." Jim clapped his hands together. "That's simple enough. You know, besides the sneaking onto a military compound and breaking out a heavily-guarded prisoner part. We'll need to put together a few supplies for me to—"

The door burst open and Kirsten and Petru came through, each carrying an armload of food.

"All right!" Nick stood up. "Food. Here, let me give you a hand." He took a box from Kirsten and placed it on the side table. "Max and I were just saying that we have to outfit him with a survival kit. What do you think he'll need, Petru?"

Petru set the cooler he was carrying on the floor. "Rope, matches, something warm for my father to wear. Something to eat. Do you have a tool to cut wire? That would be very good. Some money, of course. Cigarettes to offer guards if you run into one. Those are the basics."

"We'll need to buy a pack of cigarettes," Nick said. "The rest we have. I think there's a pair of pliers in the tool kit in the van. You can take those."

Kirsten emptied food from a box into the table. "It sounds like you two already have a plan. Are you going to let Petru and me in on it?"

"Sure," answered Nick. "Unless you see a major flaw with this idea, we'll drive south of here later this afternoon and let Max off somewhere near the military compound. He'll simply check out the situation and come back. Of course, if there's a clear opportunity, he'll help Yari to get out, but only if it's completely safe. We'll wait for him in the area, and if he's too long, then here at the hotel."

Petru reached into his pocket and withdrew a small black and white picture of his family from a worn billfold. He passed the photo to Jim. "This was taken only two years ago. That is my father between Jozef and me. You may need it in case you run into him."

Jim studied the photo for a minute then returned it to Petru. "I'll remember his face. You keep the picture." He turned to Nick. "Let me see the map, Ralph." They spread it out on the bed and bent over it. "How far is it from Brasov to Predeal? Fifteen miles?"

"Exactly fifteen." Kirsten peered over his shoulder. "How far is the compound from Predeal, Petru?"

"Maybe three miles. I will show you. They have small roads in the area that are not marked on the map." He tapped a point on the map slightly west of Predeal on Highway 73A with a large, rough finger. "It is here."

"Then later today, that's where we'll go." Jim straightened and headed for the table. "But first, we eat."

At dusk, Nick drove the van through the cold streets of Predeal, an ancient village with little more than a few hundred people, set high in the Subcarpathian mountain range. More specifically, it was set on the windswept northeast front of Mount Bucegi, which didn't seem to be a safe location for any dwelling. Nick shivered. In the long winter months, the early sunset must add to the natural chill of the atmosphere.

Petru told them a little about the area as they passed through. The village was comprised of peasants, some who scraped out their existence from the one factory in town, others who tended their farm animals, while still more commuted each day to Brasov to work in the factories there.

"For a long time, the people of Predeal were very poor." From the passenger seat, Petru swept a hand over the dashboard to indicate the entire village. From what Nick could see through the front windshield—the gaunt faces of the people walking on the street, the run-down buildings and threadbare coats—they were poor still. "Even back to the times when Vlad... how do you say... Vlad the Impaler was the ruler, they were among the first to suffer. The village has not really changed over time. A few people are more fortunate, of course, and own Dacia automobiles. Some even have black and white televisions."

Nick studied the desolate faces of the people trudging down the sidewalks.

"What a ministry one could have in this town." Kirsten leaned forward from the back seat. "If a Spirit-filled Christian came here, the possibilities for reaching a place like this would be endless."

"It is Orthodox," Petru said. "It is hard mold to break. The Orthodox do not change easily."

Nick shot him a sideways glance. "But God provides what is necessary for change, don't you think?"

"I agree," replied Petru. "But the Orthodox already believe they have proper religion. Many in the church do not want change. You must understand when you come here, that the authorities are also Orthodox. The ones who control this village are the problem. They are Orthodox and they would not like someone to come and tell the people how bad they really are. You must find a way to break in and that is not easy."

"Do you have any ideas?" asked Jim.

"Only one." Petru shifted in his seat to look back at him. "You must come to them with something to offer. If you can run programs that improve their way of living, if you can teach them work, which gives them a better life, then you might succeed. However, that is impossible now. To live in Romania, you could only come as a student or as a diplomat. Then, they will watch you very closely and sometimes follow you. There are no easy solutions."

"We need Romania to be a free country." Jim smacked the back of the seat.

"Free from what?" Nick frowned at him in the rear view mirror. "Do you really think that American influence would make this country a better place to live? Do you think American Christianity would better the Romanian church? Sure, they could use improved sound systems and more Bibles and hymnbooks. But tell me honestly, how many American churches are filled to standing room only? And how many empty seats do you see in a Romanian church?"

"It's not just a numbers game," Jim said.

"But the numbers could very well be an indication of how the Holy Spirit is moving through people's hearts."

"I've never been in a Romanian church. You know that." Jim slumped against the back of the seat.

"I have," Nick said. "And it's hard to get through the door."

Petru stared out the side window. "Change will come someday. I fear for much bloodshed in my country."

Nick drove out of the village, heading west on 73A. Petru touched his elbow. "You must go slowly now," he said quietly. "It is not far from here."

They passed a rest stop and then, slightly farther along, a turnoff that was little more than a narrow set of tracks leading up through the forest. "There it is." Petru jabbed a finger against the windshield. "That is the road that leads up to the compound. If you drive up it, you will see that it widens into a regular two lane highway. There will be other ways for Max to get there, of course."

Jim peered over the front seat. "How far is the compound from here?"

"Maybe two kilometers. I think we should let you out just ahead."

Kirsten slid to the front of the seat too. "Will you be all right, Max? I'm worried for you. It's really cold tonight."

"Pray for me." Jim tapped Nick on the shoulder. "Stop the van here, Ralph. This is where I'll get out."

Nick pulled the van carefully to the side of the road. "Are you going to be okay?"

"Sure."

"Do you have all your things?"

"Yeah, in the backpack here. I'll carry the coat for Yari."

"Don't lose that one." Nick grinned. "It's my best coat."

"I'll be careful. See you guys soon. Pray for me."

"Of course. Hey Max, do you remember that rest stop we passed a mile back down the road? We'll wait there for you for exactly four hours. After that, you're on your own."

Jim nodded and pushed open the door. After a moment's hesitation, he reached down and pulled the rubber mat off the floor, rolling it up and stuffing it in his backpack. "I might need this," he said without further explanation as he turned and disappeared into the night.

Nick strained to catch a glimpse of his friend, but couldn't see him. "It's dark tonight. Which should work in his favor."

Petru turned to him, eyes wide. "He's already gone."

Nick chuckled. "Max grew up hunting deer with his dad. It was a passion of theirs. He became quite skilled at losing himself in the woods, as I understand." He performed a three-point turn with the van and headed back to the rest stop. "If there's anyone who stands a chance at sneaking in and out of the compound, it's Max."

They returned to the rest stop and parked in the darkest corner. With luck, the police or military would not drive by in the next four hours and stop to question their presence.

Nick shut off the engine and turned to Kirsten and Petru. "Do either of you want some hot chocolate? If we're going to have to wait for a while, we might as well stay warm."

Kirsten raised her hand. "I do."

Petru nodded. "Me too."

Nick crawled over the seat into the back and set up the portable butane stove and a pot of water to boil. Within a few minutes, they had each settled under a blanket with a large mug of hot chocolate. Petru's approval was obvious. "We do not drink this very much." He smiled. "It is only sold in the Western currency stores, and is usually unavailable for us. I like it very much."

Nick smiled in return. "Petru," he began, "Cathy and I have something we want to ask." "Yes? What is it?"

Nick scrutinized him. With his unshaven face set with amiable brown eyes under a shock of brown hair, Petru Potra was a hard man to dislike. If Kirsten's instincts were correct, if Petru was an informer, Nick was struggling to detect it. What was happening in this country where as much as half the population would betray their fellow man to the *Securitate*?

And Petru? How could a man betray his own people when he seemed so concerned with the welfare of the church? What could change a man in that way? What pressures must come to bear on such a man as this that would force him to lead a double life? Nick repressed a sigh. He didn't relish the idea of finding out.

"Petru, so much of our work is based on trust. Do you understand that?" Petru nodded, lowering his mug. "Cathy and I want to ask you some questions, but there seems to be no easy way. We must be direct."

The man stiffened slightly. What did that mean? Nick studied him but couldn't interpret the emotions flickering across his face. "I am listening," Petru answered, a slight tremble in his voice.

"We are Christians, like yourself, and therefore we have to be honest with you. We also want you to understand that if you have done something that seems terrible, there is forgiveness for you, not only from God, but from us and the brothers and sisters in your church. Petru, will you be honest with us?"

"I think I know what you are going to ask me." He clasped his hands tightly around his mug. "I will try to tell you the truth."

"Did you inform the *Securitate* about your brother, your father, and the people in your church?"

Petru stared at the floor. Nick watched him. What was he thinking? Had his words—that God and all of them would forgive him—gotten through to him? Would that be enough to get him to open up to them about anything he might have done? Nick's stomach tightened. Maybe he had misspoken. He knew God would forgive Petru, and he and Jim and Kirsten certainly would, but what about his family? His church? If Petru was the one who had betrayed them, could they ever get past the fact that he had handed them over to the *Securitate*?

"Petru?" Nick reached out and gripped his arm. "What's your answer?"

Petru raised his gaze to meet Nick's. "I am ashamed; how can I reply? I am the one."

Chapter Sixteen

Yari awoke to the sound of footsteps, but kept his eyes closed. He needed time. The cold of the floor bars penetrated deep into his bones.

"Why was he brought here?"

Yari recognized the voice of Captain Andrej Grigore. The man sounded stern, commanding, and controlled, but not harsh. Unlike most of the other *Securitate* officers Yari had encountered, this one appeared to understand that his men would accomplish more for him if they liked and respected him. Many leaders failed to grasp that cruelty and shouting built defensive barriers, which in turn led to poor communication and inefficient labor.

Another man answered him. "It was the closest place that we could isolate him. We wished to inform you immediately." Yari worked to keep his breathing even. That was the voice of one of the guards he had just tangled with. No doubt the man would love to finish the job he had started outside the cell, since Yari had managed to humiliate him in the scuffle.

"Good. When he wakes up, bring him to the guard house and we'll begin our primary treatments. First, though, search him thoroughly to make sure he hasn't picked up anything to aid his escape. Or his own death. Better yet, strip him. When he wakes up, the shock will be that much greater."

Through a tiny slit in his eyelids, Yari caught a glimpse of the heel of a boot turning as the captain headed for the opening of the cage. Two different pairs of boots entered Yari's line of vision and he pressed his eyes shut. Likely the two guards who had brought him here. The men each grabbed one of his arms and dragged Yari onto the bare concrete floor outside the cage. They stripped him and hauled him back into the cage.

So they had taken his clothes. Attempting an escape without some means of warmth was only foolishness. *What will I do now?*

Before leaving, one of the guards swore loudly and drove his boot into Yari's back. He couldn't hold in a long groan of pain, although he managed to keep his eyes closed. "I hope the captain allows me to take part in the treatments of this one. I have more tricks that I can show him." The guard hissed the words so forcefully drops of spittle splattered over Yari's back.

"He overpowered you on the floor, Dan."

"He surprised me. I could kill him."

"He's an old man. You're young. Of course you could."

"It would be no trouble."

The door of the cage creaked shut and locked with a loud click. The thudding of boots grew fainter and another door slammed shut. Was he alone?

Yari wanted to curl up to conserve his body heat, but he couldn't know if it was safe. Was someone watching him through a window in the door? *Be patient. Control yourself. Don't move.* When he had heard nothing for a good ten minutes, he allowed the lids of his eyes to crack slightly open again. The room was dim. One tiny fluorescent light, high over his head, threw off a feeble light that barely penetrated the cage. Thick dusk pressed against a tiny square window. Night was fast approaching.

Footsteps sounded outside the door, a slow *tap tap* on the concrete. Yari remained frozen. The door opened and closed, followed by a vacuum of silence.

Wait. Continue to wait. He must be more patient than the guards. After a very long five minutes, his body began to tremble from the cold and damp. He needed to move. If a guard was still in the room, so be it.

Yari opened his eyes. When he saw nothing, he sat up. Pain shot through his lower back and bounced in the rear of his skull. His stomach churned violently and he nearly threw up, but somehow managed to hold himself together. He rose shakily to his feet, turning a slow circle to assess his predicament. He was alone. He let out a quivering breath. He was *alone.* They must have believed he was unconscious and therefore were waiting to take him to the guardhouse. Now the day was over. He had some time to work.

Yari turned again, more slowly this time, surveying his cell with greater concentration. His heart leapt. His clothes lay on the floor just outside the cage. Yari scrambled over and dropped to his hands and knees. He reached as far as he could, until the bars dug into his chest and shoulder, but couldn't reach the clothes. He sank to the floor, his back pressed to the bars. They had been left to torment him.

But, if he could get out of the cage, or even pry that bar loose, he could pull his clothes to him. Where was that loose bar Greceanu had spoken about?

The cage was small, perhaps seven feet high and six feet by four feet at the base. Yari clambered to his feet and reached his hand up. He could easily exert a great amount of force on the bars overhead. He methodically tested each four-foot bar; there were five of them per foot, each about an inch in diameter. *There!* One bar gave a little. Not much, perhaps only an eighth of an inch, but it was a start. He quickly tested the remaining bars, but they were solid. The loose bar was the seventh from the end. Going back to it, he used two other bars to pull himself closer to the welded joint so he could examine it for flaws. The bar rested in a type of sleeve designed to hold only about one inch of the bar. It was the sleeve itself that was welded to the main frame, not the bar.

Yari dropped back to the ground, his heart pounding. Yes, there were some cracks. Just how deep they were and how long the weld would hold he had yet to discover. With arms straight and legs only slightly bent, he gripped the bar with both hands and pushed. There was a slight movement and he pushed harder, desperately straining to ignore the pain that knifed at his kidneys. His face contorted and sweat broke out on his forehead in tiny beads. His forearms bulged from the strain, each muscle cut sharp with detail.

The bar did not move again and Yari had to stop. After a brief rest, he looked closely at the crack but it remained small. Well, perhaps a little larger. He must not give up. He could not. Maybe if he worked the bar up and down. Or side to side. The movement could create a greater break.

He straightened his body again and grasped the bar. The metal was cold on his hands and the bars on the floor froze his bare feet, a feeling he did not like at all. *And I will like it much less if I'm stuck in here for hours or even days.*

With a frenzied burst of energy, he attacked the bar, pushing up with all his might at one moment then jerking down the next. For a full minute he struggled before he finally slumped over, out of breath. *Don't give up. You can do it. You can break that bar.*

Again he pulled himself up until his face was close to the sleeve. Yes, the crack was definitely larger now. *Okay, rest a bit then try again. God, give me more strength. I need your help.*

For the third time, he strained on the bar and this time there was extra movement. *Keep pushing.*

The sleeve broke suddenly from its weld and the bar released upward. Yari yanked it from the sleeve at the opposite end, meeting only a slight resistance.

He stood in the cold cage, alone and naked, but now with a metal bar in his hands. How much longer would it take to gain his freedom from this cell? He only knew that the longer he rested, the smaller the chance would be that he would ever leave alive. It had to be now. There could be no more delays.

First he studied the bar in his hands. Ah ha! He could see why the guards believed that the cage in itself was enough security. The bar was unlike any Yari had ever seen. Actually, it was a metal bar within a pipe. Both seemed to be made of spring steel. The inside bar was set on ball bearings so that if any prisoner managed to file through the first layer, the inside bar would only rotate on the bearings and would hardly be scratched. It would have been virtually foolproof if the welders had done a more thorough job.

The pastor inserted one end of the bar through two other bars so that only two or three inches protruded on the top side. He had nearly four feet of metal to pry with and he pushed up, tentatively at first, then with increasing force as the sleeve of the second bar stubbornly held. With a snap, his pry bar forced the end of the second bar downward into the cell and he removed that bar as well and set it on the floor. *Thank you Lord.* Now he had a space of nearly eight inches. With one more bar out of the way, he could probably squeeze through and climb out of the cage.

The third bar required only slightly greater effort than the second, and Yari placed it on the floor with the other one and his pry bar.

His huge forearms lifted his body until his face rose above the top level of the cage. *The air is the same higher in the room, but now I breathe the air of freedom.* He worked one arm through and then the other and squeezed his chest through the opening.

He was out! At least, out of the cage. When he stood on top of it, he found that he could easily touch the ceiling beams. In fact, he had to duck to avoid bumping his head. Part of him longed to keep going. But first his clothes. He scrambled down and in less than a minute he was dressed. *If only I had my coat.* His wool sweater would have to suffice. It was mostly green with a little white and would blend in well in the snowy woods.

He climbed back to the top of the cage. From there, he reached for the clay roof tiles on top of a heavy wooden ceiling beam. The layered wood between the beams that held the tiles had rotted with age and already fallen away in places. In others, the tiles were wired together or to other pieces of wood. No matter.

The first tile he tested moved easily enough, only it was very heavy. They'd be covered with snow, of course, which would require a little more time and muscle to move. "Lord, put those guards to sleep. I need your help, God. I have to be free."

With another shove, he lifted the tile upward again. The thin wire retainer snapped, a piece of wood broke off, and the tile came free. Yari pushed it up through the snow and set the tile down carefully, pressing it into the snow slightly so that it would not slide all the way off and alert the guards.

Yari poked his head through the roof into open air. The cold stung his skin; the temperature had dropped well below freezing. Greceanu had warned him it would not be easy.

Off to his right, nearly a hundred yards away, Yari spotted a guard under a lamp post, his face tucked as far down into his overcoat as possible. That one would not be a problem. It was the guards he could not see that worried him. Yari shoved the thought from his mind. He would take care of them as they came along. He could not stay in this position any longer. Yari eased his tired body through the opening and into the frigid night.

Chapter Seventeen

Jim picked his way upward, blending with the trees and pausing occasionally to watch and listen. The snow was deep, up to four feet in areas where it had drifted, and he had to take care to select a route that would keep him from sinking through. If something went wrong, there would be no one to help him.

It was dark in the trees, as black as Polish coal. The moon and the stars failed to break through a tight layer of clouds, dark with the promise of snow. *Not yet.* They'd need the light later, but darkness was best for now. The temperature was plunging. Thankfully, the pines of the forest grew closely together, offering Jim shelter from the wind and—he hoped—adequate cover from creatures of the night inclined to stealth.

Like a lonely Arctic wolf, the wind howled and twisted through the trees, searching for a place to rest. Jim stood among the branches of a pine, his hands on his knees as he took a moment to catch his breath. He was warm in his sheepskin. With a wool sweater and two shirts, he could stay reasonably warm for the night. Besides that, he had the coat for Yari if he needed it. He wore a matching sheepskin hat with ear flaps that fell against his ears. He had left them loose so he could hear if anything—or anyone—moved around him. Two pairs of sweat pants covered his legs, sufficient if he kept moving. He'd packed a third pair in the backpack in case his first two got wet. Shin-high, water-proof boots with draw strings at their top to keep snow from slipping down into his socks covered his feet. They were invaluable.

He started off again, taking his time so he didn't work up a sweat. Too many people had died because they stopped to rest after traveling too quickly. Sweat would freeze to a thin icy film inside their clothing and their expended energy supply did not allow the body to recuperate. There were certain tricks to winter survival. Going slowly was one of them. Jim was glad now for the weekends he had spent with his father in the woods of the Canadian Shield. He had picked up many priceless outdoor habits there.

Jim continued to watch for any signs of movement, but saw nothing out of the ordinary. He was leaving tracks, some more than a foot deep, but that couldn't be helped. So far he hadn't encountered anyone else's. It wasn't likely that he would run into a patrol on a night such as this. Still, he had to be careful.

Were his friends still waiting at the rest stop? How much time had passed since he had left them? An hour? Maybe two? He had completely lost track. It didn't matter; he had to continue. He couldn't afford to be caught in this area during daylight hours. If he was arrested, it would not be as a Bible smuggler; it would be as a spy.

How could a country, set in the middle of modern-day Europe, allow itself to sink so low? How had the people come to accept the harsh conditions they were forced to bend their weakening backs to? Why did God allow a man like Ceauşescu to live and rule here? Jim rubbed his forehead with the side of his gloved hand. Maybe the solution was to rid the country of Nicolae and Elena Ceauşescu. Maybe they would have to go still further and remove the entire Ceauşescu clan, forty strong, who had been promoted into government positions. Would that be the answer?

He shook his head. It would be an illusion to believe that. The country would have to go much further. Change would not occur until the system that allowed the Ceauşescus to rule was changed. Communism was a barbaric form of government and it would be far more difficult to change it than to remove "The Genius of the Carpathians," as Ceauşescu referred to himself, and his family from power.

Could all the difficulties of this country be caused by one man alone? Could Ceauşescu have accomplished that by himself? Communism had to play a major role and, linked with Ceauşescu, evil flourished. What was the answer?

Jim stopped for a brief moment and pressed a glove to the trunk of a tree. "Lord, Romania needs to see your hand at work. Please do something that will give your people here the freedom to worship you openly, to share your Word with others, to receive the books that are so desperately needed."

He started walking again. The pines gradually thinned. He had to be nearing the summit. The snow was deepening in places, but he managed to avoid the drifts. It was colder, too, if that was possible, and he tugged his wool scarf higher over his mouth and nose. He would need to move more slowly, with added care. To rush now might finish him.

Wind knifed through the air, forcing his eyes to slits. Jim raised a hand to shelter his eyes and saw it. The fence! The outer perimeter of the military compound. For several seconds he stood, absolutely still, confident his body and clothing blended perfectly against an outbreak of granite and two single pines. He scanned the immediate area in front of him but could detect no human forms. Methodically, he searched an area farther out, then another, examining every jut of rock and every pine. Finally, he studied the fence and everything he could see beyond. The distance was great, more than 150 yards, but he saw no one. He had to move on. There was little time and the temperature was still dropping.

He moved closer to the perimeter, using every tree and drift of snow for cover. It took him nearly forty-five minutes to work his way to the fence. Thirty yards away, he spotted a ravine-type depression running nearly parallel to the fence, which would bring him within a stone's throw of one of the buildings in the interior. He followed the ravine. Spotting a five-foot length of branch, he picked it up as it could prove useful.

When he finally raised his head above the level of the snow, he was only five short yards from the fence. His field of vision was clear, allowing him to see a large, sparsely-lighted two-story brick building over a hundred yards to his left with flags blowing fiercely in the illuminated parade square. The building to his right was closer and smaller, only thirty yards away, and built lower to the ground. It was shrouded in blackness. With some luck, that would turn out to be the prison. Behind that were two long, low buildings, partially obstructed from his view. Were those the army barracks?

He had made it this far. What should he do? What did he *dare* do? It was essential that he not get caught. He needed to locate the guards, keep a good distance from them, and somehow find Yari Potra. To accomplish that, he had to at least get inside the fence. But where were the guards? He had been here more than five minutes, constantly alert, but had seen nothing and hadn't detected a movement from any part of the compound.

A few lights glowed in the main building and he watched those windows for several minutes. Eventually, a figure passed in front of one of the lights, creating a silhouette. So there were people here. He shifted his gaze. There, on the steps of the main building, another figure moved. The person crossed the steps into the small trees beyond and disappeared. Jim watched that spot for a few minutes, playing a game of patience with himself, hoping he would be the winner. His reward came—the faint flare of a match being struck. The guard had remained and was still awake.

Jim crouched and crept along the perimeter of the fence.

He drew closer to the small, brick building. *Please be where the prisoners are located.* More of the army barracks were visible, but cloaked in darkness. That was strange. If soldiers were living there, there should be lights. It had to be before eight o'clock in the evening and it was unlikely they would be in bed.

The two-story building was out of his line of vision now. He couldn't see the guard by the steps and hoped that meant the guard couldn't see him either. Of course, there could be others. There had to be. He would have to be patient. He could wait and watch. But he could also work.

Jim slipped the pack off his shoulders and withdrew the rubber floor mat he had brought from the car. He carefully placed this over the bottom wire of the fence in case it was electrified. He took the branch he had picked up and propped up the second wire with one end, allowing the other end to dig into the snow. That separated the wires enough for him to squeeze through the fence without touching either. It was time to explore inside. He took the backpack and pushed it deep into a snow drift until it was out of sight; he wouldn't need it inside the compound.

He slipped through the gap in the perimeter fence with ease, the coat for Yari draped over his arm. The nearest building was only a few yards away. The only way to find out if it was the prison was to move closer and inspect it.

There were several windows on the north side, but to look through them would mean exposing himself to the guard at the main building. What about the other side? Jim made his way along the western face and peered around the corner of the building. He saw no one. The army barracks were dark and quiet, like a predator lying in wait for its unsuspecting victim.

Jim stopped again, waiting, playing the game of patience once more. He could not afford to make a mistake. He *had* to be sure. If guards were in that building, his mission would be finished. A little bit longer. He could wait. He could watch. He scrutinized the windows of the building across from him, taking time with each one, making sure nothing moved behind the glass panes.

Five minutes passed. Then ten. Then twenty. He would wait no longer. Now he must move. He stepped around the corner to the south and froze at a noise behind him. *Oh, God. There's nowhere to go.* He melted back against the wall and listened.

A muffled sound drifted on the frigid air. Jim's forehead wrinkled. Was that something breaking? He held his breath at the sound of a grunt and something that might have been the crust of snow cracking. Jim peeked back around the corner, his interest getting the better of him. *Nothing.*

More sounds he couldn't quite identify broke the silence, accompanied by heavy breathing. A guard was coming and he was trapped. He wouldn't be able to move without being seen. The breathing continued, but although he expected them, he heard no footsteps. Were the sounds coming… from above?

Snow fell from the roof and Jim looked up, but the overhang obstructed his view. A moment later feet appeared at the edge of the eaves and then a body dropped the eight feet to the ground. The shock of the fall was cushioned by a thick carpet of snow.

His heart thudding against his ribs, Jim stared at the figure in front of him. A large man, maybe fifty or sixty, struggled to his feet. Even crouched over, he was clearly tall and strong. His jet-black hair was streaked with gray. Muscles bulged underneath the man's wool sweater. *Yari Potra!* His breath caught. Was it possible? Could the man he was searching for have just dropped out of the sky in front of him, as though sent straight from heaven?

Jim took a step forward and the man swung to face him; fear permeated his features. He mumbled something in Romanian. When Jim held up both hands, empty of weapons, Yatri uttered the word, "*Pace.*"

"*Pa-chay,*" Jim returned, careful to pronounce it the same way. Nick had used the word too, when greeting other Christians. "You are Yari Potra, yes? I am a friend of your two sons and I am here looking for you. Will you come with me?" He held out the coat to the pastor.

"You must be an angel!" Yari exclaimed in precise English as he grabbed the coat. "This is hard to believe."

"Not quite an angel," Jim said. "But they're probably here with us. There are gloves and a hat in the pockets."

"Thank you, my friend," said the pastor, slipping an arm into the sleeve of the coat. "Praise be to our Lord for his amazing timing. Come, standing here, we waste precious time."

Jim wasn't about to argue. "Follow me." He motioned for the prisoner to fall into step behind him. "I know a way out of this place."

Chapter Eighteen

Jim and Yari plowed down the snow-covered mountain, circling to the north as they headed in the direction of Brasov. Too much time had passed for them to return to the van. No one would be waiting now. Jim skidded to the bottom of a steep slope then turned and waited for Yari to catch up. The pastor was still remarkably fit for his age and condition. He let his momentum take him the last few feet and tumbled to the bottom. Jim grabbed hold of Yari's coat sleeves to help him with his balance and, standing close to him, looked into the pastor's eyes.

There was a fire there, a desire burning bright, a will to live and to continue on.

"Can you keep going?" A renewed energy coursed through Jim as he began to warm up. He felt as though he could go all night, but he had no idea what the man in front of him had been through the last few days.

"Of course I can." Yari extricated himself from Jim's grasp and clapped him on the shoulder. "Don't worry about me. I'll be right behind you."

Still, Jim worried. The older man's breath came in great gasps and his face was tinged with purple. Jim stared at him a few seconds longer through the white steam of his own breath, then turned and walked on at a slower but still steady pace. They both needed to conserve as much energy and body heat as possible.

He slipped his hand inside his overcoat and winced. His shirt was damp right through in places. "We'll need a fire, Pastor Potra."

The pastor frowned. "But a fire would be clearly visible in this darkness and someone on patrol might see it."

"Unless we find an ideal location. For now we need to keep moving." Looking back, Jim saw they were leaving tracks a blind man could follow. *Please God. Let it warm up a few degrees. Let it snow.*

Their first task was to put distance between themselves and the army. Once Yari's absence was discovered, it wouldn't take the guards long to bring out the dogs and begin the search. Possibly they would wait until morning, but it wasn't likely. If Yari escaped and his story made it to the West, the Romanian government would not look good. No doubt they would do anything to keep that from happening.

Maybe they did have an advantage. The guards in the compound had likely drawn the evening shift and would not be changed until at least midnight. Even if his absence was detected earlier, they might be reluctant to begin an immediate search. It had to be twenty degrees below freezing; would anyone willingly venture out in that? Jim lifted his chin. Yes, the search wouldn't begin until morning. It was a hope he staked his life on.

That left them, at best, nine hours. Nine hours to try to make it at least five miles on foot, cover their tracks, build a fire, and survive. By daylight they would have to be well hidden. No one must see them, not even the villagers.

They would need matches to make a fire. Jim stopped in his tracks. The backpack. He had left it at the fence. How could he possibly have done that? He whirled around. "Yari, I have to go back. I forgot my pack with everything we need to survive. Matches, extra clothes, food."

The pastor shook his head. "There is no time. You cannot risk it. Even now they might be coming after us. We must keep moving. We have enough clothes to keep us warm. And we can figure out how to build a fire if needed. There are tricks, you know."

Still feeling sick over his mistake, Jim turned back and trudged on. In a low voice, Yari said, "I must thank you for helping me. I do not even know who you are or where you come from. You are not Romanian. American?"

"I'm Max. I am a Canadian. I came in contact with your sons through a mutual friend and one of them, Petru, told my friends and me where you were being held. They said you were to be executed on Monday so I came up this evening to look around and you appeared. We are very fortunate that God is with us."

"*Emanuil.* God is with us, Max. He still performs miracles, yes?" He tugged on the back of Jim's coat. "How are my sons? What has happened to them?"

"Jozef escaped from prison and my friends and I found him on the road outside of Cluj. He obviously had a difficult time, but he is healing well and is with friends a few miles from here, in Codlea. Petru was set free and he is doing well. He is with my friends at the Parc Hotel in Brasov where they're waiting for our return."

"You mention friends. Who are they?"

"Their names are Cathy and Ralph. Ralph is a friend of mine from Canada. Cathy is from America."

"And how did you meet my family?" Yari stumbled and pressed a hand against Jim's back to steady himself.

Jim slowed but didn't stop. They needed to cover as much ground as possible, as quickly as they could. "We were bringing Bibles to Romania and were visiting believers in Cluj."

"Ahh. This is a good thing." His voice carried a smile. "So you are a Christian then? I would think this is obvious, but one can never tell."

"Yes, I'm a Christian. You and I," Jim ducked under the low-hanging branch of a tree, "are brothers."

"This is a good thing."

They walked in silence for another ten minutes, until Yari grabbed Jim's shoulder. "Max, look!" He pointed between two pine trees, at the side lights of five Roman diesel transport trucks. They had stumbled upon a *parkplatz*, a rest stop for automobiles along a highway. This was a different route than the one Jim had traveled a few hours before, which was likely a good thing. The more tracks the dogs had to follow, the better. The challenge now would be to figure out where they were and how to get to Codlea from here.

"I have an idea," Yari said. "Let's go."

This time the pastor led the way, his feet crunching on the crisp layer of snow. Branches and pine needles reached out and brushed their coats. Only a hundred more yards to the trucks. They had come to the edge of the forest and open ground stretched before them.

Jim's throat had gone so tight it was a challenge to draw in a breath. Was this a mistake? What if someone spotted them and called the authorities? The first ten yards held a maze of small brush and large rocks. Beyond that was a river bed that looked to be about thirty yards across and five or six feet lower than the embankment on the far side. Water gurgled under thin ice as it bounced and skipped over smooth stones and wound a narrow strip across the river bottom. As they drew closer, Jim realized the stream was only a few feet wide at the most. Still, it would be very cold and they couldn't allow themselves to get wet. They needed a good place to cross.

Beyond the river a number of large trees lined the *parkplatz*, then the trunks painted white in typical Romanian fashion. Stone picnic tables with crudely molded benches, two overflowing trash containers, and the five trucks filled the lot.

"Wait here. I'll get some matches."

Before Jim could protest, his companion was gone. He picked his way across snow-covered stones in the narrow river, and scrambled up the far embankment. Jim lost sight of Yari when he reached the trees, but caught a glimpse of him between branches when he knocked on one of the truck's doors. The door opened and a man's face appeared, illuminated by the inside glow of the cab light. The two men spoke for what seemed like an eternity. Jim shifted his weight from one foot to the other and rubbed his gloves hands together to keep his blood circulating. What could they be talking about? Yari eventually turned and walked back along the row of trucks. When he had passed the last one, he slipped quietly through the trees and headed towards Jim.

Finally. Jim met Yari in the middle of the stream bed on the snow-covered stones. Between the height of the embankment and the row of trees, they were protected from the view of the truckers.

A smile crossed Yari's face. "No problem," he said, opening his hand to show Jim a book of matches. "Let us go this way." He began to walk upstream on the slippery round rocks poking above the ice.

"Wait a minute," Jim whispered. Yari stopped and looked back. Jim held up both hands. "Where are we going? Why can't we hitch a ride with one of the truck drivers?"

"Too many post controls. Besides, I believe most drivers to be informers. Come. We must keep walking." They moved westward over the rocks, stopping now and again to back up and detour around a bend of flowing water. Overhead, the moon appeared occasionally in crescent form between layers of clouds, offering the men sufficient light to guide their way.

Is anyone following us yet? If not, they would be soon enough, so he and the pastor needed to attempt to hide their trail. The river bed would slow down both the dogs and the men for a while, but if it doubled back, they would have to leave it. What they needed was a good snowfall. And warmer temperatures. *Please God. You control the wind and the rain. Send snow and make it warmer. Please.*

"The road running beside us is a mountain road just south of Brasov." Yari looked back over his shoulder and nearly lost his balance. Jim held his breath as the pastor held his arms out to both sides and steadied himself. "We are fortunate, Brother Max, we are very close to where we can meet your friends. I would estimate about fifteen miles in a straight line or twenty if we follow the roads."

That's close? In these conditions? Jim kept the thoughts to himself. They both needed to stay positive or they would never make it.

"The one we are following now comes out on the E94 highway, which runs between Brasov and Pitesti. That won't be for at least ten miles, though. All along this road are hotels for tourists who come to ski, so we have a greater chance of being seen if we keep to this path. It would be safer to cut straight up to Brasov."

"I'm not sure about that." Jim jumped from one rock to the next. "If we don't get snow, our tracks would be way too easy to follow. I'd say it would be smarter for now to stay with this river bed as long as we can. We can even walk on the roads if necessary. If we hear a car coming, we can jump into the ditch."

Pastor Potra nodded. "All right, that is what we will do then."

After walking for another hour, Jim studied the landscape ahead, searching for a suitable place to leave the river bed and head into the forest that lay on the far side of the road. If he were following someone, he'd look for tracks leading out of the river bed in the same direction they had entered. Most escapees thought that way, trying to confuse those who would follow. He and the pastor must do the opposite, the unexpected.

Finally, he spotted the ideal exit. Jim grabbed Yari's arm and led him up a narrow sheet of rock towards the road twenty yards away. After fifteen feet, a barricade of thick bushes brought them up short. Jim pushed his way through, the pastor close behind him. Tiny thistles tugged at his clothing.

The road was close. After plowing through ten yards of brush, Jim emerged slowly, poking his head through first to make sure no one else was near. His shoulder muscles relaxed. They were alone. In just a few seconds they had cleared the road and the guard rails and had started up a steep ridge, covered with trees. They climbed up three hundred feet before reaching the top. Jim stopped and contemplated the far side of the ridge, a thick tangle of trees, brush, and crevices.

"This will be perfect." Jim began the descent, watching his feet to avoid slipping on an icy patch or tripping over a root or branch. One misstep and he'd be fortunate to stop before he plunged to the bottom.

The two made it safely down the precipice. Not more than forty yards away, another ridge rose steeply. A jumble of massive boulders lined the foot of it. Jim clapped his gloved hands together. Perhaps now they could rest.

Mass quantities of rock had long since fallen away from the ridge, leaving a natural cut in the cliff, a type of overhang with rock walls on three sides and large boulders in front. They would camp here.

Jim began dragging dry branches over that they could use for firewood and motioned for Yari to rest. "You've worked enough," Jim said. "Catch your breath and I'll put a fire together."

Jim heaved some of the larger rocks away from the overhang and shoved the rest away with his foot, leaving enough room for a fire and themselves. In the small clearing, he built a fire. Soon both men huddled close, arms stretched forward as if to pull in the warmth.

For a long time, each sat quietly. Thoughts raced through Jim's head. How many days and nights would they be out here? Would they be tracked down before they could reach safety? What would happen to a foreigner, caught aiding an escaped prisoner? In spite of the warmth of the fire, he shivered.

When the pastor finally looked over the flames at Jim, sadness filled his eyes. "Times have changed, Max. A man can't do what he wants to anymore. They took my career away from me in 1948." He scowled at the fire. "I was just getting started. Twenty years old." He sighed and leaned back against a rock. "My father had left me the family blacksmithing business. Money began to come in, but then the leaders nationalized the economy. Marxism turned the tide against us and, of course, Ceauşescu has done nothing to help." His voice dripped with contempt.

Jim tossed a small branch into the fire. "But you're a pastor. You're doing great things for God and for his people."

"Yes." Yari crossed his arms over his chest. "It is very strange how God works. I love to preach. Do you understand that? I love to. I love to serve the people. But I also love to work with my hands. Do you see these hands?" He held up both palms, the orange glow illuminating the calluses. "Look at them. They're strong. I loved my trade. It was a good feeling to have the iron shaping in my hands. It was a good thing to make something that people could appreciate and value. But to be honest, when my business was nationalized with the rest of the private enterprises, I struggled to stay motivated to work each day for an evil government. And it wasn't just me. Nobody really wanted to work. It has always been a challenge to remind myself that I must work as unto God, and not for man's sake."

Jim shook his head. "I can't imagine how frustrating that must have been."

"No, you can't, not unless you have experienced it for yourself." Yari uncrossed his arms, picked up a stick, and snapped it in half before throwing it into the flames. "We have a joke here that 'the government simulates that they pay us so we simulate that we work.'"

Jim grinned broadly. "It sounds like some of our government agencies in Canada."

Yari lifted his massive shoulders. "All government systems have problems, it's true. As Christians, we must fight not to become cynical. But it is difficult, no?"

Jim nodded. "It certainly is. And I can see how it would be more difficult for you here than in many places in the world."

Yari pulled his knees to his chest and wrapped his arms around them. "I believe it is. The goal of the Party leaders is to create citizens who are totally obedient to the Party and that do everything exactly how the Party wants. I call those people robots. And do you know how you create a person with a robot mentality?"

Jim stared into the embers of the fire, searching for an answer. "Take away their hope?" he responded tentatively.

"In what way?"

"His desire to achieve something greater and to become better off must be taken away."

"That's one way. You must also tell him there is no God. Then you must convince him that an individual doesn't have an immortal soul. Do you know why?"

"If they tell people that life is only here and now, that they are here by chance, then there's no purpose in living. Their work in life centers around satisfying their own needs and desires."

"That's right. But who in Romania satisfies all your needs?"

Jim shook an ember off his boot. "The Communist Party?"

"Right again. If you know that the Party will give you the car you need and a villa perhaps, then you will agree to whatever they want, even begin to worship them. This is their rationale. If they get rid of God, get rid of an immortal soul, essentially turn everyone into atheists who believe that life is only here and now, the people will be totally obedient to them."

Jim propped his elbows on his knees and tapped his knuckles against his chin. "That makes sense." He contemplated all the magazine and newspaper articles he'd read about Communism and Eastern Europe, and now, finally, saw the picture very clearly. This man should not be stuck out here in the middle of nowhere, he should be lecturing in the top universities in America. He had knowledge and insight and education. Of course, he was a preacher. And a teacher, clearly. The churches in America could use this man to open their eyes to the truth of what was going on in Romania.

"Of course," the pastor smiled at him over the flames, "the answer isn't any man-made system. All have their flaws as all people are essentially selfish at their core. Only a turning back to God can solve the problems in any society. As the Bible says, if a nation will turn back to Him and call on Him, He will heal them. We can talk about the ills of any political party or theory all night long, but that is truly the only solution for any country."

Jim lowered his fists to his lap. "That's it exactly. I've been trying for years to figure out which system is the best, and really, the answer is none of them. Humans are too broken and in need of a Savior." The firelight flickered and danced strange shadows over both their faces. "Now, how can I take this knowledge and use it to bring people to Christ, or to further the Kingdom of God in some way?"

The pastor selected a small branch and poked it into the fire, sending showers of tiny sparks into the air. "I'm glad you asked, because I was coming to that." He stared at the sparks, seemingly transfixed by their beauty. Jim followed his gaze to a burning ember as it wandered upwards and burned itself out into darkness overhead.

"If my faith is in God, no ruler, Communist or otherwise, can master me; I am free even in a prison cell. For many here, and all over the world, this is what they need to understand."

He leaned forward. "You must be like the apostle Paul, though, who spoke to people in the language they understood. Here in Romania, most are dissatisfied with the system. They ask, where do we go from here? What are the alternatives? They are so interested in the economics, so interested in politics, in systems, that you must try to discuss on this level. Try to show them that all human systems will fail them, that God is the answer they are looking for. Faith in God is the only viable alternative. Of course, don't talk to people who would report you to the police."

Jim's brow furrowed. "How will I know if that's who I am talking to?"

"There is a time for everything." Yari pointed up, in the direction the spark had disappeared. "The Holy Spirit will let you know if you listen carefully to His voice. I will tell you this, though. The Romanian people are ready for revolution. Now is the time to reach them. Already I have heard the prison guards outside our cell discussing rumors of dissention and riots. We have had enough of this government, and I believe that, soon now, the people will rise up. And when they do, they will need people like you and like me who can tell them there is another way, a better way." He yawned and pressed the back of his hand to his mouth.

Jim reached for a log and propped it up on another one in the center of the flames. "That should keep the fire going for a while. Why don't we get some rest?"

Yari nodded. "I admit I am ready for it. Good night, brother. And thank you again." He stretched out on his side and closed his eyes.

"Good night." Jim sat for a while staring into the flames before he, too, laid down and pulled his coat around him tightly. Tomorrow would be a long day and would come soon enough. He had no idea what difficulties they would face together. Peace flooded through him like the warmth given off by the flickering flames. Let them come. God was for them. He would give them the victory. That was all they needed to know.

Something cold and wet landed on his cheek and Jim opened his eyes. *Thank you, Lord.* A small smile crossed his face as he snuggled deeper into his coat.

It was snowing.

Chapter Nineteen

Jim woke with a start. What was that? The bright reflection of the sun off the snow blinded him and he brought his hand up to shield his eyes. Yari strode into the campsite and sank down, cross-legged, before the fire. He poked it with a long stick, clearly trying to stir some life into the cold embers, and smiled at Jim. "Good morning."

"Morning." Jim groaned and ran a hand over his face. Between the cold and the hard ground, sleep had been a little hard to come by. He glanced around. The air felt warmer this morning, thankfully. And it appeared as though several inches of snow had fallen. The land looked fresh again. In this higher altitude, the pure, dazzling white stole his breath away. He'd done research on this area before coming to the country. Throughout the years, as time had dragged its slow length along, the Transylvanian Subcarpathian mountains had changed little. Villages were built and destroyed and built again a dozen times and they, like the mountains, had learned to endure.

The pastor tossed a handful of branches onto the fire. "I have been out, looking around a little. Our tracks have been covered by the snow. We are indeed very blessed. It is a good thing to see the results of prayer."

Jim sat up, wincing as his cold, tight muscles shifted position. He, like the villages, had endured another winter night, and that alone was an accomplishment. He removed his sheepskin hat and scratched his scalp fiercely, scowling in the process. He looked up to see Yari studying him.

"I assume you are not enjoying yourself this fine morning," said the pastor. "I am sorry to involve you in my troubles."

"I've been more comfortable than this before, I admit. As much as I love the outdoors, this is not my idea of a good time." He offered Yari a rueful grin. "Still, I wouldn't be helping you unless I wanted to."

Yari nodded. "Thank you. We have a long day ahead. We must be very patient. If we move too quickly, we might be seen."

Jim stood and stretched. "What time is it?"

"You have the watch. They took mine."

Jim pulled back his sleeve and squinted at the hands. "It's 9:10. I think. For all I know, it could be upside down."

"You sleep very soundly," Yari said.

"I'm not sure if that's a curse or a blessing."

"That depends on your circumstances, I suppose."

Jim grunted. "Maybe my ability to sleep soundly shows that I have a clear conscience."

"Then you are truly fortunate. How many in this world can say that?"

Jim pressed a hand to his abdomen. "Pastor, we need food. It'll be very hard on us if we wait until the cover of dark this evening. If the weather turns bad again, we'll be in serious trouble."

"I was thinking of that. Do you think we should leave earlier? Perhaps now?"

"Now they're searching for us. For you at least, unless there are places where two sets of tracks remain. It's possible they will use helicopters."

"Even worse, the villagers will be informed and they will become our worst enemies. To hide from one helicopter will not be too complicated. The villagers will be offered great incentives to report our whereabouts. We cannot let ourselves be seen by them."

"But Yari, we must eat, or we will not make it to Codlea. We need the energy."

"I think we must pray about it. It is the Lord alone who gives us wisdom."

They sat down together before the fire and bowed their heads. "God," Yari prayed, "you alone know the best plan for us. Show us what to do. You sent the snow, we know you are watching over us. Guide us now, we ask."

After a few minutes of silence, peace flooded Jim as it had the night before. He lifted his head and looked across the flames at Yari. "I vote to go now."

"And I agree with you. We must be careful, though, or we shall be caught. I have great fear about this."

"I do, too," Jim replied. With a few handfuls of snow, he extinguished the fire. Both of them took the opportunity to pop snow into their mouths as well. The cold flakes melted on Jim's tongue and he sucked greedily on the cold liquid that remained. Then there was nothing left to do. Drawing in a deep breath, he glanced around the place that had been a gift from God as a place of refuge before turning and starting off.

The pair walked west and slightly north, moving slowly to conserve energy. Jim rested a hand on Yari's back. "When was the last time you had anything to eat?"

"Day before yesterday. Do not worry. It has happened before and it will not likely be the last time. Since my wife passed away, I have had to shop for my own food and prepare my own meals. Sometimes there has not been enough time or enough resources."

"When did your wife die?"

Yari did not answer.

Jim bit his lip. "I'm sorry. I hope I didn't bring up an uncomfortable subject."

"Of course not. I was the one who first mentioned it. The situation was very common at the time. When my sons Petru and Jozef were born, they were larger than normal babies, even though they were twins. The doctors had to cut her to bring the babies out and she did not recover. Our medicine in this country is not like that of the West, you know. There is much room for improvement."

"And you never remarried?"

"It was not possible. There was a young official in the local Communist Party headquarters who had also been in love with my wife. When I married her, he was crushed. And when she died, he was even more grieved. He started spreading rumors around the village that I was evil and that I was cursed. Then things began to happen that he said were proof."

"Such as?"

"Twice, someone attempted to electrocute me. If I had not been aware the first time, I would have been killed. Someone hooked up a live wire to the handle of my truck, but I saw it before anything happened. The second time, however, I was burned quite badly. They had put a charge through the drain pipe at the corner of my house. One night it was rattling badly, so I went out to tie it down, and a shock tore through me. I spent more than a week recovering."

Jim gaped at him. "How could anyone be that cruel?"

Yari shrugged. "Superstitions are a powerful thing, my friend. I was poisoned once, too, at the local restaurant. I had ordered a cup of coffee as a treat and I barely made it home. Apparently, it wasn't a strong enough dose to kill me. One other time, I was in a car accident and injured badly. Someone rammed my car then beat me and left me for dead."

Jim's stomach churned. "And you believe that all these things were this official's doing?"

"I am sure of it."

"And what of the police? Did they do anything to help?"

"The police?" Yari's eyebrows rose. "The Communist Party owns the police. And the police and the *Securitate* are often barely on speaking terms. We who are persecuted can only expect injustice from either of them."

"Where is this official now? Is he not frustrated that you are still alive, or has your situation improved?"

"It has not become better. The same man put me in prison. His name is Cornel Mihai Popescu."

Jim let out a low whistle. "Do you mean this animosity has been going on for forty years? When does it stop?"

"There is not much animosity on my part. God continually frees me from such feelings. For Popescu, it stops when I am dead, or when he is."

"And his putting you in prison was the beginning of the end, in his mind. Is that correct?"

"Possibly. Though he could have kept me there for years."

"I don't think so, Yari. According to Petru, today might have been your execution day."

"The day is not yet over. Take care." He pointed to a village at the bottom of the hill they were presently descending. "We'll have to circle around widely to be certain no one sees us."

"Do you know the name of the village?"

"I can only guess. I preached once in this area, but it was many years ago. Possibly it is Piriul Rece. If so, then we're still bordering highway number 73A on the northeast side. That would put us about six miles from Risnov and maybe six or seven in the other direction to Brasov as... how do you say it in English?"

"As the crow flies."

"Yes, of course. Now, if we were to cross the road and walk directly west from here, we would run into Castle Bran. Those from the West know it better as the legendary Dracula's castle."

Jim's eyes widened. "Is there really such a thing? Wasn't that just made up?"

Yari turned to the left, following a narrow wild game trail. "It is a point of dispute, whether the infamous Count Dracula actually lived there or not. There might have been another castle in this area, now destroyed, that was his actual residence. I don't think anyone really knows."

"Are you saying that this Count Dracula is an actual figure of history?"

"Correct. He was one of our folk heroes from the fifteenth century. His actual name was Vlad Țepeș and he was born in the city of Sighișoara, only seventy-five miles from here. Vlad's father, also named Vlad, was a ruling prince in this area.

Because of his bravery in battle against the Turks, the older Vlad was awarded the Order of the Dragon. The Romanian word for Dragon is *Dracul*, which also means The Devil. In this case, Vlad Dracul was *The Dragon.*"

"So that was Count Dracula's father. What happened to the son?"

"When he was young, he was taken hostage by the Turks. One year after his father's death, he escaped and assumed the throne in Walachia, a province of Romania. Vlad Ţepeş really hated the Turks and as soon as he took the throne, he put an end to the yearly tributes normally paid to the Turks. Turkish ambassadors were sent to Vlad, demanding immediate tribute. Vlad became angry when the ambassadors did not remove their turbans in his presence as a sign of respect, and he nailed the turbans to their heads. In one campaign against the Turks, Vlad and his army killed twenty thousand men. He is an incredible figure in Romanian history."

Jim walked closely behind the pastor. Around them the fir trees grew tall, acting as shields from the wind and potential watching eyes. The forest was quiet except for the faint moan of the north wind. They saw few animals, though their tracks on the snow crust were plentiful. It was extremely peaceful, ideal for conversation that distracted Jim from the dangers of the deadly terrain.

Jim tugged his hat down farther on his head. "Your hero has a bad reputation in the West."

"To many Romanians he was the hero of the people. He upheld law and order, for the most part, and he promoted Christendom, as they knew it then."

"By nailing turbans to heads?"

The pastor smiled briefly. "That, and if a person didn't align himself with the main church, he would be tortured until he did, or he could simply be executed. Sometimes whole towns would be wiped out because they did not have the same religious background." He nudged Jim in the arm. "I'm not saying it was the best way to defend Christendom—which, by the way, was much different then than it is now, without all the denominations we have today—only that in his own, somewhat twisted way, that was what he was trying to do."

"It sounds like Ceauşescu has some of Vlad's blood in him. Only maybe Ceauşescu is a little more subtle."

"It would be interesting to read what the history books say of Ceauşescu five hundred years from now."

"Maybe someone in the West will write a novel of Count Ceauşescu."

"If someone were to write of all his deeds, it could never be published. It would make the reader sick."

"Someone already had written a book along those lines called *Red Horizons*. My friend Ralph has talked to Romanians traveling in the West and they say the author, Pacepa, doesn't tell half of what happened. Ralph said that one man, who was an official in the Communist Party, told him that, in reality, his exploits were far worse."

"I could easily believe it if all the rumors that circulate are true."

Jim glanced in the direction of the castle. "Maybe I'll take a tour of Dracula's home one day."

"But it won't be today. Look. We are approaching the outskirts of Brasov."

Jim's gaze followed Yari's outstretched hand. Dull, yellowish buildings and smoke stacks appeared through a gap in the coniferous trees. "We shouldn't go much farther. Let's stop here until nightfall. That's only another three hours."

"We'll need wood for a fire. The drier it is, the less smoke it will give off." The pastor headed into the woods.

Together they dragged a number of fallen branches into a small clearing surrounded by pines. Jim shook the snow from the branches of one tree and the older man carefully crafted a fire under it. The smoke rose and filtered through the branches. Jim stepped back to watch it and it appeared to be practically invisible by the time it reached the open air.

"A person would practically have to walk straight through our campsite to discover us." Jim brushed bits of bark and dirt from his gloves. "I think we'll be safe here."

"But in three hours," replied Yari, "we'll walk right back into danger."

Dark shadows underlined the pastor's eyes and Jim's chest squeezed. How much more could the man take? They had no choice; they needed to move on. To wait another day could be life-threatening. "We have three hours to prepare ourselves. Get some rest."

Yari lowered himself to the ground beside the fire. "What will you do?"

"If you promise to rest, I promise to pray."

As dusk deepened into nightfall, Yari and Max moved slowly past the perimeter of the Panoramic station. Yari pointed to the tall poles lining the side of the hill. "See that? Cable cars used to bring tourists up here to the top of the mountain, but they stopped running a while ago. Not many tourists in Romania anymore." His throat tightened, but he pushed back the sad thoughts of the way his country used to be.

The sun had set and Yari stopped by a dilapidated, chain-link fence and looked northward over the city of Brasov, a monster with a thousand eyes.

Somewhere in the distance, the steady, low-pitched whir of a helicopter's blades pierced the silence. The noise grew louder and Yari grabbed Max's arm and pulled him from the fence to the branches of the nearest tree. Yari studied the iron bird as it buzzed over the Panorama restaurant. A halogen lamp illuminated the earth below, turning all objects that seconds before had been bathed in darkness as white as the snow.

"Watch where the light goes, Max," Yari whispered in the other man's ear. "They may be looking for us, but if we stay outside of the circle and use the glow to light our way, it can also help us down this mountain. I'm sure it will be very slippery in places."

"Let's move," Max responded. "Just keep an eye on that helicopter, in case it turns back." They watched as it flew just a few hundred yards away, hovering over the city.

"They are looking for us, I am sure." Yari stepped into a patch of snow that went up past his ankles.

"Well, we can't go back now. Watch your step." Max pointed out an area of ice-covered granite and helped Yari around it. "If we aren't back to the hotel tonight, my friends will really start to worry. So will yours. Here, follow my lead." They stepped down through the trees together, taking their time, placing each foot with care. One false step and all could be lost.

The two reached the bottom in less than an hour without incident. Yari brushed snow from his pants while Max knocked his boots against a curb, and the two of them walked out onto Filimon Sirbu Street. It was shortly after five-thirty in the evening. The pair found themselves in the crowd, moving with the majority of people as if they were a couple of men going home to dinner with their families.

"We must find the Hotel Parc." Max grasped Yari's elbow. "It's in the city center opposite Central Park. Do you know where it is?"

"Probably only five hundred yards from here." Yari glanced up and down the street, trying to get his bearings. "It's been a long time since I was there. We may have to search a little. Here, take this street." He pointed to a road, little more than a lane that led off to the left. They walked across the cobblestones, staying clear of the sidewalks. Ahead, not thirty yards away, three police officers walked towards them. Yari gulped. They were trapped. There was absolutely nowhere to go except to turn and walk the opposite way, which would certainly draw attention.

"What do we do now?" whispered Max in a low, anxious voice.

"If we turn now, they will come after us. Keep walking straight past them with your eyes on the ground. If they stop us, let me do the talking."

When the officers were just fifteen yards away, Yari lowered his gaze. Everything in him wanted to run but, with sheer force of will, he did not break stride. *God, don't let them stop us. Send your angels to protect us.*

When the policemen were only a few feet away from them, they parted slightly and the two Christians passed between them without stopping. After a few yards, Max started to look back. Yari grabbed his coat sleeve, but it was too late. Max whirled around, but his cheeks had gone pale. The policemen must have seen him. Without waiting to find out for sure, Yari pushed Max onto Castelului Street. After a few quick steps, they turned again onto Politehnicii Street, and broke into a run. Five seconds later, they made a quick turn to the right and slowed to a walk.

"We will follow this road for a few minutes," said Yari. "If we run again, there will be too many questioning eyes."

"Listen, Yari. I hear running footsteps."

"Then we are caught." His shoulders slumped. Would it really end this way? After they had come so far? He looked back. The three policemen ran down Politehnicii, only fifty yards away. Without a sideways glance, the officers kept going, as if they did not see the two of them standing on the side street.

Yari shook his head. "Come on." He started forward, in the same direction they had been heading before he looked back. Max caught up to him quickly. "God is certainly protecting us. They were so close."

"Come now. No more talk. People will hear you." A flashing blue light appeared in the distance. Could they expect another miracle? Yari tugged Jim to the sidewalk and they stood motionless against a stone building. A Militia car flashed passed them, its interior crammed with four uniformed officers. Max shot Yari a look of disbelief. Two more officers appeared on the sidewalk in front of them, running in their direction. Yari's heart beat faster. *What's happening, Lord?*

The two officers raced past them without so much as a glance. Immediately behind them ran a crowd of eight young people.

"Come with us!" a young man shouted as they rushed by. His face was flushed as he gestured for Yari and Max to join the crowd. "If you are a true Romanian, this is something you will not want to miss."

Chapter Twenty

The group of college students darted down the street at full steam. Jim stood on the sidewalk watching them, his hands shoved into both hips. *What is going on?* Overhead, the circling helicopter was joined by two others, their resplendent lights flooding each dismal corner, exposing hidden shadows and throngs of people.

"We must follow them. We must see where they are going," the pastor cried out.

Jim stood his ground. "Tell me what's happening. Please. I feel like running the other way."

"Max, listen to me. On November 15, two years ago, there were demonstrations and protests here in Brasov. People were demanding better conditions and better food. Thousands of people, factory workers, and young people, came to the city center to protest. Some were killed."

Jim bit his lower lip. So far the pastor had not convinced him to join the throngs.

Yari clapped his hands together. "This is it, Max. This protest looks far greater. This could be the revolution our country needs. That helicopter wasn't coming for us. It had more important business to take care of. Max, I am a Romanian. Like that young person said, I must be a true Romanian. I cannot miss this."

Jim frowned. "And what of me? Where do I fit in?"

"You have other responsibilities to this country. But come and observe. If we get separated, I will come to the Parc Hotel and meet you and your friends there."

"I have an idea. Why don't we stop at the hotel first and see if they are there? They'll be very anxious to know if we're safe. Perhaps they can tell us what's going on in this city. If this protest is truly large, it'll continue for a few hours and we won't miss all of it."

Yari hesitated. He turned his head in the direction the young people had disappeared, then back towards the city center. He looked torn, undecided.

"We will go to the hotel." He nodded once, curtly. "It is only a few blocks from here. If your friends are there with Petru, we can talk with them for a few minutes, but only long enough to understand the situation. Then I must join those who are gathering. For my country. For my people. I belong with them. I must show them my solidarity."

They ran up the street, passing growing numbers of excited young people, all rushing in the opposite direction. A distant roar of rhythmical, chanting voices could be heard over the drum of the helicopters.

"*TIMISOARA! TIMISOARA!*"

Jim stopped running and tore off his hat. "Listen. What are they saying?"

"They are shouting the name *Timisoara*. It's a city near the Hungarian and Yugoslavian borders. Something must have happened there. Come, Max, we must hurry. This is much bigger than I had imagined. The demonstration goes beyond Brasov. It must be in Timisoara also."

"Maybe there are other cities, too." Jim pulled his hat back on. They ran across Gheorghe Gheorghiu-Dej Boulevard, following Yari's pointing finger, then over the snow covering the May 8th Park. Jim sucked in huge amounts of cold air and his lungs groaned for relief. How was the pastor faring? How much longer could they keep running at this pace? As he was about to slow to a walk, the Hotel Parc came into view across the park, on the corner of the street. *Thank you, Lord.* They had made it back to their friends. *Please let them be here.* Jim followed Yari into the parking lot, taking just enough time to see if the *P* sign was bent to a forty-five degree angle. It was not, which meant that Nick and Kirsten had no cause to warn him away.

The two crossed the street. Jim forced himself to slow to a walk to avoid attracting attention as they mounted the steps and entered the front doors of the hotel. The reception desk was empty so they bounded up the stairs to their floor, taking them two at a time. At the door of the room, Jim knocked and entered, not waiting for a reply. Nick, Kirsten, and Petru sat around a small radio they'd placed on a coffee table.

"You're back!" Kirsten jumped up from her seat and ran into Jim's arms. "I'm so glad you're safe." She stepped away and looked up at him, still holding his arms. "We wondered if you'd ever show up. We've been praying for you."

Nick stood behind her and he stepped forward now and gave Jim a high-five greeting and an uncharacteristic quick hug. "Good to see you, Max," he said, emphasizing the use of Jim's code name. "When you didn't turn up at the *parkplatz*, we knew you were on to something."

"Hi Ralph. Meet Pastor Yari Potra."

Jim turned to the pastor. He had pulled Petru into a strong bear hug. Both men had tears running down their cheeks. Yari moved back and slid an arm around his son's shoulders. He stretched out his free hand to greet Nick and Kirsten.

"I am Yari Potra. I thank you for helping me. And I thank you for befriending my sons."

Nick gripped his hand. "My name is Ralph. And this is our friend, Cathy." He punched Jim in the shoulder. "How in the world did you manage to find each other and escape from the compound?"

Jim removed his hat and stuck it in the pocket of his coat. "That's a long story for another time. Right now, Yari just wants to find out what's going on at the city center, and maybe go join in."

Nick led them into the room. "It's true. Incredible events have been happening in this country while you've been gone."

"Timisoara?" The pastor whirled towards his son. "What has happened in that city?"

"Three days ago, on the fifteenth, protests began in Timisoara. It started when a few hundred ethnic Hungarians surrounded the church of the Hungarian Reformed Pastor László Tőkés."

"László Tőkés!" Yari pressed his palm to Petru's chest. "He is a friend of mine. I mean, I know him. We preached together at a group of meetings in Oradea two years ago. Why did they surround his church?"

Nick flopped into an armchair. "The pastor had challenged the authorities regarding their human rights policies and the ways in which ethnic minorities were treated. The authorities wanted to evict him and his family, but his people stood around him and his church in protest."

Petru led his father over to one of the beds and they both sat down. "The next day, several thousand people, mostly ethnic Romanians, joined the protestors around Tőkés' church."

Yari's mouth dropped open. "That's truly amazing. Romanians and Hungarians together."

"And Serbians, too. They all went from the church through the city singing revolutionary songs and chanting slogans against Ceaușescu. They burned his and Elena's portraits and the books of his speeches and cut out the communist symbol from the center of the flag. That night the army troops, *Securitate* forces, and the local militia attacked the protestors with truncheons and water cannons and tear gas."

"And the radio said that some used bayonets." Kirsten sank down on the other bed. "It reported that many were brutally beaten and some were tortured."

"The radio?" Yari's eyes grew wide. "It is telling you this?"

"Radio Free Europe," clarified Nick. "Petru translated for us."

"So that's why the crowds are chanting Timisoara. They have heard this on the radio, too."

"Wait, there's more." Petru rested a hand on his father's arm. "Yesterday, as the crowds in Timisoara grew, the army and *Securitate* were shipped in by large numbers. They massacred hundreds of people. Maybe even thousands. Armored vehicles ran down the protesters. We are still waiting for more reports to hear if the killing has stopped."

Jim settled in the arm chair across from Nick. "That must be why there were hardly any soldiers at the military base when I came looking for you. Most of them had been shipped to Timisoara."

"Oh, Lord," Yari dropped his face into his hands, "my heart is torn for my countrymen. Please don't allow this revolution to fail." He straightened up and faced Petru. "Son, we have to join them. Let us go now."

"I'd like to come with you." Everyone turned to Kirsten. Jim's eyebrows rose. When did she get so bold?

Kirsten stood up. "Come on, you guys. What did you say about putting your life on the line for these people? Now's a good time, don't you think?"

"We will go now," Yari pressed his hands together, "but first we must pray. We need the Lord tonight, as no other night before. Ralph, I would like to hear you pray for us."

Nick nodded. "God, I have to admit that I'm more than a little afraid right now. I ask you, God, to protect us this evening, and throughout the coming days. And we pray that we will act wisely. In Jesus' name. Amen."

"Amen," everyone agreed.

"While you guys put on your coats," Jim clambered to his feet. His entire body ached and he wanted nothing more than to crawl under the covers and sleep for a week, "Yari and I are going to grab a quick bite to eat. We're starving."

Nick cocked his head. "We packed you lots of food."

"Sorry, I forgot the backpack at the prison," Jim explained with a sheepish grin. He put together two sandwiches, thick with sliced processed meats, and gave one to Yari before dropping two small boxes of fruit juice into his pockets. The five of them filed through the door and Nick locked it behind them.

"What of my son, Jozef?" Yari asked suddenly. "When will we see him?"

"We can drive there tomorrow if it's safe to do so," replied Nick. "Although something tells me we'll have to wait a few more days."

They left the hotel together and followed the deep, reverberating roar of chanting throngs of people. The sound, mixed with a cacophony of drumming helicopters and whining police sirens, sent adrenaline coursing through Jim.

"If anything happens," the pastor shouted above the din, "return to the hotel room. Max, you and your friends come back every three hours to check in."

"Follow me." Petru broke into a jog." We are going to the square called the 23rd of August. This is the central point."

They walked down the streets, moving quickly, yet taking time to observe the activity on the streets. Many people ran past them, a few merchants still in their aprons, a surprising number of wrinkled old men, clearly rejuvenated with excitement, but mostly young men and women in their teens and early twenties. All raced in one direction to the center of the action, obviously anxious to join their fellow Romanians at the square. The roar of the mob swelled and Jim strained to make out the words.

"DOWN WITH CEAUȘESCU! GOD IS ALIVE!"

A helicopter buzzed directly overhead and a thousand white papers fluttered to the streets. Jim stopped long enough to stoop down and grab one. He handed it to Yari to translate.

"It is a warning to disperse." The pastor crumpled up the paper and tossed it into the gutter. "Ignore it. We must continue on."

They picked up their pace, half-walking, half-running, caught up by the momentum of dozens of others running in the same direction.

The chanting of the multitude hypnotized and propelled their steps. They began to run to the square.

"DOWN WITH CEAUȘESCU! DOWN WITH DICTATORSHIP! FREEDOM FOR ALL!"

A fresh burst of energy seized Jim. "Faster," he cried out. "We can't miss anything. Run." He sprinted another block then forced himself to stop and wait for the others to catch up. "Hurry!" he shouted back to them.

"FREEDOM! FREEDOM! DEMOCRACY! FREE ELECTIONS FOR ALL!"

Once the others had joined him, Jim led them to the edge of the main square. It was packed. Half the city seemed to want to participate in this radical event.

"Remain on the fringes," Yari shouted. "If the army comes in, run back to the hotel and stay in your room. You can help us more if you are alive."

Kirsten grabbed Jim's arm and shouted in his ear. "What did he say? I couldn't hear."

Jim repeated Yari's instructions. Before he had finished, Yari had been swept towards the center of the mob as if some unknown force propelled him inward.

"*LIBERTATE!*" the mob chanted. "*LIBERTATE!* WE WANT FREEDOM!"

Jim spun to face Nick and Kirsten. "Isn't this wild? Let's move closer."

Three helicopters circled directly overhead, not more than two hundred feet above the ground. All eyes in the crowd seemed transfixed on them. Jim tipped back his head. What would they do next? Silence gradually overcame the people, as though everyone held his breath. The beating of the flying scorpions' propellers drowned out every other sound. Kirsten's fingers tightened around Jim's arm.

The first echo of a gunshot pierced the dizzying tension of the night. A woman screamed and the protesters roared like an erupting volcano.

Soon thereafter, death marched in.

Chapter Twenty-One

Petru Potra ran through the square, fighting against the flow of the masses, trying to follow his father. A long staccato burst of machine gun fire erupted from one of the helicopters. Seconds later it was joined by a similar burst from the other. The two helicopters dropped lower and hung motionless in the sky, not far above the tallest buildings. Bullets continued to rain down upon the people and the 23rd of August Square began to clear. Some people fled in a desperate attempt to save their lives. Others stood in defiance. Many sprawled on the ground in lifeless abandon, like discarded children's toys.

As Petru passed by, a young woman who looked to be a university student took two bullets in the chest and crumpled to the ground. Directly beside her, another girl's neck was shattered by a bullet and she fell to the cobblestones. The frightened mob trampled her.

Petru tripped over the crumpled body of the second woman and he stopped and stared at her, heat crawling up his neck and flooding his face. "O God, what are they doing?" he cried. He dragged the trampled woman to the edge of a building and into a doorway already crammed with frightened people.

"Move aside," he screamed. "She's badly hurt." Men and women gave way before him and he pulled her body through the doorway into the *Cerbul Carpatin* restaurant. A bullet ricocheted through the glass, hitting a wall then tearing its way into the ceiling. Petru ignored it and dragged the woman to the back of the room.

"She won't make it," someone said. "Look, even now she is dead."

"No," Petru cried. "No, this is not right. They can't do this." He lowered the woman's head gently onto the carpet before rushing to the doorway and pushing his way into the square, overcome by the guilt of his own recent betrayals. Few people remained in the open. About a dozen fallen figures were stretched out on the ground, their bodies soaked and lying in pools of blood.

His stomach churning, Petru ran past the dead woman from the university into the center of the clearing. The shooting stopped suddenly. People around the square focused their attention on him. From the corner of his eye he caught a glimpse of Jim, Nick, and Kirsten on the steps of a building, the *Strada Ciucas*, a hundred yards away, staring in his direction. *Where is my father?* He scanned the square and his heart skittered wildly. Yari stood on the far side of the square in a group of at least twenty men.

A blinding light from one of the helicopters caught Petru in its circle and the group of men all turned in his direction.

Petru stretched out his hand toward the light. "Stop it! What do you think you are doing? Are you going to kill everyone?" His shouts were barely audible above the whirr of the helicopters. "Look. We are not fighting you. We desire peace. Would you shoot me, too?" He reached down and flung open his overcoat, ripping the buttons away in the process. With his chest bared to the sky, he shouted, "Are you going to kill me? What will that accomplish?"

A grumble rippled through the crowd and the helicopters backed off, circling higher into the air. Petru sensed a victory and raised a fist, shaking it at the twin helicopters. Eventually, he turned back to the crowd, his fist still raised, adrenaline pumping. He was a hero.

But no one moved. *What is wrong?* Why weren't they cheering him? What could they be thinking? The earth shook behind him and his chest tightened as he turned around. A line of six armored personnel carriers rumbled into the square from Gheorghe Baritiu Street.

Petru did not move. He could not. He was transfixed, his feet rooted to the cobblestones. The adrenaline that had been propelling him to action faded and his body shook, but he pushed back his shoulders and stared down the advancing troops. "Are you the ones who will allow this?" His voice trembled slightly. He swept an arm around the square. "Look at these people you've killed. They are your countrymen. Don't you even care?"

He was met by silence. Behind the armored carriers filed a number of soldiers, row after row until hundreds were lined up on the cobblestones.

"Are you going to kill everyone?" Petru spread his arms out, baring his chest again. "Then start with me. Kill me too."

In a single, sudden fierce barrage, bullets raked across his body. Darts of fire ripped through him. *No. They wouldn't. Father.* Petru dropped to his knees. An intense cold gripped his chest and spread down his arms. He fell backwards, slamming against the cobblestones. His vision blurred. *Father. Jozef. I'm sorry.*

Petru closed his eyes and gave in to the darkness.

⚒

From the steps of a building across the square, Nick watched in horror as Petru shouted at the soldiers. When the shots rang out, he started forward, but Jim wrapped an arm around his chest from behind and pulled him back. "There's nothing you can do. They'll shoot you too."

Nick's hands closed into fists. Jim was right, but it drove him nearly out of his mind to stand back and watch what was happening and not at least try to help. Movement caught his attention and his mouth dropped open. The people who had vacated the square earlier were trickling back in now. One or two at first, but they were soon joined by others pouring out of buildings and streaming in from side streets.

Kirsten grabbed his arm. "Nick, look!"

Nick's heart sank. Yari ran towards Petru. Would they kill him too?

"That's my son!" Yari shouted, his voice echoing around the city center. "Oh dear God, my son has given his life. Oh Petru. Petru." The haggard pastor tried to fight his way through the crowds, but was swept away to the perimeter of the square.

"Timisoara!" one man cried out.

Thousands rallied the cry. "TIMISOARA! TIMISOARA!" They surged forward, moving as a mass towards the soldiers, either forgetting or not caring about the bedlam the helicopters has just wreaked. Yari had stopped within ten feet of the soldiers and he stood with several hundred others facing the grim faces of young, uniformed men with their fearsome AK-47 weapons.

The soldiers held their fire and Yari Potra moved closer, dropping to his knees. "Please do not shoot us," he pleaded. "Can't you see? We are Romanian. We are just like you. Please do not kill us. You do not have to shoot us."

The town clock chimed twelve times, its midnight call. A brief silence followed, then a man yelled, "Down with Ceaușescu! Down with the tyrant!"

The crowd, spurred to a frenzy, took up the chant. "DOWN WITH THE TYRANT!"

Someone grabbed a flag from a nearby building, cut the communist symbol from it, and walked around the square, waving it as he went. Like a pied piper, he attracted others and thousands joined with him. "LIBERTATE! LIBERTATE!" Yari turned from the soldiers and struggled through the crowd.

Within seconds, Nick lost sight of him. "Lord, protect your servant!"

Along with several strangers, Jim, Kirsten, and Nick remained in the shadows of *Strada Ciucas*. Part of Nick longed to run down and join the throngs, but it would accomplish little to put himself in that kind of danger. For an hour, they watched the throbbing crowds and the restrained army and militia playing mind games. Finally Jim, who'd been leaning back against the wall of the building, smacked both palms on the stone. "We're not doing anyone any good here. Let's head back to the hotel. Yari said he'd meet us there."

Once in their room, Jim flopped onto one of the beds. Kirsten stretched out on the other and Nick slouched in an armchair, his heavy leather coat on the carpet next to him, where he'd dropped it. The room was silent. Jim folded his hands behind his head and stared up at the ceiling. Nick pretended to doze but, like Jim probably was, he, too, was deep in thought. Kirsten fidgeted, as though what she had just seen prevented sleep from coming to her. The distant strain of the chanting throngs filtered into their room, a keen reminder of the reality of the revolution before them.

Finally, Kirsten sat up. "Do you think Petru is dead?"

"I'm pretty sure." Nick straightened in his chair. "And we shouldn't be sitting here like this; we should be on our knees praying."

They knelt beside the beds and prayed silently for what seemed like an hour. Over and over, Nick begged God to intervene for His people.

They were interrupted by a knock on the door. Nick scrambled to his feet as Yari entered.

"Good," he said quietly, his shoulders sagging. Deep lines were grooved across his face. He appeared to have aged a decade in the last few hours. "I see you have not neglected your most important duty."

Nick strode across the room and grasped both of the pastor's arms. "What has happened?"

"Petru has disappeared. His body, I mean. When I turned from the soldiers and went to find him, he was no longer where he had fallen." Yari's voice broke. "I should have gone straight to him. Perhaps there was a chance he might have been saved. Oh Lord, my Petru is gone."

Jim rose from his knees and crossed the floor to Yari. Nick let go of the pastor and moved out of Jim's way. He had spent a lot of time with Yari and his presence might be a comfort. "There was no chance." Jim rested his hands on the big Romanian's shoulders. "Even from where we stood, we could see. He died a very brave man."

Kirsten came up to stand beside Jim. "Are you thinking of going back to the square?"

"I will wait until morning." The pastor ran his fingers through his disheveled hair. "Now I feel very ancient and very tired. It is time for this old man to sleep."

"Can you sleep after what you just witnessed?" Nick reached for the hotel room key Petru had left on the table by the door.

"I don't know if my mind will allow my body to sleep, but I must try. I need to be able to think clearly tomorrow."

"Petru had the room across the hall." Nick held out his hand. "Here's the key. Take that if you want. Then you won't be disturbed."

"This is good. Will you call me in six hours?"

"Of course." Nick led Yari into the hall and waited until he had opened the door and gone into his room. When the door had shut and the key turned loudly in the lock, Nick turned back to his own door. In the corner of his eye a shadow moved slightly and he whipped his head in that direction. Nothing.

Slowly, he walked down the length of the hall, the only lights coming from the cracks underneath the doorways. "Who is it?" he asked, his eyes straining to catch a glimpse of any movement. "Who's there?" He reached the end of the hall without finding anything. He stopped in front of a large window and stared out. The distant lights of the helicopters glowed in the sky, and he caught the faint noise of the chanting masses. The window had been left open and the curtain stirred slightly in the breeze. *Is that what I saw?*

Nick headed back down the hallway. *Pretty sure it was something else, but if someone was here, they're gone now.* His stomach tightened. Were Jim and Kirsten okay? Lengthening his strides, he reached their door in a few seconds and pushed into the room, Kirsten appeared to have drifted off on one of the beds and Jim was running the bath water. He offered Nick a tired smile through a crack in the door. "It's been a long couple of days."

"I'll bet. Still want to hear that story, but have your bath first. You've earned it."

"Thanks."

Nick nodded and pulled the door shut tight. He made his way across the room and sank down on the edge of the bed across from Kirsten.

She must have sensed his presence, because she opened her eyes and sat up. "Oh Nick, I can't believe what we just witnessed. I mean, you see these things on TV, but it's different in real life. All this for freedom. Freedom that I take for granted in the States."

Nick moved over to her bed and slid an arm around her shoulders. "I'm glad you're with me."

"Me too. But did you hear what I said?"

"Yes. And I agree. I take freedom for granted too. What I saw today also made me realize how important you are to me. I'd hate to lose you."

She rested her head on his shoulder. "I'd hate to lose you, too."

He tightened his hold and whispered into her ear, "I think I love you."

She opened her mouth, but a loud knock on the door kept her from answering.

"Who is that?" Nick let her go, reluctantly, and scowled as he walked towards the door. *Whatever this is, it better be important.*

"Be careful, Nick," Kirsten whispered. Nick nodded, hesitated a moment, then unlocked their door and opened it a crack. Peering out, he recognized Cristea, Jozef, and Carl.

"Come in, come in." Nick swung the door open wide and stepped back. "It's good to see you. "*Grüss Gott, Jozef,*" he added in German. Jozef nodded but didn't speak. His face was ashen and he looked nearly as old as his father. *Does he know about Petru?* "What are you all doing here? You were going to wait for us."

The three of them filed past Nick into the room. Before closing the door behind them, he stuck his head into the hallway and checked in both directions. Nothing moved. Blowing out a breath, Nick closed the door and turned to face his friends.

"It is good to see you, Ralph," Cristea said quietly. "We had to come." She waved at Kirsten. "Hello Cathy. How have you been?"

"I'm a little shaken by everything that's going on, but I'm okay." Kirsten climbed off the bed and hugged Cristea.

Cristea rubbed Kirsten's back. "Of course you are. Were you at the square today?" She held Kirsten out at arms' length. "Did you see what happened?"

Kirsten nodded.

Cristea pulled her back into an embrace. "Poor thing. That must have been terrible."

"It was."

Nick's legs suddenly felt weak and he sank onto a chair. He held out an arm to the others. "Please, sit."

Cristea took the chair across from him as the men settled on one of the beds. Kirsten stayed on her feet, but leaned back against the wall. "Where is Max?" asked Cristea. "Is he back yet? Did he succeed?"

If Nick's emotions hadn't been in such turmoil, he might have smiled. *Pretty sure her interest in Jim goes beyond the plight of his mission to rescue Yari.* "Max is having a bath. We haven't heard how yet, but he was able to find Yari and get him out. He returned earlier this evening. Right now, Yari is sleeping in the room across the hall."

Cristea translated for Jozef. He started to get off the bed, but Nick held up a hand. "I know you want to see him, but we should let him sleep. He looked terrible when he got back here from the square."

Jozef said something in Romanian to Cristea, who turned to Nick. "He wonders if his father knows about Petru, that he is dead."

Nick exchanged a look with Kirsten before shifting to the front of his seat and resting his hands on his knees. "You know then."

"Yes." Cristea's eyes misted. "We were at the square. We saw Petru sacrifice his life. Some men came and took his body and threw it in the back of a truck, along with the others who died."

"A truck!" Kirsten covered her mouth with her hand. "Why?"

"We don't know this. We only saw the driver close the doors on the bodies and drive away. We don't know where he took them."

Nick pressed his eyes shut for a few seconds. When he opened them, Cristea was watching him. "Yes." It required all the energy he had left to get the words out. "Yari knows. He was there too."

He pushed to his feet and went over to the portable stove to boil water for tea. "Why did you come to Brasov? You were going to wait for us in Codlea."

"It was impossible for us to stay." Cristea gripped the armrests of the chair. "A man drove through the town this evening and told everyone that demonstrations were beginning in the city. He said all true Romanians would join in. We could not remain in our friend's apartment knowing that others were putting their lives on the line for our country. We have listened to the Radio Free Europe broadcasts and they tell us everything about Timisoara. And then today, Radio Budapest reported that 60,000 to 70,000 people have been killed so far in the revolution. We could not sit and wait."

All the color drained from Kirsten's face and she swayed on her feet. Alarmed, Nick started for her, but she shook her head. "That many?" The words came out in a raspy whisper.

"I'm afraid so." Cristea got up and went to her. She wrapped one arm around her and Kirsten rested her head against Cristea's. After a moment, she lifted her head and managed to offer Nick a wan smile.

He wasn't convinced, but he went back to making tea, knowing they all needed a little fortification.

"How is your shoulder, Jozef?" Kirsten asked. Cristea translated quickly and Jozef offered a short response.

"He says his shoulder is better. I don't think he is thinking about it right now; he has too many other things on his mind."

"Of course he does."

"We all do." Nick handed both Cristea and Kirsten a cup of tea. "I'm sure we have a lot of questions for each other, but maybe those should wait until morning. We could really use some sleep now." He poured boiling water into more cups.

Cristea set her cup on the table between the beds and stood. "You're right, we do."

Jim stumbled from the bathroom in sweat pants and a T-shirt. At the sight of the others, he stepped forward to greet them. He met Cristea first and gave her a warm hug. "It's good to see you."

"I know." Her cheeks flushed. "I mean, I am very glad you are safe."

Nick caught the lingering glance between them. *Interesting.*

Jim touched her arm. "Can we talk in the morning, just you and me?"

"Please."

He turned to Nick. "Where will we all sleep?"

"This is no problem." Cristea picked up her cup. "We have purchased rooms for ourselves. With the tension in the city, the clerk did not even bother to ask for our identification." Nick handed a cup of tea to each of the men and they carried them to the door. Cristea followed them. "If you need us, we are directly below you on the bottom floor. Good night."

"Good night. Sleep well," said Nick as the Romanians filed from the room.

"God night," tried Jozef.

Nick shut the door, locked it, and left the key in the lock from habit. As he walked back across the room, a feeling of dread suddenly struck him. He stopped in front of the television set. "Did it occur to anyone tonight," he tapped the top of the television with his fingernail, "that our room still might be monitored by the *Securitate*?"

Jim and Kirsten stared at him before all three of them shifted their gazes to the little cassette player. It sat on the table in the corner, silent, as it had been since they had returned from the square.

Nick swallowed hard. They'd have to pray hard that their oversight hadn't just made a terrible day a whole lot worse.

Chapter Twenty-Two

Yari Potra lay in his bed, not quite asleep, but not yet awake, half-listening to the distant roar of the excited mob in the city center. Or was that a dream? He couldn't tell. He'd had similar dreams before, but this seemed different. *WE ARE READY TO DIE! WE ARE READY TO DIE!* What? He wasn't yet ready. He was anxious to live a while longer. *TIMISOARA! TIMISOARA!* The cries of his dream people continued.

He shifted nervously, trying to awaken, yet overcome by exhaustion. Other senses, fine-tuned over the years from the frequent threat of peril, detected a movement closer, something in his room. His eyes opened wide as the cold metal of a gun-barrel touched his lips.

"You could not stay away, could you?"

Yari focused on the cigarette-stained fingers holding the gun before shifting his gaze to a pair of sinister brown-black eyes, a hawk-like nose, hair combed back over a balding scalp and a cruel smile.

"You are very quiet, Colonel Popescu. My congratulations to you."

"You are fortunate that you slept well. It will be the last time, I am sure."

"I am dead then."

"Not yet. Believe me, it will take some time." The colonel turned and signaled the men behind him. "Take him upstairs."

Two of his officers, Nuvelei and Elanului, stepped forward and pulled the pastor from his bed.

Jim woke with a start at exactly 9:05 the next morning. The noise of the chanting revolutionaries still filtered through the double-pane glass windows. He flung back the covers and sat up. It was time to wake Yari. He was late even, but it should not matter. The old man certainly had needed the sleep.

Jim climbed out of bed and tugged on his pants and a sweater as it was cold in the room. Nick stirred, opening one eye to look at Jim before closing it again and pulling the blanket over his head. "Yari," was all Jim explained before leaving the room and closing the door behind him. Across the hall, he knocked on the pastor's door, then waited, scanning the hallway for suspicious on-lookers. He saw no one. He knocked again, this time louder, and tried the doorknob. To his surprise, it turned easily and the heavy wooden door swung open.

The bed to his left was empty and unmade. The bathroom directly in front of him was also vacant. Jim searched the small room before walking out and closing the door again. What should he do? He ran down the hall to his left, descended a flight of stairs to the first floor, then slowed to a walk, searching for Cristea's room. *There, on the left.*

Jim knocked loudly. A moment later, Carl opened the door, his eyes still heavy with sleep.

Jim didn't bother with small talk. "Is Yari here?"

Carl pointed across the hall. "Cristea," he said.

Jim banged on Cristea's door. Thirty seconds later the door opened and a smile flashed across Cristea's face. She looked much better-rested than Carl. Jim would have given anything to sit down and enjoy a leisurely breakfast with her, share everything that was on his heart. Now was not the time. "Have you seen Yari this morning?"

"He has not come here." Her forehead wrinkled. "How would he even know we are here?"

"You're right. Then he's disappeared."

Cristea pressed both hands to her cheeks. "But where could he have gone? To the protests?"

Jim shook his head. "I don't think so. We had planned to meet up first."

"Then something has happened to him. We must think the best and prepare for the worst. We will come to your room in fifteen minutes. Then we will decide what should be done."

An officer on either side of him, Yari had been dragged up three flights of stairs to the top floor of the Hotel Parc. At the far end of the hallway, a cleaning woman with her mop and trolley of clean linens continued to work in spite of the demonstrations. Was she afraid of the communist regime, the one that had the power to give or take away her job? How much terror had been inflicted upon her or her family by the dictators of the past? Yari cast her a longing look as he was bustled through a doorway.

The officers shoved him into the room, one of normal size, void of furniture except for a television, a bed, and two heavy armchairs. The latter were set in the center of the room, their backs to each other with a space of about three or four feet between them. The legs had been nailed into the carpet. Yari stared at the stains on the carpet as he walked over them. Was that blood? His stomach tightened.

Greceanu's words drifted back to him. *They can take your life, but they can't steal your soul. Don't let them steal your soul, Yari. If they kill you, they only send you to glory.*

Officers Nuvelei and Elanului still held his arms. A third officer, one Yari remembered from the night he was arrested, Mumuleanu, appeared in the doorway in a well-fitting navy suit. He drew instant looks of contempt from his counterparts. "Quickly," they shouted, "shut the door." Mumuleanu closed and locked it, then walked over to Yari, pulling two black socks from his pocket as he approached. One he stuffed into Yari's mouth. The other he tied over his mouth and around his neck.

"Sit on the floor," Popescu ordered. Nuvelei kicked the prisoner to his knees then shoved him again with his foot, so that Yari was sitting. "Clasp your hands around your ankles," the colonel demanded. Yari did so and Nuvelei tied Yari's hands tightly to his feet. Popescu then took an iron bar, five feet in length and an inch in diameter, and passed it through the space between Yari's elbows and his knees. Nuvelei and Elanului picked the bar up with Yari hanging in the middle and set him between the two armchairs. The bar was free to roll over the backs of the chairs and Yari swung like an awkward pendulum between them, his head bumping on the carpet when he dared relax his neck muscles.

"I can't watch this." Mumuleanu shook his head. "This is not our work here. I refuse to be a part of wasting our time. This is your own personal vendetta. Not mine." He stalked to the door.

"Woman!" Nuvelei said. "Get back here."

Popescu raised a hand. "Let him go. There'll be enough of him for each of us." He came over to stand beside Yari as the door slammed behind Mumuleanu. "You've caused me much grief in my life, Comrade Potra. Now it is my turn to reciprocate.

We will play a little game. Every time your head hits the floor, you will be kicked. If you hold yourself up, you may save yourself. But only for a time."

Yari pulled his head from the floor, blocking his surroundings from his senses. From the outside, the furor of the demonstrations reached his ears. A gunshot sounded close by, then a tirade of automatic fire. Yari turned his eyes to the window, searching for hope.

"Don't even think of receiving help." Popescu laughed. "No one knows you're here. Listen to the guns. Soon we will crush these revolutionaries. If you do not cause us too much trouble, we may let you live to see the protests fail. Then," he snapped his fingers, "you will disappear like the rest." He turned to his officers. "Rock him," he ordered.

Yari began his first spin on the bar.

Nick sat in their hotel room with Kirsten and Jim and their Romanian friends, drinking coffee at the small table and discussing possible courses of action.

"He could be at the demonstrations." Cristea wrapped her fingers around her cup. "We could look for him there."

Nick shook his head. "He wouldn't have gone by himself."

"It's a possibility, though." Jim scooped sugar into his coffee and stirred it with a plastic spoon. "The problem is finding him among all the people. There must be over 100,000 of them."

"Closer to 300,000, I'd guess." Kirsten turned away from the window she had been staring out of. "Even from here, we can see the streets are full of people. How would we find one man?"

"Certainly not by sitting here." Jim tossed the spoon in the garbage.

Jozef spoke up, talking rapidly in his native language. When he had finished, Cristea translated. "Jozef asks if you would please stay here. You don't know the city, and could get lost and we would have to search for you too. And if you ask for directions, everyone would know you are foreigners, which could cause trouble."

"But …" Nick started to get up.

Jozef clapped a hand on his shoulder and Nick sat back down. "Please."

"Fine." Jim threw his arms up, clearly as agitated as Nick at the thought of being cooped up in their room while everyone else was out doing something. "Is there anything we can do while we're here waiting?"

Cristea flashed him a smile. "Yes, Max. It is what every Christian must do in times such as this. Pray. And when you have finished praying," her face flushed with passion, "pray some more. You have many Christian brothers and sisters out there risking their lives."

"Of course." Jim smiled back at her.

"Lunch will be in four hours." Kirsten tapped her watch. "Meet back here and tell us what you have found out. Be positive. We have God on our side. Nothing will happen to Yari that God does not allow."

Jim looked across the small table again at Cristea. "We only have until Sunday. We are expected for Christmas at our friends' home in Austria. If we don't come, they'll be very worried. Especially since they will have heard what is happening here on the news."

"The Poplawskis are *always* worrying about us." Nick smacked his hand on the arm of the chair. "I think this time we can risk their worry for the sake of a man's life. We're staying until we know that Yari is okay."

Cristea nodded and started for the door, the Romanians following her.

"Cristea," Nick strode after her and gripped her elbow. "If Yari doesn't return by tonight, we must consider that someone found out where he was. Maybe that Colonel Popescu."

She covered his hand with hers. "If that is so, then there is nothing for us to do but pray."

Yari had been standing for over six hours, a small respite after hours of torture. His feet cried out for relief, but none was to be found. It was early Thursday afternoon now, and he had been a prisoner for more than two days. December 21 would not be a day he would care to remember in the future. If he had a future. Last night there had been no real sleep and no break in his punishment. How long could he endure? He was too old. How much longer?

This morning he had regained consciousness from a brief blackout, a result of the beatings the days before. Popescu had left early the night before and the other two were clumsy with their torture, each vying for a kick or punch, constantly in each other's way. A stray boot had connected with Yari's temple and he blacked out. He remembered little that happened after that, until this morning.

Six hours ago, when he first dared to open his eyes, Popescu stood in front of him. He yanked Yari to his feet. The colonel kicked Yari's legs wide apart and secured his ankles to the bed posts with barbed wire. He secured Yari's hands behind his back with a cord. Now, even a small shift in his position and the bleeding would restart. His ankles were numb from the swelling, but the balls of his feet yearned for a respite.

"How did you escape?" The colonel spat the first question at him.

"It was easy. God helped me."

Popescu struck Yari in the stomach with a hard fist. "Leave God out of this!" He shook out his hand. "Give me a straight answer."

"I cannot leave God out of this. Without Him, I would still be in my cell."

"Tell me, does God carry a backpack? Did God leave a car mat at the perimeter fence? Did God leave the second set of footprints in the snow? Is it possible that your God works for the CIA?"

Yari ignored the question. "You are Orthodox, yes? Can I tell you the essential difference between you as an Orthodox and me?"

Popescu, infuriated, drove his foot into Yari's groin. "I am a communist!" he screamed as Yari sank to the floor. The flesh on his ankles tore from the barbs. "I am a communist!"

Yari tilted his head back, his teeth clenched against the pain. "But Jesus still loves you."

Gunfire erupted close to the Hotel Parc and Jim flinched. He lunged for the window and peered cautiously into the street, just in time to see uniformed soldiers running for the hotel's front door.

"The soldiers are coming in. Quick, let's barricade the door." He and Nick dragged a bed into the narrow space between the door and the bathroom. It fit with only inches to spare.

"Both of you grab the end of the other bed. Let's put it on top." All three of them worked together to cram the second bed into the same narrow space. "Stay back here, I'll see what's happening."

Crouching down, Jim made his way to the window. He pressed his back against the wall and peeked out through the bottom of the glass. A fusillade of bullets ricocheted in the streets below and two people dropped to the ground. One appeared to be a student, the other an old man cowering in a doorway, both unluckily in the wrong place at the wrong time. The stutter of an AK-47 rattled sharply in Jim's ears and he looked up. Did that come from a floor above them? His stomach lurched. Were soldiers hunting people down in the hotel now?

Jim crawled back to his friends. "I think this might be a good time to do that praying Cristea mentioned earlier."

Kirsten swallowed hard. "I agree."

Jim lowered himself to the floor and leaned back against the beds. Nick stood in front of them and looked at his watch. "We're going to be a while. Tea, anyone?"

Kirsten managed a weak smile. "I'll help."

Jim watched the two of them as they crossed the room—keeping to one side to avoid walking in front of the window—and began preparing tea. While this was definitely not a situation Jim would have wanted them to be in, since they had to be holed up here with a war raging all around them, there was no one he would rather be with at the moment than his two best friends.

⚒

Colonel Popescu turned the television so Yari could see it clearly. "In a few minutes, our most inspired leader will give a speech in front of the Central Committee Building in Bucharest." He grabbed Yari's chin with his right hand, lifting the pastor's weary head. "Keep your eyes open, Comrade. You will not miss any of this. You will watch and learn how our great leader controls the population."

Yari turned his tired eyes to the colonel. "While we wait, tell me why you hate me so much. How have I wronged you?"

"You don't deserve that answer."

"You have been consumed with years of hatred. When I die, do you think you will be free from that?"

Popescu turned to his other officers. "Leave the room." They hesitated for a moment. "Now!" he screamed.

When they had gone, he locked the door and returned to Yari. "When you die, I can focus my energies for the good of the Party."

"What has the Party done for you?"

Popescu gaped at Yari as if he couldn't believe the question. "The Party has given me my life. How dare you ask such a question?"

"Life?" Yari cocked his head. "The Party has totally ruined this country and President Ceauşescu has accelerated the process."

"How dare you?" Popescu hurled the words at him, barely inches from Yari's face. "How dare you? You cannot talk in such a manner."

"Colonel, my life matters little to me now. I am concerned for you. When you kill this body, I go to heaven to live forever. And I shall be very happy. You, Colonel, will remain in Romania and suffer at the hands of the leaders who hold you in this terrible situation. Even your privileged position in the *Securitate* cannot compare to what God offers."

Popescu did not respond.

"Do you have children?" Yari pressed. "Do you want them to grow up in this country where everything will be so hard for them?"

"Leave my children out of this," Popescu snarled, turning on Yari.

"What if you died today, Colonel?" Yari persisted. "Would the country provide for your children?"

The colonel paced the carpet for a few seconds, apparently deep in thought. Approaching Yari, he whispered in low tones. "Let us assume a hypothetical situation. Let us assume that Austria was taken over by an evil person leading an evil force. What do you think should be done?"

Yari forced a smile. "Hypothetically speaking, it wouldn't be enough to be rid of the evil leader. The system that allows such a man to rule is at fault and that system must be cast away before positive changes can occur."

"What are the alternatives?"

"Many people believe democracy."

"And you?"

"Whatever change comes to Romania, it will take too many years to turn this nation into one of economic prosperity. You and I are old. We might live ten or fifteen years more and I doubt we will see much change. You must prepare for the eternal, for life after death."

Popescu pointed to the television. "Ceaușescu is about to make his speech. We will listen and see what he has to say." A minute passed and then television cameras scanned the crowds of youth holding banners revealing pro-Communist slogans and portraits of Nicolae Ceaușescu and his wife Elena.

"How do I prepare for the eternal?" Popescu asked suddenly.

"It is only through Jesus Christ," Yari answered. "You must repent of your sins and follow the example that he set for us to live. There comes a time in every man s life when he must take a stand and choose to walk God's way."

Popescu waved away the suggestion. "Watch the television now."

The screen came in and out of focus and Yari blinked until it settled. The nation's leader stood with his wife and officials on the front balcony of the Central Committee Building. Popescu reached for the volume control and turned it up.

"Recent events in Timisoara have been the result of hooligans, of pro-Hungarian terrorists intending to advance their territorial boundaries. They are illegal forces at work, irredentist madmen."

"You see?" Popescu grinned as his mentor twisted what had happened to undermine the attempts at revolution. "He's a genius."

"... I promise that you will receive increased rations. I promise that..."

Shrill whistling came from the back of the immense crowd. In seconds it grew in volume. Ceaușescu raised his hands in an attempt to calm the hecklers. It had no effect. The whistling only grew louder. Ceaușescu turned his back on the crowd and left the balcony for the safety of the building.

Popescu's mouth hung open. The filming was disrupted as the camera swung wildly, ending up on a shot of the top of another building and the open sky. The camera man had either fled or joined the crowd.

"Your time is coming to a close, Colonel," Yari stated quietly as audio from the television continued to pick up the increasing furor of the Bucharest young people.

Gunfire from a room on what sounded like the same floor of the hotel prevented him from saying more.

Popescu looked Yari squarely in the face. "I'm not finished yet. Much can still be done."

He picked up his coat and walked to the door. "I'll return with my men. Be sure of it."

"And what of your future in eternity?" Yari ventured with fading hope.

"Not quite, Comrade. You have not yet persuaded me to become a Christian."

Chapter Twenty-Three

O n the evening of December 21, Jim paced the floor of the hotel room in a rare display of impatience. Nick and Kirsten sat on one of the beds, still positioned against the door as a makeshift barricade, playing Uno, their favorite card game.

"I can't believe we have to just sit here and wait." Jim whirled towards them. "There's got to be something we can do. Make some phone calls or something."

A knock sounded at the door and Kirsten jumped up. "Who is it?"

"It's Cristea. Open quickly, please."

They hauled the beds away from the door and flung it open, ushering in Carl, Cristea, and Jozef. As soon as everyone was inside, Jim locked the door and he and Nick shoved the beds back into place.

"The shooting has mostly stopped now." Cristea removed her coat and hung it over the back of a chair.

Jim's stomach rumbled. When was the last time they had eaten? He headed for the small kitchen area to see what he could find for supper. Kirsten joined him.

"Be careful," replied Nick. "It may only be for a time. We saw about twenty armored personnel carriers go by the hotel today. In all my trips to Romania in the past, I've never even seen one. I think they could be positioning for a major offensive against the people."

"There were soldiers in the lobby this time. They looked at my papers. We told them we were on vacation here."

Kirsten looked up from the pot of water she was about to heat to cook pasta. "And they believed you?"

Cristea shrugged. "They let us go. We prayed they would."

"Were you followed?"

"No. Carl remained at the end of the hall until we reached your door to make sure."

Jim dumped a bag of pasta into the water and went to get a chair for Cristea to sit in. When he pulled it up to her, she smiled warmly at him. "You are a gentleman."

Warmth rushed into Jim's cheeks. "I try." He retreated back to the kitchen. Cristea wandered over and stood near him, watching. Likely she and her friends were hungry too.

Jim stirred the pasta. "We must leave tomorrow."

"It will not be safe."

"It could get worse if we stay."

"Will you come back soon?"

"I'm not sure. It depends if things stabilize here. Ralph mentioned that he has materials to deliver to a Christian brother in Czechoslovakia. I can't say now what our schedule will be."

Cristea's smile faded. "I am very sad."

Jim leaned across the corner of the table and took both of her hands in his. "And I am very sorry."

Nick cleared his throat. "Max, can I see you for a minute?"

Jim gave Cristea's hands an extra squeeze before he let them go.

"Sure, Ralph."

He joined Nick by the window and they looked out over the darkened streets together. Snow began to fall gently, temporarily purifying the streets. By morning, the snow would have turned to dirty slush. Now, though, it was a beautiful sight, almost holy. Especially with the Christmas music drifting from the cassette player.

Nick nudged Jim in the ribs. "We need to tell them our plan."

"You've got to tell *me* your plan first." The corners of Jim's mouth twitched. They had discussed little about the future, distracted by everything happening in the present.

Nick turned to the others in the room. "Friends." He lifted a hand to get their attention, not wanting to raise his voice above the music in case anyone was listening in on them. "Max and I want to tell you our plans for tomorrow." The others moved closer so they could hear him. "We would like to leave here by ten o'clock. If you wish, we will give you a ride back to Cluj."

Cristea shook her head. "We will stay and continue to look for Yari."

Jim frowned. "I'm sorry, Cristea. I just don't think there is anything left for us to do here. It's been more than two days since we've seen Yari and we still have no clue as to his whereabouts. Our visas expire soon and our friends in Austria will be anxious for us."

"I understand."

Jim studied her. Did she understand? Did she have any idea how badly he wanted to stay, to spend more time with her so they could find out if what was happening between them was real and might actually go somewhere?

As though she could read his mind, her face softened and she reached for his hand. "Please. Let us pray together one more time."

Yari awoke in the middle of the night, his legs weak and shaking from hours of half-standing. His whole body ached. He was alone still. Popescu and his officers had failed to return, even late into yesterday. Perhaps they would never come back. His shoulders sagged. Popescu wasn't the type to give up. That would be too much to ask. Or was it? Through his pain and exhaustion, Yari prayed.

He opened his eyes. He was still there, still tied to the end of the bed, his hands bound tightly behind his back. Could he untie the cords? His fingers strained to reach the knots. For several minutes he struggled, until his fingers cramped and he nearly cried out from the pain. It was no use. He would remain in his semi-upright position until Popescu returned. Unless someone else found him first.

Yari did his best to shut out the sensations assaulting every part of his body. "Father." He lifted his face to the ceiling. "I don't understand you. You said in your Word that you desire the best for your children. Yet you allow evil men to subdue me. Lord, I desire to live. I desire to preach your Word again to the Romanian people. Please don't allow this revolution to fail. May your justice be found in this land. May your Holy Spirit move through this people. Lord I praise your name."

At 9:30 the next morning, after breakfast with the others, Nick and Kirsten headed for the lobby. The night had been noisy. Intermittent gunfire erupted around the city, and a few times in their own building. The two trudged down the stairs, partly from exhaustion, partly from apprehension. Nick's chest was tight. Would they be able to leave the city safely?

When they came through the door into the lobby, soldiers were everywhere. Nick grabbed Kirsten's hand and pulled her to his side. "The army's here. Be careful what you say."

Her eyes had gone wide. "There's so many. Let's go back to the room."

"It's too late." Nick hesitated a moment then moved forward, desperately trying to appear nonchalant. He ignored the soldiers and walked straight to the front desk.

"We would like to pay for our room, please." He held up a coupon.

The clerk shot a nervous look at the soldiers and suddenly stepped back from the counter. A barrel-chested officer in military-style uniform, slightly different from those the army wore, appeared at Nick's side. Nick whirled around and stared into the barrels of four machine guns.

"Who are you?" the officer barked. "What are you doing here?"

They handed the officer their passports. "We are tourists." Nick willed his voice to remain steady. "We came to Brasov, this very beautiful city, and all this fighting started. So we stayed in our room."

"Which room were you in?" the officer snapped, leafing through the pages in each passport.

Nick hesitated a moment. Would telling the truth put the others in danger? He saw no point in delaying; the hotel had their records.

"Room 319."

The officer in command uttered an order to two other soldiers who came forward instantly. "You will go with these men," the leader said. "We will talk with you for a while."

"Wait a minute." Nick frowned. "We're not going anywhere with you. I'm a Canadian. We—"

The officer snapped his fingers and the soldiers hurried the two into the vacant hotel dining room. Soldiers pushed them into the first chairs they came to then moved back six feet and pointed their AK-47s at the hostages.

Nick nudged Kirsten's knee with his. "Looks like we aren't moving."

"Not for a while. The first man took our passports. What about the others?"

"They'll wait. What else can they do?"

"Ho!" one soldier exclaimed, waving his machine gun.

Kirsten's eyes narrowed. "What?"

"He wants us to shut up." Nick stood and approached the soldier. "Hey look. Let me explain."

The soldier stepped forward and jabbed Nick in the chest with his rifle barrel. Nick let out a cry of pain and sat back down.

"Nick." Kirsten clutched his leg. "Are you okay?"

Not really. He nodded.

The officer in charge came running in with his other men.

"What is going on here?" he demanded. The young soldier spoke rapidly and pointed at Nick. The leader asked another question and the soldier shook his head.

"You said you were tourists." The one who appeared to be in charge strode over and stopped in front of Nick. "I don't believe you."

"There's not much I can do about that, is there?"

The officer glared at him a moment then his face twisted into a smirk. "But there is something I can do." He approached Kirsten and twisted her blonde hair in his fingers. "You have very beautiful hair. Almost unusual, I might say."

Nick started to his feet, but a soldier behind him grasped his shoulders and shoved him back down.

Kirsten squirmed.

A tall officer walked over to them. The officer let go of Kirsten and said, "Mumuleanu, tell me again what you saw."

"She was in Bratislava, Colonel Popescu."

A second officer jumped in. "She's a spy. I know it. She's a spy."

"No, I'm not," Kirsten protested. "Where did you see me? I'm not a spy."

"Don't play games with me," Popescu snarled at her. "We could keep you here a very long time."

"I doubt it," Nick retorted, trying to sound more certain than he felt. "I'm a Canadian. She's American. You can't do that."

Popescu shook his fist at Nick. "Who do you think you are? You are not in Canada or America. You are in Romania. You will do what I tell you. Times are changing here. Perhaps no one will know if you disappeared or not."

The hotel clerk came running into the restaurant. "Colonel, the phone. Quickly!"

With a last, heated glare at Nick, the officer turned and left the restaurant.

Now's as good a time as any. Kirsten's hand still rested on his leg and Nick took it in his. "The more I realize I could lose you, the more I want to spend the rest of my life with you."

Her mouth fell open slightly. "Is this a proposal?"

"Do you think it's possible, you and me? There'll be no white picket fence. That's a guarantee."

"I'll take adventure with you and God any day over a picket fence. Though right now I'm not entirely convinced I feel that way." She offered him a wry grin.

Nick felt the quiet affirmation deep inside him. A woman who could grin at him that way, under these circumstances, was definitely the woman for him.

The sound of Popescu's enraged shouting ended the conversation. The colonel stormed back into the room, yanking his pistol from its holster as he headed straight for Nick and Kirsten.

Jim was talking quietly with his Romanian friends when a loud knocking on the door interrupted their conversation.

"I'll get it." Still wary, Jim crossed the room and opened the door a crack. He blinked at the sight of the cleaning woman in the hallway.

"We'll only be one hour." Jim pointed at his watch and held up one finger. The woman shook her head and leaned around him to look at the others in the room as she spoke rapidly in low tones. Jim didn't understand what she said, but the others obviously did. They all jumped out of their chairs and rushed to the woman. After they'd conversed for a few seconds, Carl pulled the cleaning woman into the room and closed the door.

Cristea turned to Jim and clasped her hands together in front of her chest. "She has seen Yari. She knows where he is."

Jim grabbed her by the shoulders. "Where? Where?"

"That's the problem. She said it is very hard to make a living and she is taking a risk in telling us. She has many children to feed and her husband is sick. We must make it worth her while."

Jim looked wildly around the room. *What can we give her?* "We have no more coffee."

"Max," Cristea rested a hand on his arm, "She will take almost anything you own. This is Romania. We do not have."

Jim crossed the room to his small suitcase. From a plastic bag he pulled a pair of white and blue Reebok running shoes, examined them, and took them to the cleaning lady. The lady grabbed them, compared them against her own boots, and smiled. She muttered a few words to Cristea and walked out the door.

"What did she say?" Jim could barely draw in a breath.

Cristea was already heading for the hall. "There is an old man in Room 625. He is alone now."

Nick froze as the colonel made a beeline for him, his knuckles white around the handle of his pistol. "Oh Lord, help us," was all Nick managed, before the colonel reached him and shoved the barrel of the weapon into his forehead. Nick closed his eyes and held his breath. *God, give me strength.*

Beside him, Kirsten cried out.

Nick slowly opened his eyes, looking squarely into those of the colonel's. "Why?" he asked. He'd heard they never killed foreigners here, that it was unheard of, but it appeared as though that was exactly what the man in front of him had in mind.

The colonel drew in a deep breath. "General Milea of Bucharest, the commander-in-chief of the armed forces, just sent a telex to the army commanders here in Brasov. He ordered them to stop firing on citizens. The army is siding with the people!" A maniacal look swept across his eyes. "Do you understand me?" In an ice-cold voice, he pushed the words out through clenched teeth. "Milea is a traitor. The army is betraying its country. It has sided with the revolution."

The colonel spun suddenly to one of the soldiers, pulling the trigger without aiming. The first bullet dropped a young soldier to the ground like a rock. The second soldier was also caught off guard. With his jaw agape, he took the first bullet in the throat, the second and third in his stomach.

Kirsten threw herself at Nick and he wrapped his arms around her tightly. His ears rang from the sound of the blasts. *God help us. God help us. Keep her safe.*

The violent explosions echoed in the brief aftermath of silence. The colonel whirled on Nick and Kirsten. "You are very fortunate that I have no time to question you further." He stalked to the restaurant door, to a tall officer standing guard. "Mumuleanu. Eliminate Potra. Then find the others. Quickly! We must flee."

He stopped at the door and turned back, his gaze meeting Nick's. "You are indeed very fortunate that I have no more time." He flipped their passports to the floor, spun on his heel, and walked from the room without a backward glance.

Yari slouched at the end of the bed. *Take me home. I'm ready.* He barely had the mental energy left to form the prayer. He groaned when someone flung open the door of the hotel room. *No more.*

"Father!"

Yari lifted his pounding head. Was that…? "My son. You've found me. Oh, thank you Lord!"

Jozef sprinted across the room and began tugging at the cords. "Oh God, what have they done to you?" As Yari's hands came free, he tottered, nearly falling forward. Jozef caught his father.

"My feet, Jozef. Untie my feet. Carefully."

Jozef bent down, moaning as he untwisted the barbed wire. "Father, what else did they do to you?"

"Not now. It is enough that I am alive."

The door creaked behind Jozef and he spun around, crouched and prepared to fight. A tall officer in a military-like uniform approached slowly. "I, too, am glad he's alive."

"What have you done to him?" Jozef cried out. "What are you doing?"

The officer came closer, drawing his pistol from its holster.

"My name is Officer Mumuleanu. I was a member of the Security Forces, D4 units." White-hot rage slashed through Jozef and he clenched his fists. Before he could lunge at the man, the officer tossed the pistol on the bed. "The army has just sided with the people." A smile crossed his lips. "I am now the people. Allow me to help you."

Chapter Twenty-Four

Jim clutched the steering wheel as he drove the group from Brasov to Cluj-Napoca. None of the eight spoke unless it was absolutely necessary. The van was crammed with bodies and luggage. The atmosphere was mixed. The passengers were partly elated that their mission had been accomplished and that the revolutionaries seemed to be winning, yet they were still mourning Petru's death. The peril of the twisting icy roads was further shadowed by the continued threat of roving *Securitate* bands. Forces loyal to President Ceauşescu wreaked havoc across the nation, concentrating their acts of terrorism in a few of the major cities: Bucharest, Timisoara, Brasov, Arad, Cluj.

Cluj. The city to which they were headed. A city where the killing continued. Cristea pointed to it on the open map. "We must reach Cluj by nightfall or our danger will increase many times. A Western vehicle in the middle of the country will be an easy target for the rebel *Securitate* forces."

By the grace of God, they completed their journey without incident, other than having to pass through a total of twelve barricades set up by military personnel looking for *Securitate* agents, and once a haphazard collection of peasants armed with sticks and farming tools in search of the same people. That group symbolized nearly the entire Romanian population. They had caught a glimpse of their freedom; they would not give up without a fight.

At the city limits of Cluj, where Highway 1 from Turda turned into Calea Turzii, they encountered their final road block for the day. Two armored personnel carriers waited side by side on the uneven pavement, their cannons pointed in opposite directions. Obviously intrigued by the Western van, an officer hurried out to take control. "Passports!" he barked. Jim handed the officer their three passports and the others' documents.

"It is not safe. Where are you going?" the officer asked, his tone a little friendlier.

Cristea leaned over from the passenger seat. "I live on Calea Manastur. We are all staying there."

Should we be that obvious about our connection with the Romanian Christians? Jim kept his features neutral. It mattered little now. It was done. God was in control of even the small details of the revolution.

They were escorted by four soldiers in a jeep across the city to Cristea's house. Upon their arrival, one of the soldiers jumped out and ran back to the van.

Cristea translated his ecstatic announcement as he spoke. "It was just announced," he sputtered in Romanian, "President Ceaușescu and his wife have fled the country."

"It is not good enough," Yari said, loud enough for the soldier to hear him. "He should be brought to trial for all the evil he has done against our country!"

"Trial?" A second soldier had come up behind the first, and he spat on the ground. "If I could get my hands on him, I would cut his body into little pieces, feed them to the dogs, then burn the dogs."

When Cristea translated, Jim nodded. While he didn't condone the violence, he understood the reasoning, and he'd never even had to live under the man's rule.

"Your chance is gone, Douru," his mate countered. "Come now, we must return."

Jim maneuvered the van into the courtyard, and they entered the empty house. Yari was unable to walk because of his wounds, so Jim and Carl lifted him awkwardly into a bed. Yari smiled his thanks as he settled his body into a comfortable position.

One on each side of the bed, Kirsten and Cristea tugged the blankets up to his chin. Cristea straightened and looked at Jim and Nick. "You will stay the night?"

Warmth rushed through Jim's chest at the hope in her voice. He caught Nick's eye and nodded.

"We will if it's all right," his friend replied. Jim could have hugged him. "But we will need to leave early tomorrow."

Yari beckoned the three couriers to come closer. When they approached, he shook their hands. "I hope to see you again. You have been very kind to us. What will you do now?"

"Now that Romania is being liberated," Jim said, "maybe Albania will be next. I think I'd like to spend some time there. They let Canadians in, at least." He glanced at Cristea. "Nothing's decided yet, though."

"How about you, Ralph?"

Nick squeezed Kirsten's hand. "Cathy and I have been talking about working full time in Romania. We're going to think and pray about it."

Yari clapped his hands. "Oh, that would be marvelous."

"It has been an honor to know you," said Kirsten. "I hope we see you again soon." She kissed him lightly on the cheek.

Tears came to Yari's eyes. "We thank you so much. I sense that God has great plans in store for all of you. We will remember you in our prayers."

"This is a good time of year, Yari." Jim rested a hand on the man's shoulder. "In three days it will be Christmas. With Ceauşescu gone, there is reason to celebrate."

"With my son gone, it is a time to mourn."

"Yes, that's true. And for you to heal. And when you have, what will you do?" Nick crossed his arms over his chest.

"Then I will preach. Perhaps even this Christmas."

"Christmas!" Kirsten smacked her forehead. "That reminds me." She turned and raced for the door. When she returned a minute later, she held her hand behind her back.

"Cristea, I have a Christmas present for you." Kirsten held up a wrinkled pink dress she had pulled from her suitcase. "I want you to have this."

Cristea's eyes widened. "It is so beautiful. Are you sure?"

Kirsten nodded, smiling. "Come," she said, pulling Cristea into the bedroom, "let's see if it fits you."

Jim stared after the two girls. Was he supposed to let Cristea go? Peace settled over him. It was the right thing to do. For now. He could wait. There was certainly no hurry.

Yari beckoned Jim and Carl to his side. "It is different in Romania. For the young people, I mean."

"In many ways," Jim agreed.

"I am speaking about young men and women and their relationships. In America, in Canada, if a man sees a woman he likes, he asks her to go out and spend time with him. I have heard this is true, yes?"

Jim nodded. *Where is he going with this?*

"Romania is different. When a young man in the church sees a girl he wants to marry, he will pray and ask God if she is the right one. If he believes God has said 'Yes', then he will ask the girl to marry him."

"Wow, I couldn't do that."

Yari nodded. "The girl will take his proposal, pray also, and if she believes God has given his blessing, she will accept the young man's proposal."

Jim's brow furrowed. "And that works?"

"Of course. God does not trick us."

What is he saying, that I should pray about whether or not to ask Cristea to marry me? He shot a look at the young man beside him. If so, why did he ask Carl to come over as well? A sudden, horrible thought struck Jim. Did Carl think Cristea was the woman God wanted him to marry? How could that be? Jim had felt so sure… Yari's words floated through his mind. *God doesn't trick us.* Jim pushed back his shoulders. He would have to wait, as he felt led to do, and trust that God would show all three of them the way He would have them go.

Yari grasped Carl's forearm. "Carl, our brother here, has been praying about Cristea. He knows you are leaving and he asks for your blessing before he goes any further."

God, help me to let her go. If she comes to me, we will both know it is your will for us to be together. And if not, then I pray only that Carl will make her happy and take good care of her. Summoning every ounce of strength he had, Jim reached for Carl's hand and looked him in the eye. "You have my blessing to try."

Two days before Christmas, at high noon, the van rolled under the covered inspection area of the Romanian border crossing, just outside the village of Bars. Apart from two army jeeps, theirs was the only vehicle present. Guards emerged to take their passports and exit cards.

"Where have you been?"

"Brasov. Cluj," Nick replied.

"Why did you come here?"

"It says on the visa. Hey, all this fighting started and we just want to leave."

The guards searched the van quickly but thoroughly then allowed the three to leave. On the Hungarian side, Nick jumped out to expedite their visa process. They were going home, or to the guesthouse of the Poplawskis, at least, as much a home as they would enjoy for another year. With good roads and their smooth-running van, they should be there in time for Christmas. Unless something else went wrong.

Two men came out of the office. The first, a long, lean, thirty-something who looked Swedish, or maybe Dutch, carried a microphone. The other man, shorter and with dark hair, trailed after him, a massive camera on his shoulder. The tall man approached the driver's side and Jim rolled down his window.

"Hey, my name is Pete De Vries and I'm with KBBC. We're a Christian network out of California. What cities did you come from? Did you see the revolution? What's happening in there?"

Jim tugged on his growing mustache. They did have stories to tell, and this might be the best way to get the word out about what the Christians in Romania were going through and let people know how they could pray. "Look, I'm happy to talk to you, but I've been driving for hours. Could we maybe do this interview over lunch?"

"Absolutely. There's a great restaurant up the road in Debrecen. We'll meet you there." The reporter started to turn away then stopped and gripped the window frame. "Have you heard the latest news?"

"I've *lived* the news," Jim replied. "What else has happened?"

"Ceaușescu and his wife have been captured. They're holding them for trial."

"I thought they'd fled the country."

"So did we. There were tons of stories going around here. This is really it, though."

"That's good news. Thanks for telling me."

The man nodded. "See you in a few minutes." He and the cameraman headed for their car.

Nick opened the passenger door and slid onto the seat. "Who was that?"

"A reporter from a Christian station. Wants to interview us about everything we've just been through. Are you okay with that?"

Nick shrugged. "Good chance to get the truth out there."

"That's what I thought." Jim glanced from him to Kirsten in the back. "I could always talk to them, and the two of you could have lunch at another table, spend a bit of time alone."

Nick peered over the back seat. "That sounds pretty good, actually."

"Yes it does." Kirsten smiled, her cheeks pink.

Jim punched Nick lightly in the arm. "I guess a lot more happened on this trip than I realized," he teased. "That's great Nick. Just when the Romanians get their freedom, you run off and give up yours."

Kirsten grabbed Nick's arm. "Nick's not giving up his freedom. He'll be sharing it with me. After all, 'He who finds a wife finds a good thing.' That's what Proverbs says."

"Yeah. Every girl memorizes that one."

Nick shook his head. "All right, let's go. I'm hungry."

Jim started the engine. He thought about what Kirsten had said. It *was* a good thing to find a wife, he knew that. And he thought he had… He straightened in his seat as he drove the van through the border crossing. God was in control. Jim was content to wait and see what God would do in his life and in Cristea's.

Peace flooded through him as he pressed down on the accelerator and headed for the restaurant.

Chapter Twenty-Five

The February north wind blew cold through the Transylvanian Basin, stirring tiny white particles of snow over barren fields. Yari hobbled from his house to a large shed around the side. Eerie shadows, formed from the flickering light of the lantern in his hand, danced weirdly across the old sign, POTRA AND SONS—BLACKSMITHS. Even as a pang of sorrow shot through him at the loss of one of those sons, he smiled. *Ahhh, it's good to be home.* And tonight his new friend Greceanu would join him for dinner.

He reflected back on the past seven weeks, the rest he had earned and the good changes his struggling Romania desperately had craved and were beginning to find. Even Mama Angelina's life had taken an abrupt swing—a fatal heart attack as she watched the capture of Nicolae and Elena Ceaușescu on her small black and white television. Although he wouldn't wish anyone dead, her absence was an added small victory for the people of the Jablonec and Olcea villages.

Last week he had preached his third sermon. Believers across the land focused their attention on reaching their own people in this new-found openness. There would be hope for Romania yet and hope for his son, Jozef. *And his son's sons too.*

He checked the lock on the shed door and had just started back to the house when a noise stopped him. A car approached, its headlights expelling darkness from the narrow laneway. Yari frowned. Greceanu wouldn't arrive for another hour. *Who could be visiting at this time of night?*

The car came to a stop and a man got out. Yari waited patiently for him to step forward.

"Yari Potra! It has been a long time, yes?"

Chills ran down his spine. That voice. The evil. It isn't possible. "Popescu?"

"You are indeed correct," the colonel answered, laughing softly.

"What do you want?" Yari's jaw tightened. "You can't harm me now. We have a new government."

The colonel didn't answer, just walked towards him, a smile on his face.

"You are still the *Securitate*?" Yari took a step back.

"That's why I'm here." The colonel reached Yari and grasped him by both shoulders. "My dear Yari. The government has given me a new role. You don't have to worry. I've been sent to *protect* you." He squeezed Yari's shoulders and lowered his head. "And… I've come to see if maybe you can find a way to forgive a bitter, angry man who's been punishing you for forty years when your only crime was falling in love with a woman I mistakenly supposed I had a right to." He shook his head. "I've been fighting on the wrong side, old friend. I know that now."

Yari searched the dark eyes that met his. The cold, demonic Popescu had vanished. The face before him held genuine sadness and contrition. Could he forgive his old enemy for everything he had done? He shook his head. No, he couldn't. Not in his own strength. Thankfully, after everything he'd gone through the last months, he knew one thing to be absolutely true: when he didn't have the strength, God did.

God, help me to let go of my hatred and anger. Help me to forgive, as you have forgiven me. He nodded at the colonel as the weight he'd carried around for years slid from his shoulders. "We can talk. Let's see how it goes."

Popescu let out a heavy breath, as though he'd been holding it. He slid an arm around Yari's shoulders and guided him towards the house. "And maybe, while we are at it, you can tell me a little more about this Jesus of yours, yes?"

Epilogue

On December 25, 1989, the day Christians around the world celebrate the anniversary of the birth of their Lord Jesus Christ, President Nicolae Ceauşescu and his wife, the Comrade Academician Doctor Engineer Elena Ceauşescu, were led before a firing squad. The charges against them had been brought before a secret military tribunal: genocide of more than 60,000 victims; undermining the power of the state through armed action against the people and state powers; causing material damage through demolition and explosions in cities; undermining the national economy; and attempting to flee the country by taking advantage of more than one billion dollars deposited in foreign banks.

Three volunteers, picked out of a squad of eighty soldiers, were tasked with performing the execution. All eighty men had put their hands up. Three were chosen, and they slaughtered the Ceauşescus even before the command was given and before the cameras were in place.

Across the country, an ever-diminishing number of fanatical *Securitate* members roamed the streets, committing acts of terrorism. The army eventually gained complete control. The D5 branch of the *Securitate*, responsible for Ceauşescu's protection, faded into the woodwork. A few were captured and sentenced to prison terms while others escaped the country. Still more assumed new identities, a simple process expedited by those carrying second and third identification cards.

Ion Iliescu took control of a temporary government on December 22, leading what was called the Council of the National Salvation Front. Iliescu was an ex-government leader who had opposed Ceauşescu publicly in the past. He remained a communist.

Also on December 22, Radio Bucharest reported that General Vasile Milea shot himself after being exposed as a "traitor to his country". Mr. Silviu Brucan, acting as the post-revolution Vice President, reported that Milea was murdered, perhaps by Ceauşescu himself, for commanding the army to stop firing on the people.

On December 26, many changes were immediately wrought by the Council. Eleven of them are worth noting:

1. The rural resettlement program was halted.
2. The restrictions on the right to choose one's domicile were canceled.
3. The strict anti-abortion policy was reversed.
4. Norms for per capita consumption of food and calories were abolished.
5. Citizens were no longer required to report any conversation with a foreigner within twenty-four hours.
6. Citizens could now play host to foreigners.
7. Citizens now had the right to free movement.
8. Citizens could stay abroad without fear of retaliation.
9. Cancellation of forced and unpaid (patriotic) labor
10. A regulation was passed allowing most Romanians to attain passports.
11. The death penalty was abolished.

In Bucharest and in Sibiu, a network of underground tunnels was discovered through which *Securitate* agents had been able to maneuver around the city without detection. A Christian man in Bucharest, once an architect on the tunnels, approached the authorities to tell of their existence. The army began a process of sealing certain entrances and flooding the tunnels with water, forcing thousands of agents to the surface.

On December 24, Radio Budapest from Hungary quoted "authoritative sources" by announcing that seventy thousand to eighty thousand people had died so far in the revolution and that the number of injured reached 300,000. On February 8, Silviu Brucan more accurately declared that only ten thousand died in the revolution and that fifty thousand more had been killed in the past twenty-four years of Ceauşescu's regime.

On January 27, 1990, the National Salvation Front issued a decree ordering penalties of one to five years for those who verbally or physically assaulted the police or members of the *Securitate*. Government officials tried to make the public believe that the *Securitate's* role in the revolution was limited to "just a few unrepentant bad guys".

Those chanting "*Ole, Ole, Ole, Ole, Ceauşescu nu mai e*," meaning "Ceauşescu is no more," changed their tune. Their new song became "*Ceauşescu nu fi trist, Iliescu-i Comunist*" or "Ceauşescu don't be sad. Iliescu is a communist."

On April 13, citizens from Brasov claimed that *Securitate* agents captured while firing on a crowd had been simply set free; there were no statements from witnesses to their arrests, nor any record of their cases. Subsequent threats had frightened the population to the point that no one dared to speak out any more. They were told that the arrests of *Securitate* people were a result of false accusations. None of the authorities in Brasov could explain who had killed a number of the town's citizens during the fighting.

No one knows the exact number of people killed in the revolution. Estimates of between one hundred and four thousand were reported for the city of Timisoara. On Elena Ceauşescu's orders, forty bodies were transported from Timisoara to Bucharest for cremation to make identification impossible. While the townspeople reported one figure, the government denied it and agreed to a much lower number. In the city of Brasov, the government reported that sixty-eight people had died. The citizens claimed that the number was 113.

Distrust of President Iliescu grew. On March 11, several members of Timisoara's civil and intellectual groups composed a dramatic declaration, transcribed here only in part:

> The Communist Party has gone so far as to commit genocide; as a result, it has excluded itself definitively from society. We shall not tolerate it either in principle or in practice, regardless of the name under which it tries to resurrect itself.
>
> We were in the streets of Timisoara during the days of the revolution and know that the number of deaths was higher than that officially reported.
>
> This has been a genuine revolution, and not a coup d'état.
>
> People did not die in Timisoara so that second- or third-rate communist activists could move to the front.
>
> Do not consider that the revolution has been concluded. We shall continue it peacefully but firmly. After defying and defeating without anybody's help one of the strongest repressive systems in the world, no one and nothing can intimidate us anymore.

Peaceful demonstrations continued daily in Bucharest. On June 14, President Iliescu bused in club-wielding miners to combat the protesters. At least five people died and well over four hundred people were injured. Offices of the two political opposition parties were destroyed along with the office of an opposition newspaper.

Through all the political changes, an open door remained for the Gospel of Jesus Christ to be preached. Courier groups across Europe brought in Christian literature and Bibles by the thousands, declaring them without problems to the border customs officers. Teams of missionaries entered Romania and preached the Good News to thousands more. On December 27, just days after the Revolution, the author entered Romania with an open load of Bibles, food, medicine, and clothing. At the border, he encountered the same guard who had searched his vehicle so thoroughly the week before. When he asked the guard why the searches had been so intense, the guard replied, "We had to. The *Securitate* were watching us."

American Josh McDowell traveled with a team and preached the Word to thousands of students and professors, and thousands claimed Christ as their Savior for the first time. South American evangelist Luis Palau preached the Gospel in a week-long crusade and an estimated 46,000 trusted God with the good news of salvation. Many believe over one million people trusted Christ as their Savior in 1990.

The land of Romania still needs your prayers, perhaps more than ever. Operation World (http://www.operationworld.org) reports that a moral vacuum exists *"with every kind of social evil. Substance abuse, prostitution, pornography, human trafficking and challenges to child welfare are widespread. Romania has one of the highest abortion rates in the world, with three or more abortions for every child born. Poverty is still common, with widespread unemployment and economic instability, caused to a large degree by rampant and entrenched corruption."*

Let us continue to pray for Romania and for God's church that stands in the trenches every day to shine a brighter light.

Author's Notes

For two years I travelled behind the Iron Curtain delivering Bibles, Christian literature, food, clothing, medicine, and money. Although the storyline of *In His Majesty's Secret Service* is fictional, many of the actual experiences or conversations that are included in this book were mine or those of my teammates.

For example, the meeting with Jan Mirolek in the first chapter was my own adventure and is duplicated faithfully. The border crossings of the couriers into Romania were typical of the intensity that Bible couriers experienced at that time (although the customs location in Chapter Four is fictional). The return of the food to Stan Dumitresti is true, but many details have been changed to protect his identity.

The most common question people asked me upon my return to North America was, "How did you actually smuggle the Bibles in?" Invariably, my answer was, "You'll have to join a team to find out." Even though the Iron Curtain has crumbled, for the sake of possible future missions to countries closed to the Gospel, I have deliberately simplified the smuggling technique. Until some former smuggler breaches a trust, the true methods will remain on a need-to-know basis.

The startling events at the end of Chapter Six and the beginning of Chapter Seven seem unrealistic, but I was there. They happened to me and I recorded everything with only a minor change in details.

The details that Cristea provided about her father's arrest at the end of Chapter Eight were taken almost verbatim from a conversation I had with a young believer.

The military stockade south of Brasov is fictional.

Colonel General Iulian Vlad was the head of the *Securitate* in 1989, just as Nicolae and Elena Ceauşescu were the leaders of Romania. The Palace of the People was under construction in 1989 and was unoccupied at the time of the novel.

After the revolution in December of 1989, I had the opportunity to talk with a young man who had been in prison for attempting escape from Romania. His tortures were similar to those that Pastor Potra experienced in the final chapters; he informed me that to tell more was too difficult for him.

Details given by the media during the revolution were sporadically unreliable. For example, through Radio Budapest the world learned that Ceauşescu had killed up to 70,000 people during the course of the revolution. The statistic was later altered to include the toll for his whole lifetime.

The death toll for Timisoara has been reported to be anywhere from 120 to over 10,000. I was interviewed by a CBS news team only days after the revolution and they claimed that they had not seen any bodies and they believed all reports to be grossly exaggerated. Since facts surrounding the revolution have been suppressed, I simply added my own details to the official reports and the video reports, which were displayed worldwide.

Most characters in this novel are fictional.

To contact Patrick for media interviews, In His Majesty's Secret Service curriculum resources, or with any questions, please email:

patrick@patrickbooks.com